NO FEAR

NO FEAR

No Justice Series: Book 6

NOLON KING

DAVID W. WRIGHT

STERLING & STONE

To YOU, the reader.
Thank you for your support.
Thank you for the wonderful emails.
Thank you for the thoughtful reviews.
Thank you for reading and loving our stories.

Prologue

McKenna Shaw hated the Sundays when their usual babysitter, Cami, had to work her other job. Cami always kept Alice occupied.

It was McKenna's last day of freedom before going back to school, but she had no freedom at all. Not only was she was forced to wake up early for church then spend half the morning there, she also had to watch her little sister after while her mom worked.

The whole entire day, shot.

It wasn't fair.

McKenna was fourteen. She was supposed to be out having fun with friends, not babysitting. Alice was eleven, more than old enough to look after herself, or at least to walk the few blocks home from church.

She walked ahead of McKenna, humming a song from *Hamilton* — annoying because Alice only liked the musical because McKenna and her friends were into it. Why couldn't she ever find her own thing? Why'd she always have to be such a try-hard?

McKenna looked down at her phone. Her friend, Lexi was texting.

Lexi: Can I come over? Got some tea to spill.

McKenna: What's it about?

Lexi: I'll tell you when I get there.

No way, Lexi.

McKenna: Oh, come on. Just a hint?

Lexi: Patience!

McKenna: You suck. I'm on the way home from church. Should be there in five.

McKenna picked up her pace. When she caught up to Alice, she said, "Lexi's coming over."

Alice smiled. "Oh?"

"Yes, but you can't hang out. She wants to talk."

"Oh." Alice looked down at the ground.

McKenna delighted in deflating her sister, even though she knew it was wrong. But it was Alice's fault for being their parents' favorite and *always* getting her way. McKenna had to include her sister in everything, and she shouldn't be punished because her sister didn't have her own friends. It wasn't *her* fault.

McKenna was usually nice enough to Alice. But there was something about her sister that made her want to act unkind for no discernible reason. Still, she never hit Alice or teased her. McKenna just ignored or shut her out whenever she got too cloying.

Cloying, like Carly Jenkins said I am.

That was the first time McKenna had ever heard the word. She looked it up and was disappointed by what her last best friend had called her. McKenna wouldn't make that mistake with Lexi, though.

She'd play it cool, and that meant not having Alice around. Because her sister was definitely cloying. Desperate for people to like her, enough that it reeked.

Maybe cloying was contagious, and it had made McKenna a bit desperate herself. When Alice hung out with the annoying kid down the road, she turned into somewhat of a pest herself.

Alice walked in silence, the song gone from her voice. McKenna began to feel guilty. Maybe she'd let her sister hang out with them after Lexi spilled the tea.

Maybe.

McKenna noticed something white moving slowly in the street at the edges of her vision.

She turned to see a van slowing down, an overweight man in the driver's seat looking at them both. A creeper — the kind of guy McKenna and her friends sometimes saw passing by the bus stop or staring at them in the mall. They would laugh, sometimes even flirt with the pedos before mocking them. Not McKenna, though. The creepers scared her too much.

The van stopped, and the guy lowered his window. "Excuse me, have either of you seen a white poodle around here?"

Alice started walking toward the van.

McKenna reached out and grabbed her sister's arm. "Alice! We have to get home."

"Just take a look." The creeper held up a printed photo of a dog. From this distance, McKenna could only make out two things under the photo: *LOST* and *REWARD $50.*

She looked at the man's face. He was still big and creepy looking, but not as threatening as she'd first thought.

"My name is John Franks. I live on the next street. You're Al and Maryann's kids, right?"

"Yeah," Alice said.

McKenna squeezed her sister's arm and whispered, "Don't talk to him."

"He's our neighbor." She pulled away from McKenna and moved toward the truck.

She walked beside Alice, straightening her back, glaring at John Franks, trying to intimidate the man, just in case.

He moved over to the passenger seat, leaned out the window, and offered them the paper. "If you can just keep an eye out for Sparky and call the number at the bottom if you see her?"

Alice reached out to grab the paper.

And John Franks grabbed her by the wrist.

Alice let out a surprised squeal as the van's door opened, moving Alice with the door, him clutching her wrist through the open window.

What is he doing?

It was all happening too fast. She knew about Stranger Danger and how to respond, but in the moment, McKenna remembered nothing.

Shock and fear overwhelmed her.

"Help!" McKenna screamed, running toward the man with balled fists.

If she hit him hard enough, he would let go of Alice.

He might grab her, but she at least had a better chance of fighting him off. Alice was too young and small.

When McKenna was inches away from him, she saw what was in the man's other hand.

Then John Franks fired his gun.

Chapter 1 - Mallory Black

MAL SAT in the hospital waiting room, thinking about was how much Alice Shaw reminded her of Jessi Price. Not just Jessi, but Ashley as well. She pictured a bright blue sky, like she had taught herself to start doing whenever her daughter's death came to mind. It was the best way to bar the crime scene photos from haunting her with images of Ashley's naked body, dumped in a drainage ditch.

Are we going to find Alice's body too? Dumped like fucking trash?

Her partner, Mike, was at the Shaws' house with the girls' aunt looking for any clues to who might have abducted her. Mal was sitting with their mother, Sheila, while waiting for the older daughter, McKenna, to come out of surgery.

Sheila was thirty-five, though she looked closer to forty. Her eyes seemed even older, dulled by heartache and pain. They were a washed-out blue, bloodshot, with smudges of mascara blending into the dark circles beneath and making her look like a racoon. She wore her blonde hair pulled back into a tight ponytail, and she'd chewed her fingernails down to the pinks. Her work clothes — black pants and a shirt with a bright red tie, same as all the servers at Creek County Steak House — seemed to hang on her thin, frail frame.

Mal had questioned Sheila at length, and while the woman could barely manage a pair of sentences in a row without starting to sob, nothing about her actions indicated deception, or that she knew anything about who took one daughter and put a bullet into the other. Sheila had no boyfriends, estranged lovers, or anyone else in her life that had given the girl an unnatural amount of attention.

She was a single mom working two jobs and hadn't really dated anyone since the girls' father killed himself nine years ago. Sheila was doing her best with a shitty situation — making an effort, which was more than Mal could say about a lot of people she came into contact with while on the job.

"Who would do such a thing?" Sheila asked.

"That's what we hope to find out. Do your kids usually go to church alone?"

"Cami usually takes them. She's our sitter, but sometimes she has to work her other job Sunday mornings."

"Where does she work?"

"Crescent, that new restaurant on the beach."

"I'll need her number."

Sheila handed it over, and Mal added it to the list on her scratchpad.

"And the girls haven't said anything about anyone at school, maybe the bus stop — anyone else who might have approached them?"

"They know better than to talk to strangers. No offense, but shouldn't you be out there looking for Alice? You've already asked me a million questions. I know what they say about there being a window when someone goes missing. The longer we're sitting here, the less likely she is to be found."

"Believe me, our officers are looking. My asking you these questions helps us know where to look and who to look at. Narrowing down the list of people helps immensely. But I believe I've got everything I need here. If you think of something else or remember anything at all, please call me. Anytime."

Sheila took the card and thanked her.

As Mal departed, she ran smack into two of her least favorite people in the department.

Captain Bill Lummock was the new head of Special Crimes. He was a recent hire brought in when Sheriff Barry cleaned house of all who were too loyal to Gloria. Lummock came from Daytona Beach and had a decent track record overseeing Special Crimes there. He was a red-faced, barrel-chested, old-school cop with an alcoholic's nose, a splotchy face, and dusty blond-going-gray hair. The guy was loud and obnoxious, always telling crude jokes and calling people snowflakes.

Walking side-by-side with Lummock was Cameron Ford, the ex-journalist, ex-blogger Mal hated more than pretty much anyone other than the sheriff. The asshole helped Barry get elected and earned himself a position as the Sheriff's Public Information Officer.

Lummock asked for an update. She gave it to him as quickly as she could.

"Thank you. We're going to have a media briefing downstairs once the Sheriff gets here."

Cameron, who always seemed to go out of his way to annoy the fuck out of Mal, said, "Good job, detective."

She looked at him blankly, barely hiding her contempt. "Gee, thanks."

He looked down at his feet, avoiding eye contact like the coward he was.

"If that'll be all, I need to follow up on some leads."

Lummock nodded.

Mal walked away, fast as she could, suffering a shortness of breath. Her skin felt clammy, her stomach churned. She needed to find a bathroom.

She raced to the restroom, burst through the door, then into a stall where she vomited.

A sheen of cold sweat covered her. She felt awful. Her heart still pounded, and she continued to retch, but she had nothing left inside her to puke.

When her pulse slowed and her breathing settled, Mal washed up then left the restroom.

On her way to the elevators, she passed a couple of men, including the last face in the world she expected to see — Paul Dodd, the man who murdered her daughter.

The man she killed in Mexico more than six months ago.

She spun around, hand on her gun, ready to draw when she realized that it wasn't Dodd. It didn't look anything like him. These two men were Indian and both wearing doctor's scrubs.

They looked at Mal like she was tripping. Fortunately, she hadn't drawn her weapon.

What the fuck?

Why did I just imagine Paul Fucking Dodd?

A tightness in her chest made it harder to breathe. Dizzy and weak, Mal leaned against the wall, trying to calm herself. Her heart was racing faster than before, and she could hear her pulse.

She reached and patted her pocket, soothed by the familiar shape of her two Just In Case pain pills. Addicts were supposed to get rid of their drug of choice to keep temptation away. But carrying the pills had offered Mal some sense of comfort in the six months since she'd quit, some sense of control over her addiction.

Knowing she *could* take them meant she didn't *have* to.

That had been working. Until now.

No, no, no. I am NOT gonna relapse. Not now.

Mal clutched at her chest, the tight ache spreading as she gasped for air. Surely she was about to die by either heart attack or suffocation.

Her vision blurred as she lost her footing, even though she was already leaning on the wall.

A rush of movement came at her.

"Are you—"

She didn't hear what else the woman was about to say.

Instead, Mal collapsed and found the darkness again.

Chapter 2 - Jasper Parish

JASPER WOULD GIVE anything for a moment of silence.

Unfortunately, his podmate refused to shut the fuck up. Jasper lay on the top bunk, eyes closed, just trying to sleep. It was too damned late for this nonsense.

Wally was a light-skinned black guy in his twenties with a tight afro, tattoos up and down both his wiry arms, and a few rather unfortunate ones on his face. The kind of guy who wanted you to think he was tough but was actually nothing more than a big mouth. Those flapping gums got him beef with a rival gang, and now he was doing time for a drive-by that not only killed some of his rivals but also an innocent child caught in the crossfire.

"Way I see it, this whole thing was rigged from the get-go. Folks in power say we choose this life, but we don't choose where we born, ya' know? You take the same kid grow up where I was and put him in with some rich family in one of them neighborhoods with green grass, and I guarantee he's gonna make some different ass choices, ya' know?"

Jasper didn't want to argue, but he hated when people

drowned in their pity, blaming everybody but themselves for their choices.

"Yeah, well *I* grew up in the hood and sure as hell didn't go around robbing people or dealing drugs."

He stopped there, failing to articulate his chosen profession. Being a cop in gen-pop was a death sentence. No one knew who he was, sentenced to a prison in Georgia with an assumed identity as part of his plea. Malcolm "Mac" White.

It wasn't quite protective custody, but there was no way in hell he would ever get that, especially since the District Attorney was friends with Oliver Kozack.

"Yeah? So why the fuck you in here with me then? What is it you did? You killed someone or you wouldn't be up in here. Old Mac preaching to *me* about morality." Wally gave him a thin and raspy laugh. "Tell me your life wouldn't be different if you grew up somewhere else and with different parents."

"I *chose* my path. Nobody to blame but me. And the people I killed ... well, they deserved it."

Jasper stopped short of adding that his killing didn't result in the death of an innocent child. No reason to make an enemy of his podmate. Wally wasn't an awful person to be stuck with for the most part. He could have been much worse and wasn't a threat.

"Yeah, you just keep tellin' yourself that story, Pops."

Pops.

That reminded him of the young man, Tyrell, who died trying to protect Spider. He wondered how she was, if there'd been any change in her condition. Last Jasper had heard from his lawyer, she was still in a coma.

That was two weeks ago. The whole thing was his fault. Her in a coma, Tyrell and others who had aided him in his pursuit now gone forever. So much death he was responsible for, all the more tragic when it wasn't by his own hand.

And for what?

Revenge, his daughter had said. Accused him of being driven by revenge.

The prison guards made sure that Jasper took his meds every night before lights out, so now he never saw her. The pain of Jordyn's absence was almost unbearable.

But he'd made his bed, and it was his to lie in. He chose to forgo a trial, to confess his crimes. He was fine with prison, he just hadn't considered the consequences of being medicated for his condition.

Just as well. Jasper didn't think he could look into his daughter's eyes right now. She warned him not to kill Calum Kozack or pursue Victor Forbes and the pedophile network. It was dangerous, and there were other options with Forbes. The network would have been exposed without him.

But Jasper had wanted revenge, so others paid the price.

Now *he* was paying the tax for his bloodlust. Stuck in prison with Wally Talks Too Much.

After a long moment of quiet where Jasper felt hopeful that Wally was either going to sleep or jerk off, his podmate piped up again.

"Man, you seem smarter than most the cats in here. How'd they catch you?"

"I confessed."

"Confessed? Why the fuck you do that?"

"Because I'm tired of running. I did the crime. I'm doing the time. No sense in fighting it."

"I would never confess to shit. Never, hell no, uh-fuck-ing-uh."

Jasper didn't say anything.

Eventually, he heard Wally beating off.

He turned over, faced the wall, and tried to ignore the sound.

∼

AFTER BREAKFAST, it was time to hit the yard for fifty minutes of "recreation."

The recreation yard at Lennox State Penn involved two different areas with weights and benches, a basketball court, a handball court, and a track that circled the yard. Forty-three prisoners were there at once, with four corrections officers keeping watch on the ground and one in the tower, holding a rifle and overlooking the yard.

Jasper stood alone with his back to a squat concrete shed at the far end of the track, enjoying the wash of sunlight on his face. He'd once made the mistake of leaning against the fence, before Wally told him, *You can't do that, man. They'll think you're trying to break off a piece for a shiv.*

The sun was warm, and the breeze wasn't bitter. Days like this he missed freedom and thought of Alicia and Ophelia. Imagined a life where he settled down with her and started over. But a normal life was never in the cards for him. Even when he'd tried to aim for the straight and narrow, trouble followed him and threatened the lives of those he loved.

Jasper wondered how Mallory Black was doing. How Jessi Price was. How were those girls down in Mexico?

He felt no guilt for the people he killed protecting them. Those killings had been for the right reasons. They weren't revenge.

Jasper should've kept it to that, saving people instead of enacting the justice that had twisted him into something he could no longer face in the mirror or even live with. But there was no running from all those crimes that haunted him nightly. Even if he could, He was tired of fleeing from the things he'd done and the person he'd become.

He'd flirted with fighting the case in hopes of getting the death penalty instead of settling for a miserable existence in prison. But Jasper deserved the time. Penance and death would only be cheating justice.

As he eyed the flock of birds flying in formation overhead, he heard footsteps coming toward him. More than a single set. He turned, looked. Bit back a sigh.

Two buff white dudes. One tall and bald, the other short with slicked back dark hair and lots of ink on his arms — Aryans.

The shorter one, Kenn Faber, looked Jasper up and down. "Word is you're a cop."

Fuck.

Jasper didn't know if the man was fishing or if he knew. He suspected the latter and said nothing.

"That true?" Kenn asked.

"No."

"Well, some people are talking about shivving you. Personally, I don't care one way or another. One less n— well, you know. But we just might be able to help each other out."

"*Oh?*"

"Your cellmate needs to go. And since you're already a lifer, you oughtta do it."

"You want him dead, why don't you do it?"

"It ain't *me* who wants him dead. I'm just fulfilling someone else's request. My boys do it, and it's a race riot. But ain't no one gonna do shit to you. One more black dude killin' a black dude, ain't no one gonna blink. You probably won't get more than a few days in the hole."

"And what do I get for doing your work?" Jasper had no intentions of killing Wally.

"You have protection."

"From the Aryans? What about the others?"

"Protection from *all* the people who matter. Ain't nothin' that happens in here without going through me or Young Luther."

Young Luther was a rising rap star a few years back who took the gang thing too far and got in over his head. Went to prison and brought his 904 Mafia gang thing behind bars. It was the 904 Mafia, White Nation, and Muerte Boyz all vying for the top spot on the food chain.

"*Young Luther?* You and he are, what, knitting buddies?"

Kenn smiled, his canines filed sharp. "Nah, but we have a working arrangement. Same with Hector and the spics. We all agree you're safe, then shit, you might as well be sleeping in church. But first you gotta do this thing for us."

"I'll think about it," Jasper said.

"You've got forty-eight hours. Otherwise, someone else'll do the job and *you'll* be next."

Kenn smiled and walked away with his pet behemoth.

Jasper leaned back against the shed wall, eventually glancing over to where his podmate was lifting weights with another dude.

Wally looked suspicious.

This time, Jasper did sigh.

He knew what he had to do.

Chapter 3 - Mallory Black

BEING STUCK in a hospital bed waiting for the doctor to return with a prognosis was a purgatory Mal needed to get the fuck out of.

It had felt like she was having a heart attack. She had passed out. But now, everything was back to normal. Except for her skull-crushing headache.

Mal wanted to detach from the machines reading her oxygen level, heart rate, and blood pressure. Wanted to get up and out of the hospital gown and back into her clothes.

It sucked being sidelined in a hospital bed while some sick fuck was doing the unthinkable to a little girl. She needed to be there when McKenna woke up. Needed to find the bastard before it was too late and Alice Shaw was just another dead kid.

She grabbed her phone and texted her partner.

Mal: Any news?

Mike: No. You okay?

Mal: No. Doc said it's bad.

Mike: WHAT??

Mal smiled.

Mal: Yeah, said I've caught a case of the Asshole Virus. Must've been from my partner.

Mike: Fuck you. Seriously. What's wrong?

Mal: Still waiting to find out. Not ruling out the Asshole Virus, though.

She could picture him shaking his head.

Mike: Okay. I'm gonna swing by. Fill you in on the latest.

Mal: Can't wait.

A knock sounded at the door, then it opened to Dr. Patel — an Indian woman in her late forties, with big warm brown eyes behind thick glasses and long hair pulled back into a bun.

"Hello, Mal. How are you feeling?"

"Top notch, Doc. So, what's the verdict? Am I gonna die?"

"No." She smiled and looked down at her chart. "But based on your responses, I think you had a panic attack."

"Ah."

"Have you had them before?"

"No?" But as Mal cycled through the past few months, there were a few similar instances, just not as extreme. She told the doctor about that, then asked, "So, what does that mean? Is this a thing I'm gonna have to deal with from now on?"

"Not necessarily. But it's possible. I know you have a stressful job, and ... well, you've been through a lot these past couple of years."

She's bringing up Ashley, my abduction. Is VICTIM all anybody sees when they look at me?

Mal nodded, looking down at her hands in a braid on her stomach.

"Are you seeing anybody?"

"You asking me out, Doc?"

The doctor gave Mal a polite laugh. "I meant a therapist."

"No. Not really. I mean, I have, but no, not ongoing."

"It might do you some good. Meanwhile, I'm going to prescribe .25 milligrams Alprazolam."

"Xanax?"

"Yes. Only take it if you feel another attack coming on. I'm prescribing the lowest dose. Start with one pill and see how you respond. You can bump it to two if one isn't working."

The doctor went on about the medication, but all Mal could think was, *Great, another fucking pill.*

She'd been sober for six months. The notion of taking a pill so many people abused made her feel weak and even more afraid of a relapse. Plenty of people died from mixing Xanax and opiates, maybe being on Xanax would make her less likely to take the pain pills again. Choking to death on her own vomit wasn't how Mal planned to leave this world.

The doctor detached the sensors then left.

Mike arrived a few minutes later. He looked at Mal like she was a sick kid or a wounded puppy.

The pity made her want to punch glass. "Don't look at me like that."

"Like what?"

"I'm fine. Just a panic attack. No big deal."

Mike began to ask questions.

Mal took off her top.

"Jesus." Mike shielded his eyes. "Could warn a guy."

"Do my tits offend thee?"

"Fuck you," he said, still looking elsewhere as she put on her bra.

"It's okay, my offensive tits are now covered." Mal grabbed her shirt and started to put it on. She was still in her underwear, but Mike didn't turn away. At least he wasn't a total prude.

He kept asking her questions.

She continued dodging them, then fired back, "You're supposed to be updating me on the Alice Shaw case. Where are we?"

"Yeah, about that …" Mike looked sheepishly away.

"What?"

"Sheriff took you off of it."

"What?"

"He heard you fainted on the scene and thought maybe it was a bit too close to all the shit you'd gone through."

"And who'd he put on it?"

"Me and Skippy are leads."

"Fucking Skippy? You let him put *fucking Skippy* on it?"

"It's not like I had a choice, Mal!"

"Did you at least fight for me?"

Mike said nothing.

"What the hell, Mike?

"I thought you had a heart attack! What was I supposed to do? I'll ask him to—"

"No." Mal grabbed her coat, shoved her arms through, then her holstered gun which she slipped onto her belt. She strode past Mike and into the hallway with a shake of her head, unsure of where she was going but knowing she needed to get away from him.

"Seriously, it's no big deal. I'll ask him to put you back on." Mike followed her out of the room.

Mal reached the elevator just as the doors opened and a pair of orderlies stepped out. She got on, then met her partner's gaze. "You should've fought for me, Mike."

She stabbed the button. The elevator doors slid shut.

Mal wanted to scream.

Sheriff Claude Barry had been waiting for the moment to fuck her over, and this was his excuse. He was taking her off the case. How long before he tried to make an argument that she was ill-suited for duty?

This was revenge for her backing Gloria Bell when she ran against him and got him out of office. Not only had Barry attacked her through his proxy — that fucking coward, Cameron Ford, and his stupid blog — he'd tried derailing her several times since returning to office. Someone must've said something, because he backed off for a bit. Even went so far as to publicly praise her. He wasn't an idiot, and Mal was adored by the press for all she'd been through. It would be too obvious if he cleaned house immediately.

But now he had legitimate cause, calling her fitness to serve into question.

Barry was the main reason she hadn't taken any pills. If she slipped up and used, he'd find out and would fire her on the spot for sure. Might even arrest her.

I can't take Xanax.

He'll say I'm a liability in the field.

Fuck!

The doors opened.

Mal got off the elevator as her phone started ringing.

It was a dispatcher. "I've got a man on the line saying he needs to talk to you. It's about the missing girl."

"Put him through." Mal stepped outside the hospital, looking for a quiet spot just outside the entrance.

A fountain in the distance sprayed water in rhythmic spurts, and her mind flashed on a little girl's severed neck, her carotid artery sprinkling blood like a Bellagio water show.

"Is this Mallory Black?" A man's voice streamed suddenly in her ear, snapping her back to reality.

"Yes, who is this?"

"I'm the one you're looking for."

"Who is this?"

"The one who took Alice. Write down this number if you want to find her: BR60C3A866." He vented a heavy breath, then said, "Good luck, detective. And don't be late."

The call went dead and Mal grabbed her notebook, jotting the number down.

But what the hell was it? Too short for a VIN. She typed the number into her browser then did a search to see if anything useful popped up.

Nothing.

What the fuck?

Mal stared at the numbers, trying to make sense of them. She flashed back to her time researching for school, and later on the job, thinking that maybe the numbers were something from the Dewey Decimal System.

A quick search of the Library of Congress's website still yielded nothing.

She stared at the numbers. If it was a book, maybe some of the numbers referenced a specific page.

Mal typed in the digits, a few at a time until she saw a title: *The Confessions of Augustine.*

A religious book and a crime involving two girls walking home from church seemed to line up. The only extra numbers, if they were indeed for this book, were the numerals 66.

She went online and saw several editions of the book, including a few public domain freebies. She bought a digital edition, but there weren't any page numbers.

Fuck.

She went to another online store and found an edition

that *did* have page numbers, and bought that. But page sixty-six offered no clues.

Mal stared at the numbers again, trying to think of what else they might be.

Why did he say, 'don't be late?'

Then the answer hit her smack in the face — the library.

There were two in town. She called Mike and told him about the call, asking him to hit the library in Butler while she took the county library.

She called Butler and spoke to a librarian named Pam. After confirming the book was there, she told her not to touch it or let anyone else near it.

Pam met her at the door then led her to the book in question.

Mal slipped on her gloves, removed the book from the shelf, then flipped to page sixty-six.

There in the margins, almost obscured unless she opened it all the way, Mal found a local address written in red ink.

She called Mike, bagged the book for evidence, then raced out of the library.

The second Mal hopped in her SUV, she tore out of the parking lot, hitting her lights and siren.

Chapter 4 - Jasper Parish

"LIGHTS OUT IN FIFTEEN," said a Corrections Officer over the intercom.

Time for the guard to go on his rounds, checking the pods and making sure Jasper took his meds.

The door buzzed open.

Tonight's CO was Officer Ramón Hernandez, a stout man in his mid-thirties who looked like he had hit the weights hard before letting himself go. Though he had a baby face, his dark eyes, with darker circles beneath, betrayed any softness. He wasn't the hardest of hardasses on the block, but he was all business, with little tolerance for nonsense. He'd taken Wally to the hole twice since Jasper's arrival, both times for being a smartass.

In one blue-gloved hand, Hernandez held a small paper cup with Jasper's three pills inside.

He opened his mouth and in went the pills.

Hernandez gave Jasper the cup which he used to fill with water from the sink over their toilet to wash them down. Then he opened his mouth for inspection. Sometimes Hernandez would pull Jasper's tongue to the side to check, but this time he didn't.

Hernandez left without a word.

Jasper laid down on his bunk, closing his eyes as he wondered how long it would take Wally to bring up that he'd seen Jasper talking to the Aryans.

"So, what's those pills for, anyway? Keep you from shivving me?" Wally asked instead.

An interesting choice of words. Did he know someone green-lit him?

Jasper decided to be direct. "The Aryans asked me to kill you. Gave me two days to decide."

Wally was uncharacteristically quiet. Then he sighed. No asking why or freaking out like Jasper had imagined.

"And? Are ya?"

"No."

"Then they'll find someone else to do it."

"So, you saying *I should?*"

Wally shook his head. "No."

"Why do they want you dead? *Who* wants you dead?"

"Someone's spreadin' shit how I *might'a* snitched on someone outside. A friend of Young Luther. But I didn't say shit."

"You should request protective custody."

"They ain't gonna give me protective custody 'cuz I ain't told them shit. See, I think the cops who questioned me are hoping I'll talk. They're spreading rumors, thinking I'll go to them."

"Then maybe you should. If you've got something they want, trade it."

"I ain't no snitch."

"They're gonna kill you, Wally."

"Then at least I ain't died a rat. Rather die with honor than live being a snitch bitch."

"That's just stupid."

"All a man's got is his name."

"What good is your name on a gravestone?"

"It's about legacy, man. I want my name to mean something to my sons. Don't want my boys thinkin' their old man was a fink."

"But people already think you did it, though. So, what's the point? Why not tell the cops what they want to know and get protective custody."

"Ain't you listening? I got kids. I run to the cops, someone might take a shot at my lady or my boys. They wanna come at me, let 'em, but I ain't havin' other people get hit over my bullshit."

Jasper shook his head. He could understand wanting to protect people on the outside. But resigning yourself to dying because someone else thinks you gave them up was losing your life without a fight.

His efforts to fly under the radar were now null and void. He was on these fuckers' radars with his own shit to deal with. If he refused to kill Wally, the bull's-eye landed on his back. How long until someone shivved him in the yard, mess hall, or shower?

How long before he had to sleep with one eye open because his next podmate got the same offer? Most people couldn't be blamed for seeing that offer for exactly what it was — one that couldn't be refused.

Jasper was in the rare position of not knowing what to do. Worse, he couldn't talk to his wife, his daughter, or his old mentor, Lenny Barnes. His meds were clouding his thoughts, blocking his visions.

While the pills were in his system, he was on his own.

∿

JASPER LEANED against the shed wall and watched everybody from a distance.

An overwhelming sense of dread washed over him, like something awful was seconds away. But his meds had dulled his perception so much, he also barely knew up from down.

One of the COs, a big, strapping country boy named Dalton Springs, walked the yard with his hands on his belt like a cowboy, waiting for someone to give him a reason to whip out his baton.

Dalton Springs was square-jawed with a dirty blond crewcut and icy blue eyes that always seemed a bit hazy, if not red. Always chewing on a pen cap, though if Jasper had to guess, the man preferred tobacco.

As Dalton walked past some of the men in the 904 Mafia who were working out at the weights, he cast a threatening stare at them.

A couple of the guys shot him sideways glares, but nobody directly challenged him. Dalton had a rep for knocking heads whenever violence erupted. Any excuse to whoop some ass.

Jasper saw movement in his peripheral vision, someone approaching him on the track.

He flinched then relaxed. It was only Crazy Gary, an insane-looking old white dude with long, straggly gray hair, a meth face, and matching teeth. The guy was forever talking to himself.

He looked at Jasper, stopped dead in his tracks, and narrowed his eyes. "What?"

Jasper looked side to side, as though Crazy Gary might be talking to someone else. In all his time here, the crazy fuck hadn't said anything to him. In fact, he'd never seen the guy talking to anyone but himself or the voices in his head.

"What?" Jasper asked, confused.

"Not you. Her."

Her?

Jasper turned, half expecting to see a woman, but there was nobody near him.

Crazy Gary stared for a long moment then finally smiled, nice and wide, like the two of them were co-conspirators agreeing on a mutual lie.

"Ah, okay, pal. I gotchya." He winked then went on his way.

"Whatever, crazy fuck," Jasper muttered under his breath.

Someone else was approaching.

Jasper turned to see Kenn coming, slowly, casually.

"So, what's it gonna be?"

Jasper looked the man up and down before settling on his eyes, burning with hate and smug with power. He was untouchable in here. He wasn't used to people saying no.

"Do I have a choice?" Jasper asked.

Kenn shook his head.

"No," Jasper said.

Kenn gave him an uncomfortable smile. "You sure about that?"

"Positive."

Kenn laughed, then turned.

Jasper struck, quickly — shiv at the man's neck, in and out, too fast for Kenn to do shit about it. He was already slipping down, blood spurting everywhere.

A sense of movement preceded the shouts — the Aryans raced over to intervene. Jasper tightened his grip on the shiv as the first came at him.

The man collapsed before he could connect. Behind him stood an officer with a stun gun. A half-dozen more followed, moving in to prevent a riot and subdue Jasper.

He dropped the shiv and fell to the ground in surrender.

Dalton got there first, swinging his baton on Jasper's back and ribs, hard enough to break something.

He crawled into a ball, trying to make it clear that he wasn't fighting back.

"I'm workin' a double and you pull this shit?" Hernandez grabbed Jasper, so rough it only compounded the pain in his already aching back and ribs. Still, yanking him out of there probably saved Jasper from an even more brutal beating from Dalton.

Hernandez brought him to the hole, a row of cells away from all the others and under tighter security.

Mission accomplished. Jasper would be safe. For a while.

A lockdown might give him a few more days, but not much beyond that.

Now he was living on borrowed time.

Chapter 5 - Mallory Black

"WHERE THE FUCK IS THIS PLACE?" Mal muttered to herself as the SUV bounced hard on a pothole, the road neglected and bumpy. It was the only paved street in Desanto, a tiny and mostly abandoned town.

Mal passed a poverty-stricken, dirt-covered kid in flip-flops standing in front of his run-down house. The boy was staring at Mal, disinterested enough to make her wonder if he'd ever known joy. He held a deflated red ball in his right hand. An old woman sat on a swing behind him, knitting.

The kid met Mal's gaze. His expression conveyed the desperation of a boy born in the wrong place to the wrong parents, maybe stuck here forever. It pained her to drive past.

Though the town was called Desanto, Mal always thought it should've been called Despair. It was one of the older towns in Creek County, barely a dot on the map. Once home to a hundred and fifty or so cement plant workers, anyone with any sense fled the shitburg after the plant closed a quarter century ago. Remaining residents were either stubborn, delusional in hopes life might one day return, or had surrendered in full. The only trait they all shared was that they were stuck, in both a time and place that had passed them by long ago.

On the vary rare occasions when Mal had driven through town, it felt like she was passing through a fading sepia memory. One main street with old storefronts shuttered long ago. A handful of homes further down, most left to rot or torn to lumber. The cemetery was filled with ancient death and too many weeds.

Her address was a boarded-up church at the end of the street.

Mal arrived first. As she climbed out of her car, Mike pulled up. Skippy was calling it in when she met them at their vehicle.

She drew her gun and approached the church entrance. Mike and Skippy split up, heading around to the rear.

They communicated via radio. Mike reported a board torn away from one of the windows.

Mal and Skippy met up with him.

He nodded, taking the lead as he crawled inside the church through the remnants of a window, shotgun with mounted light piercing the darkness ahead.

Skippy took a position outside in case the suspect was still there and decided to make a run for it.

Mal followed Mike through the window, flashlight in her left hand, right hand aiming her pistol, turning the beam toward the rear of the church as Mike took the front.

She raked her light over a debris-littered floor, broken pews, then a graffitti-covered wall to her right before she heard Mike gasp.

Mal spun east, toward the front of the church and the altar, where her beam blended with her partner's.

Horrified, she froze. Yelped without meaning to. Her

throat washed in copper, her pulse burned with the tears in her eyes.

Any hope of finding Alice alive was gone in one cold shot to the gut.

The young girl was nailed to a large wooden cross, naked, arms spread like the Messiah, legs bound with cord or rope or something dark. She'd been cut open from chest to crotch, and her guts spilled onto the stage. A red candle burned in each of her eyes.

Mal spun around, searching for any sign of the sick fuck responsible for this. Mike was already on his radio, asking Skippy if anyone had come out of the church.

No one had.

Mike called in the murder in as Mal finished sweeping the interior, careful not to destroy any evidence. She headed toward the narthex, making certain their suspect wasn't hiding in the vestibule.

She searched for the killer or evidence, her mind strobing with images of Jessi and Ashley, her daughter murdered by a monster and Jessi traumatized forever.

Even after all this time on the job, even after having such horrible violence personally affect her, Mal still couldn't fathom what could make someone hurt another person. Especially a child, and especially in such a gruesome way. Not that understanding could ever prevent the atrocity.

It wasn't as if these demons walked around announcing their intentions or even looked like the ogres they were. These monsters hid among men. Neighbors, doctors, politicians, teachers, and camp counselors — they could be anyone.

Parents couldn't exactly hide their children from the world.

But still, Mal wished she'd held a tighter leash. She

should have never let Ashley walk home, even with a friend. She should have picked her up from school, or Ray could have done it.

They left their daughter vulnerable instead.

In the end, it was Mal's fault Ashley had been murdered, and there was nothing she could do to ever pretend otherwise or get over her pain.

Mal returned to the nave. She joined Mike and Skippy at the altar, where they were taking preliminary crime scene photos before the forensics team arrived.

Standing among the pews, she couldn't take her eyes off the horror nailed to the cross. This child, who had been a person just hours ago, was now reduced to some sick fuck's prop. One of them would have to tell Alice's mother the horrible news. Part of Mal would rather die.

"What the hell are *these things* on her?" Skippy took a closer look at the girl's side.

Mal couldn't see what he was staring at and started toward the altar.

"Looks like some kind of symbols," Mike said. "This guy a Satanist or something?"

A musical chime, thin and tinny, startled her. She spun around, gun still drawn, then realized it was a ringing. Had the killer dropped his phone?

Could they be so lucky?

She followed the tone to one of the pews where she found a phone sitting on a piece of paper with large black letters.

DETECTIVE BLACK.

What the fuck?

She grabbed it and answered.

"Do you like what I've done with the place?" It was the same man from earlier.

Mal wanted to jump through the phone and rip out his

fucking throat with her teeth. "You said we'd find her alive!"

An infected, raspy laugh. "I said you had to hurry."

"Bullshit. She was dead when you called." Mal was making an assumption, of course. She hadn't examined the body, but it seemed unlikely he was able to stage such a scene, make the call, and get away in such a short amount of time. Unless he'd done everything but gut her.

Had they really just missed saving the girl?

She wanted to vomit, but Mal had to engage with the killer, not show him she was shaken. "What is this? A statement?"

"This is merely the beginning."

"The beginning of what?" Mal asked him.

Is he planning to kill more people? More kids? Stage more horror shows like this?

The monster paused, either for drama or thought, before he finally answered. "This, Detective Black is the beginning of the end. Where the boundaries fall, and all will be revealed."

"When what—" Mal started.

But the monster was already gone.

Chapter 6 - Howard Loomis

TWO WEEKS AGO ...

HOWARD ONLY HAD twenty minutes for lunch before his next appointment. His last install had gone an hour over, and he had another two ahead of his next break. He was starving and, of course, the line at Sloppy's drive-thru was insanely long.

He sighed as he pulled his Titan Security van into a parking spot. After climbing out of the vehicle and stretching his aching back, he shuffled inside the joint then got in line.

There were only two groups in front of him — an elderly couple at the register and a pair of petite college-aged girls. A black girl wearing tight jeans and a tank top stood next to a tanned brunette in denim shorts and an itty-bitty red bikini top. They chatted to each other while scrolling bullshit on their phones.

Howard looked down at the brunette, admiring the tan

lines peeking out from under her top. He wanted to see more, wished he could reach out and pull her shirt aside.

The brunette absentmindedly adjusted her top as she scrolled through her LiveLyfe feed, pulling it out and up a bit, giving him a glimpse of more white flesh and a blushing nipple. Her tits were big, begging for his gaze.

Howard felt a rush of excitement as she continued adjusting the top. He imagined her turning to him, taking it off, then begging him to grab her tits.

What I wouldn't give to just touch them.

He would play this fantasy in his head when masturbating later, before descending into a shame spiral in which his mother would scold him for being such a wicked little masturbator, reminding him yet again that he was doomed to spend an eternity in hell.

Howard wished he could pull out his camera and capture a photo or video to help him remember her better, but he was in his work uniform, and civilized society viewed men sneaking creep shots as disgusting or, in the case of men attempting to get upskirts, as lawbreakers.

If only polite society knew how many of his customers' webcams he accessed from his home, how many he watched as he imagined the things he would do to them. How many women had their most intimate moments recorded by him while they were alone or in bed with their lovers.

Howard wanted to remember this girl, to record her. But he couldn't. He needed his job too much for a bust. So, he stared instead, doing his best to commit her perfect tits to memory.

Until she turned and caught him.

Damn it.

Time froze as the brunette stared him up and down,

the slow crawl of her gaze allowing her to document his shame and horror in morbid detail.

Her mouth distorted in a disgusted snarl, her eyebrow arched. "Yuck."

The black girl looked at her friend then at Howard. They laughed before moving up to the register.

Howard turned away, his cheeks hot with anger and embarrassment. Anger at the level of disgust she had for him and her contemptuous laugh. Embarrassment that he'd been caught practically drooling like a weak-minded idiot.

Who the hell does she think she *is?*

She was young, fit, tan, and beautiful. He wasn't even close to her type, or *anyone's*. At six foot six and four hundred and nine pounds, Howard Loomis was an unsightly giant.

His greasy dark hair was thinning, and he had a fat face. His piggish nose drew ridicule from girls and had ever since childhood. Coke-bottle glasses made his brown eyes look cartoonishly large. He was practically the poster child for Fat Virgin Thirty-Something Losers. He had a job and a house, but the gig was unfulfilling and the home wasn't his. He still lived with his mother in a shitheap that looked ancient a decade ago.

The brunette wasn't the kind of girl who would ever give Howard a chance. Judging by her appearance, the superficial chatter with her friend, and the way she was glued to her phone, she was just another moron in a world that reveled in stupidity.

But that world was about to change.

The End was coming, and girls like this would be wise to be kind to Howard. Because when The End came, he would be one of the few to thrive.

Howard wasn't sure when The End was coming. Mister

K said it would be soon. But he'd been promising that for many years. For now, he was meant to suffer and to learn, to prepare himself, to follow Mister K's teachings. His suffering would end soon, and his loyalty would be rewarded. Howard would thrive in this new world and see his righteousness rewarded.

He smiled, imagining girls like these writhing in misery as the demons spilled forth from the depths of Hell and split them where they stood. See how their silly little iPhones and their overpriced lattes would help them then.

The brunette glanced back to see if Howard was looking as her friend ordered, but he refused to give her the pleasure. He no longer found her attractive. The girl's ugly demeanor had twisted her into a troll. He wouldn't let her suck his dick if she begged.

They moved to the side, waiting for their food as Howard stepped up to place his order.

Two True Americans, a large fry, and two large Cokes.

He heard the girls giggling as they filled their drinks at the station, could feel them looking at him, probably making fun of his unhealthy order.

"Oh, my God, could you imagine?" one of them said.

Imagine what? Screwing me?

Bitches.

He got his cups then walked over to the beverage dispenser.

The brunette stood in his way, pretending not to see him as she sipped her soda and talked to her friend.

"Excuse me," he said.

She looked back and up at him before moving without a word.

The cashier called them to pick up their order. As the girls got their food, Howard filled the first cup with ice and Coke. He put on the lid then set it aside. One Coke for now and another for later. While he filled the second, the girls sat at a table near the front. When the cashier announced his order was up, he slapped a lid on his second drink then grabbed both cups.

On his way to the counter, one of the lids slipped off. He tried to right it, but the cup slipped from his hand. In an instinctive attempt to catch it before it hit the floor and made a mess, Howard also lost his hold on the second cup.

They hit the ground and exploded, spraying soda and ice all over his pants and the floor.

The girls burst into laughter.

"What a fucking loser," one of them said.

Howard was burning hot, panic swelling inside him. If anything else happened, he was going to lose his shit.

He looked at the cashier behind the counter, who looked annoyed at the mess she would have to clean up.

His face grew hotter. His hands began to tremble. He had to get out. Now.

Howard didn't even wait for his food. Instead, he rushed through the doors then out to his van, the sound of the girls laughing like the soundtrack to his nightmares playing behind him.

He closed his eyes inside the van. Turned the engine, cranked the AC.

Relax.

Just relax.

Howard wished he had his mask, but he never brought it to work. He only wore it at home or when peeping through windows. He'd have to get calm on his own.

They'd shaken him from the confidence he managed to carry at work, and he hated them for it. If he didn't calm down, he'd be a stumbling, bumbling mess when he got to his next call.

He counted backward from fifty until he felt a little

calmer. Then he opened his eyes and turned on the radio. Voices crackled as the station's signal got lost in static.

Howard heard a voice, the one he'd known since he was a teenager.

Mister K was the *something* that had been missing from his life, the something that promised to give him the answers he so desperately needed.

"Hello, Howard."

Even now, the deep, distorted voice still unnerved him.

With a tremble even evident in his words, he said, "Hello?"

"Why do you let them mock you? Laugh at you?"

"I don't know. It doesn't matter."

"It *does* matter. If you refuse to command their respect, then you are not worthy of my knowledge."

"Please," Howard said, too aware he was groveling and Mister K hated his weakness. "I will command respect."

"How?"

"I don't know. Next time I'll say something."

"*Next time?* Yes, I suppose you can wait until next time to stand up for yourself and be a man." Laughter got lost in the static. It sounded like his mother, but that was impossible.

He felt ashamed, insignificant, and small. "It's too late to do anything about it now."

Silence. Then the radio resumed the talk show, and Mister K was gone.

Howard had disappointed the entity.

He hated himself even more.

Sitting in the van, he glared at the entrance to Sloppy's, the girls' laughter echoing in his mind.

He should have stood up for himself.

Howard watched as the doors opened. The girls came out carrying drinks and chatting as they walked toward a white Ford Fiesta. Of course they didn't notice him sitting in his van. They were too self-absorbed in themselves and their phones.

They didn't seem to notice him as he followed their car out of the lot. Nor did they seem to notice him as he pulled up behind them at their gated community.

Of course they didn't.

After they used their key card to get through security gate, Howard waited long enough so they wouldn't notice him following but moved fast enough to pass through before the panel swung shut.

He trailed them through the parking lot as they made their way to Building 10 in the back of the complex. When they parked, Howard kept driving, slowly, keeping an eye on them as they got out of their Fiesta then walked to their first-floor apartment. He noted the number for another time.

He would return to command their respect and prove himself worthy.

Chapter 7 - Jasper Parish

JASPER REALIZED something on his third day in the hall —
he needed to be around people.

Odd, given he'd been virtually alone ever since Jordyn's
death. He'd felt alone most of his life, except for when he
had a wife and then a daughter. But even though Jordyn
was gone, she had visited him countless times, along with
Carissa and his old mentor, Lenny Barnes.

Until prison.

The forced medications kept them away and made him
truly alone. He had to pay for his sins, for the deaths of
innocents and Spider's coma. He needed to be punished.
But hadn't thought through this part of his imprisonment.

Now Jordyn, Carissa, and Lenny were gone.

There was some debate as to whether they visited him
or were manifestations of his altered personalities. Shrinks
thought they were all in his head. Jasper thought something else.

He wasn't sure if they were ghosts, echoes of energy
left behind, or something else he couldn't understand. But
he didn't think they were in his head. That was a narrow

viewpoint. Unexplainable phenomena didn't mean impossible. His psychic abilities shouldn't exist, yet he routinely predicted events that nobody could randomly guess. Jasper could win the lottery for Mallory Black and place enough bets to make a nice little nest egg to fund his vigilante activities.

Unexplainable, sure, but he refused to believe his relationship with Jordyn was gone. He couldn't access her in a medicated state and needed to do something about that.

But what?

The guards were assholes when it came to forcing his meds. He might be able to occasionally fool one of them, but there were never more than a couple of days in a row without one of them shoving gloved fingers into his mouth to prove that he'd swallowed them.

The hole wasn't all that different from his usual pod, save for a few differences. It had its own shower that was turned on for ten minutes every other day. Had only one bunk instead of two. And there was the undiluted loneliness broken only by the two meals that came through a slot in the door and some face time while he was forced to take his pills.

Jasper paced and tried to steer his mind from the void that threatened to swallow him. Instead of dwelling on the pills and what they did to his mind, he focused on his body and every step he took.

But that only worked if he kept moving. And no matter how fit a man was, he couldn't walk forever.

After just three days, he was desperate for contact. It shouldn't be so easy to break a man.

You were already broken, dumbass.

The thought was his, but it came in Lenny's voice.

Jasper looked around the pod, but he saw only the same four fucking walls. The lights would soon die for the night, plunging him into a darkness that felt eternal in the hole, leaving him alone with his thoughts and regrets.

Hell.

He listened, waiting for another message. If he could hear Lenny, maybe Jordyn would be next. Carissa might finally talk to him again. But how could he convince his jailers to not medicate him? How could he get them to break the rules? What was in it for them?

A buzzing preceded the release of locks.

"Stay on your bunk," Hernandez said.

Jasper sat and waited.

Hernandez entered for the second night in a row.

"You get transferred to Mac duty?" Jasper asked, making a light attempt at conversation.

He held out a gloved hand with the cup of pills. "Open up, *Mac.*"

It was the first indication Hernandez was aware of his true identity. Only the warden, and perhaps a few other higher-ups, were supposed to know. But Kenn called him out on being a cop, and Hernandez seemed to know something, as well.

"I need to ask you something."

"Come on, I got shit to do," Hernandez said.

"Do you know who I am?"

"Yeah, prisoner oh-four-six-seven—"

"You know who I am and what I did. *Right?*"

"You gonna tell me you're not guilty or some shit? Or threaten me?" He looked about ten seconds from drawing his baton.

"I'm psychic. You heard that, right?"

Hernandez stared at him, impatiently waiting for Jasper to find his point.

He had to rush through the next part, telling the corrections officer how he was able to know that Jessi Price was in danger, how he knew other men he'd admitted to killing had done what they'd done, even after getting away with their crimes. It was a lot to get through, and Jasper had to rush, thoroughly botching it and coming off like a desperate lunatic.

"So, what's your point? You want me to treat you special because you killed bad guys? You're still a killer."

"That's not what I'm saying."

"What do you want? You're on my last nerve."

"I can help you."

Hernandez rolled his eyes. "Open up and take your meds."

"Let me go a couple days, maybe three, and I guarantee I can help you."

"Help me with what?"

"I can't access my abilities while I'm on the meds, so I don't know yet."

"I don't need your help. Now, take your meds. Or I'm gonna make it difficult."

Jasper swallowed his pills.

Hernandez left, the door buzzed and locked, then the lights went out, casting Jasper into another dark and lonely night.

A regular thought came calling.

Maybe it would have been better if Kenn had just killed me.

Chapter 8 - Mallory Black

CLAUDE BARRY LEANED back in his huge desk with his gaudy cowboy boots propped up on it like he was the redneck king of Creek County instead of its sheriff. The man was tall with broad shoulders and a long face, big ears and droopy jowls to match his low hanging eyes. The aged spawn of a Bulldog and a human.

Mike was bringing him up to speed on the Alice Shaw case. Mal and Skippy stood silently behind him.

"So, you're sayin' we got some Satanist serial killer out there? What the fuck?"

"I don't know if he's a Satanist, per se," Mike said. "I've put in a call to a professor from University of Florida to ask him to look at some of the symbols carved into the body. We're also reviewing security footage from the library, but they only keep back-ups for a week, so I'm not counting on anything. No prints or anything from the book itself."

"And have you informed the girl's mother yet?"

"No, sir."

"Mal, you handle that while the boys go and talk to the people around that church and whatnot," Barry said.

"Sir, I think I'd be better in the field. Can't you have Reynolds inform her?"

"No." Barry brought his feet down and sat up. "The news should come from a woman. Besides, I'm sure you can use the rest, what with the panic attacks. Inform the mother, then take the rest of the day—"

"Are you serious? There's a potential serial killer out there who contacted *me directly*. I don't need to rest, boss. I'm fine."

"She's right, sir. Stan can inform Mrs. Shaw. I think Mal's experience is invaluable here."

Barry glared at Mike. He didn't like Mal talking back to him, and certainly didn't like a second deputy questioning him, especially in front of a younger deputy.

"This isn't up for debate. I've made my decision."

"Yes, sir," Mike said, turning to leave.

Mal wasn't sure what she expected her partner to say, but she was pissed that he didn't make more of an effort to bring her on board. Skippy nodded at Barry then followed Mike out.

Mal turned to follow then stopped short of the door. She closed it and turned around.

Barry looked up at her, surprise raising his eyebrows. "Yes, Miss Black?"

"What's your problem with me?"

Denial, feigned shock at the accusation, or for Barry to laugh it off — Mal wasn't sure what she expected, but whatever it was, she wasn't prepared for what he did instead.

"I don't much like you, Miss Black," he said, meeting her gaze with a cold stare. "Not only were you a traitor going behind my back when I hired you to campaign for

Bell, you disgraced this department with your hysterics, drunken behavior, and unending sense of entitlement. The only reason you still have a job is because Mike vouched for you and promised to keep you on a short leash. But you're skating on very thin ice, young lady. And I suggest you simmer down and learn your place, or I'll bounce your ass out of here so fast you won't even know what hit you. And before you get any bright ideas of going to the media or trying to oust me, know this. *I've enough dirt to bury you twice.*"

Mal stared back at him, dumbstruck. Not at his candor. She knew Barry hated her. She was stunned that Mike had agreed to keep her "in check."

Was that a lie to sow dissension between Mal and her partner, or was Barry telling the truth? She thought back on how he'd backed down, and about how he'd been different with her lately, taking the lead in investigations and interrogations when he'd always been more laid back, letting whoever had the ball take the lead.

Is he keeping me in check?

She also wondered what "dirt" Barry might have. Had he been having her followed? Did Cameron Ford find something?

Does someone know I killed Dodd?

Do they know of my conversations with Jasper?

Both seemed unlikely. That knowledge would've come out and been used against her already.

Unless they're saving it for blackmail, get me to play ball on something big.

Her chest tightened. Pulse raced as the walls closed in around her.

Fuck, not now, not now!

Barry took Mal's silence as his cue to dismiss her. "I've got work to do if there's nothing else. Maybe you ought to tell that poor girl's parents before the news, don't ya' think?"

Mal left without another word. The panic attack was making her feel weak, like she'd allowed him to win. She wanted to blow up at him, tell him to come at her or back the fuck off, but she'd flown off the handle far too many times in the past and was working to be less volatile. To prove she was better.

Who knew what would happen if she exploded while having a panic attack?

She went to the restroom, dug into her jacket for the Xanax, then swallowed one dry, hating that her first response to stress was to take yet another pill. From painkillers to Xanax, Mal was an addict.

Not that she was taking enough to get high. Mal wasn't even sure she'd like the Xanax high, and she wasn't dumb enough to mix it with other shit. God only knew what would happen then. Plus, she was committed to staying sober.

Mal left the station in silence. Got in her car and pounded the wheel with her fists. Just once, not a full-on assault this time. She backed out then headed to the hospital to deliver a round of terrible news. With any luck, McKenna Shaw would be out of her coma and maybe would have something to help them find her sister's killer.

But Mal wasn't feeling hopeful.

The Xanax would kick in soon. Then she would feel even less.

～

MAL WAS TOO LATE.

By the time she arrived at the hospital, news had already broken that Alice's body had been discovered and crucified. The story was picked up from the local CBS affiliate by national media outlets and was everywhere immediately. Mal wanted to find out who the hell had leaked the news, but it was pointless now.

Sheila was in a full meltdown by the time Mal found her.

"What did he do to my daughter?" Sheila wailed as she approached the waiting room.

There were about twelve other people in the waiting room, including a family of five with three young kids. All of them watching.

"Why don't we take a walk?" Mal suggested.

"No! Tell me what happened. Did they really ..."

Sheila couldn't finish, stopping to sob in her arms instead.

Mal was numbed by the pill, but even so, she still felt a terrible aching for the woman. She'd delivered this news before, but Mal had also been the recipient — *your daughter's body has been found.*

It never got any easier.

"Come." Mal led Sheila from the waiting room then down the hall toward a quiet second-story walkway between two buildings.

She delivered the details, leaving out the more gruesome ones and hoping no one would leak any crime scene photos. No mother should have to see their kid dead on blogs or message boards or LiveLyfe.

Mal allowed her to cry and answered all of Sheila's questions she could before steering the conversation toward her own. "Any news on McKenna yet?"

"No." Sheila blew her nose and stared out the window.

"Is there anyone you can think of who might have done this to Alice?"

"Who would do this?" Sheila looked back at Mal,

perplexed and shaking her head. "No. I can't think of anyone so sick and twisted."

"The girls were walking home from church, right? Is your family very religious?"

"*Very religious?* No. We're believers but not Bible thumpers, if that's what you're asking. If I were more religious, maybe I would have been in church instead of working on a Sunday." Sheila started crying again.

"You're a single mom working to keep food on the table. Can't beat yourself up about that. I'm sure God doesn't mind."

"Why do you ask?" Sheila asked after catching her breath.

"The religious nature of the crime. We're exploring all possibilities. Is there anyone at church you've had disagreements with or who paid an inordinate amount of attention to your girls?"

Sheila kept staring out the window, thinking. "Not that I can think of. It's a small church. Everybody's nice there. No problems."

"Is there anyone else you can think of? Neighbors? People who worked at your house? Anyone who seemed a bit off?"

"I can't think of anybody … I've already answered all of this."

"I'm sorry. Sometimes it helps to ask questions a few times. The mind tends to remember things later that it might not in the moment."

Mal kept talking to her, mining as many details as possible about the girls without adding further stress to their mother. Fifteen minutes later, she got a call on her police-issued phone then excused herself, adding distance between her and Sheila before taking the call.

"Detective Black," she answered.

"Hey, it's Deputy Travers. I've got a girl over at Coleman's that got nabbed for shoplifting. I recognized her as one of your prior cases and thought I'd give you a call."

"Who is it?"

"Katie Turner."

She swallowed and sighed. "I'll be right there."

Chapter 9 - Jasper Parish

JASPER'S HEAD KEPT BUZZING. He felt like someone or something kept squeezing it to send fresh waves of stabbing pain into his brain.

He paced his cell, feeling itchy, antsy. Like his clothes were biting into his skin. He ripped off his shirt and grunted as he tossed it onto the bed.

Get a hold of yourself, damn it. You're fine.

"Lenny?" Jasper called out, spinning around, searching for his old coach but finding himself still alone.

The walls shuddered as an ear-piercing buzz sent him to his knees. He covered his ears, feeling like his head might explode, painting his brain all over the walls and floor.

Gritting his teeth, Jasper tried to brace himself against the intensifying pain.

The door unlocked. Time for his meds.

"Sit on your bed," Hernandez said.

Jasper sat, his cheeks wet with tears. He covered his face, ashamed of the pain, thinking Hernandez would think he was faking or had lost his few remaining marbles.

Maybe they'd shove him in a mental hospital, and maybe that would be better.

Except then you'll never see them again.

Now his own voice instead of Lenny's warned Jasper to keep his shit together.

"What's the problem?" Hernandez asked.

"Please," he looked up, crying. "Don't make me take the meds."

Hernandez was quiet.

A moment of hope swelled inside Jasper.

"I looked into your case," Hernandez said. "How did you know?"

"I told you, I see things."

"Fucking psychic?"

"Come on. I'm not a threat to anyone. I can only convince you if you give me a chance. Keep me locked in the hole as long as you need, I don't care. Just ... don't make me take the meds."

"Why'd you kill Kenn?"

"He was trying to force me to kill Wally."

Hernandez's face shifted ever so slightly.

Fuck, someone had gotten to Wally.

"Did ... something happen to him?"

"Yeah, another prisoner got him in the mess hall."

"You know who did it?"

"Nope. Nobody's talking. It was in the middle of a ruckus. Don't think it was the Aryans, though."

"They were doing a job for someone else."

"Who?"

"Will you let me go a few days without making me take the pills if I tell you?"

Hernandez shook his head and sighed. "Why'd you kill that businessman's kid and the girl?"

"I didn't kill the girl. Calum did. But she facilitated my

daughter's rape, made her life a hell until she killed herself."

Hernandez nodded.

The man shared his pain, Jasper could feel it. Maybe not a daughter, but he'd lost someone, and in a similar way. He considered pressing but backed off, knowing how easily it might backfire. Nobody liked having their loved ones used as pieces in a game. He could wait Hernandez out.

"I never killed anyone who didn't deserve it."

"Then why confess? You didn't put up a fight at all, admitted to shit we didn't even have on you. Why?"

"Because I caused a lot of innocent people pain. I don't deny that I need to be punished. I … I just can't take these pills. Let me prove it. I can help you."

"Help me, *how*?"

"You play the lottery?"

"You can tell me the winning lotto numbers?" Hernandez laughed.

"Guessed 'em before."

"Bullshit. You've won the lotto?"

Jasper couldn't tell him that he gave Mallory the winning ticket. Hernandez probably didn't even know her, but it wouldn't take long to tie Mallory to him and likely ruin her life.

"I was a ghost, remember? Faked being dead. Would've been hard to cash in a ticket, but I've guessed the winning numbers too many times to be a coincidence."

"No." Hernandez stared at Jasper then shook his head. "No fucking way. You guessed the winning numbers multiple times and didn't find a way to cash in a ticket or get someone else to do it for you?"

"I didn't say I didn't make *any* money. I found other ways — mostly bets. But I just needed enough to live off the grid and do what I was doing. It was never about the money."

"So, you're gonna give me winning lotto numbers if I help you?"

"I can't promise that, but I guarantee I'll find some way to help you right back. Stuff just comes to me. And if I don't help you, then put me back on the pills. No harm, no foul. Not like I'm gonna hurt anyone from here even if I did go fully mental."

"Man, I don't know. And besides, I don't even work every night. *If* I do this, I'm not letting anyone else know. You're gonna have to take the meds on nights I don't got rounds, unless you can find a way to avoid swallowing 'em."

"Whatever, man. Just … please."

Hernandez stared for a long, quiet moment. Jasper could tell the guard clearly didn't trust him. But he could also see belief. Something deep inside this man had been convinced by something he'd found out or that Jasper had said. Maybe he was in a desperate situation he really needed help with.

But Hernandez had a job to do and didn't seem in the least bit corrupt. He took pride in his work, in doing the right thing. Jasper had once been a lot like this man.

He didn't beg or plead anymore. He would have to battle it out in his mind.

Hernandez stepped toward Jasper with the cup.

Fuck. He's gonna make me take—

But then he kept walking, dumping the pills into the toilet.

He raised a finger to shhh the prisoner. *Our little secret.*

"Now, tell me what you know about the hit on Wally."

Jasper snitched and told him everything he knew.

"You've got four days to prove yourself," Hernandez said before leaving.

Jasper closed his eyes, hoping something would come to him in time.

If not, he'd probably never see Carissa or Jordyn again.

Chapter 10 - Mallory Black

MAL ARRIVED at the department store where Deputy Will Travers was waiting outside in his cruiser. He sat in the front seat on his laptop. Katie waited in the back, looking a lot different than the last time Mal had seen her. Then she'd been a scrawny, fifteen-year-old blonde, dressed only in long and modest dresses that would have been old when ordered from a Sears Catalogue decades ago.

Now she looked like the average fifteen or sixteen-year-old girl, trying to overcome a lifetime of being forced to dress conservatively by her overly religious parents by going the other way. Too much makeup, hair dyed with pink and purple streaks. Heavy eyeliner and ravines of mascara. Mal couldn't see what else she was wearing beyond her black leather jacket, but figured her whole outfit was probably designed to piss her foster parents right the fuck off.

After years of oppression under an abusive and overly religious father, Katie was probably finally feeling some hyper version of her teenage rebellion.

Mal felt bad for not having checked on the girl since

her father had murdered her mother. She told herself it was best not to check directly with Katie since the girl blamed Mal for her mother's death. Katie felt Mal should never have pressed so hard for her mother to leave.

Fuck. First Katie then Maggie and Emma.

Every time I try to help someone, I only make things worse and get good people killed.

Still, Mal could have checked with Katie's foster parents. The Andersons were good people, from what Carrie Thompson in Victim Services had told her.

Travers got out of the car as Mal approached on foot. "How's it going?"

"Okay," Mal said. "Thanks for calling. What happened?"

"Got caught stealing a watch."

"A watch? For what?"

"Wouldn't say. Was lucky to get a name out of her. She looks tough, but you can tell she's terrified, so I figured I'd call you."

"Does the store want to press charges?"

"I think they can be persuaded not to."

"Can you do that while I talk to her?"

"Sure thing. You want to bring her home and talk to her parents, or should I?"

"I've got it. Thank you," Mal said as Travers opened the door.

Katie looked at Mal and shook her head, pursing her lips. After she climbed out of the back seat, Travers removed her cuffs.

"Detective Black is going to take you home."

Katie wouldn't even look at her and seemed a hiccup from crying.

"Let's go," Mal said, walking Katie to her unmarked SUV.

She opened the door then Katie got in, still not looking at her or saying a word.

Mal drew a deep breath and shut the door, then she circled around to the driver's side. "Where do the Andersons live?"

"Oh, I don't live with them."

"What?"

"It wasn't working out."

"What happened?" Mal seemed to remember Carrie saying they were at their limit already with three fosters and two of their own *before* Katie.

"I guess the problem is me." Katie looked down at her hands, at the cuts on her right wrist. When she saw Mal looking, she tugged her sleeve down to cover it.

"Self-harm or suicide attempt?"

"Does it matter?" Katie turned away to stare out the window.

"You've been through a lot. Do you have anybody to talk to?"

"They made me see a doctor, but it wasn't working out. She just wanted to put me on drugs."

Mal had to be careful. She wanted to find out what was happening but had no relationship with Katie other than being the person who fucked up her life. She had to establish a bond.

"Do you mind if we make a pit stop? I haven't eaten anything, and I'm starving."

"Sure ... I guess."

"You hungry?"

"I could eat."

"What are you in the mood for?" Mal asked.

"Whatever. I don't have any money, though."

Mal wanted to ask what she was doing in a store

without any money, but attacking the girl now would only shut her down.

Terrazzo's had big private booths. "Like Italian?"

"Yeah," Katie said.

So, Terrazzo's it was.

～

TERRAZZO'S WAS RELATIVELY quiet for dinnertime on a Sunday. They were sitting in a high-backed booth with the closest patrons two empty tables away. The aroma of freshly baked garlic rolls made Mal's mouth water before she was even seated.

Katie spoke only to order her single slice of pepperoni. Mal ordered a slice of cheese and a half-dozen garlic rolls. After several minutes of silence, Mal finally broached the obvious topic while they waited for their food to arrive.

"So, what happened at the store?"

Katie sipped at her Dr. Pepper and shrugged. "I put it in my jacket and forgot. It was an accident." She looked down at her fingers, folding the straw wrapper into ever smaller and tighter squares.

"Bullshit."

Katie looked up, eyes wide for just a moment before her gaze fell back on the table. She crossed her arms then looked back up at Mal. "I dunno."

"So, you don't know why you stole it?"

"It doesn't matter. You won't believe me, anyway."

"Try me."

Katie sighed.

Mal took a drink of her Coke. "Seriously. You can talk to me."

Her jaw clenched. Katie wanted to say something but bit her tongue.

"What is it?"

"Last time I talked to you, my dad killed my mom."

"I'm sorry about that."

"I trusted you. I thought you were going to help. But you *didn't*. You got my mom killed instead. You … should've just let things be."

"I'm sorry about what happened. I truly am, Katie. But you know as well as I do that your father was always dangerous. Whatever you're going through, you don't have to feel alone, I promise you can talk to me. That you can trust—"

The server brought their food.

Katie wiped at her eyes and looked away from the girl as she set their plates on the table.

"Anything else I can get you? Need red pepper or garlic or anything?"

Mal waited a moment, but Katie didn't respond. "No. We're good. Thank you."

The server left, and Mal grabbed a garlic roll. She tore it apart and watched the steam rise from it, inhaling the buttery garlic aroma. "Have you had their rolls before?"

"Never been here."

"Try them." Mal knew she ran the risk of coming off like she wasn't taking Katie seriously enough, but she needed to settle the mood.

Katie grabbed a roll and took a bite.

"Good, am I right?"

Katie nodded and offered her a half-hearted, "Yeah."

They ate in silence. Mal was letting the girl decide when to start talking.

It took a while, but she eventually said, "I took the watch for a guy I like."

"Oh? Who is he?"

"Just a guy. He's nice."

"How'd you meet?"

"He works at Hill of Beans. I go in there after school."

"You two dating?"

"We've hung out a few times." Katie looked away. Clearly, she felt some shame, but Mal couldn't be certain if it was because the guy was a piece of shit or if Katie was feeling guilty thanks to being raised by such an overbearing religious father.

"Did he ask you to take the watch?"

"No. I just wanted to give him something nice for his birthday."

"How old is he?"

Again, she looked away.

Mal feared the worst. Katie had been groomed by her soccer coach when she was fourteen, lured into a sexual relationship she couldn't legally consent to. Was another older man grooming her? Was Katie trying to fill that void in her life with another abusive man?

"How old is he?" Mal repeated.

"Relax. He's a few years older than me. I don't have money or a way to earn any. Ben took my allowance away."

"That your foster father? Why'd he do that?"

"Because my grades are bad. I … I really don't fit in at school. The few friends I did make weren't good enough for Ben and Sarah. They said they were 'bad influences.' They're almost as controlling as my dad was."

"That sucks. So, you don't have any friends?"

"Only James."

"James, being the guy you like?"

"Yeah."

"He go to your school?"

"I think he dropped out."

Mal wasn't buying it, but she also wasn't about to press

Katie on it now. After a few bites of pizza, she nodded at her wrists. "Is that cutting or did you try killing yourself?"

Katie shifted in her seat. "I tried to end it. That's why the first family kicked me out."

"Damn."

"They were afraid to have me around after that. Not sure if they were scared I'd try it again or that I'd hurt one of the other kids."

"Did you get along with those kids?"

"No, not really. They weren't mean or anything, but they didn't like me. I'm not like most kids my age."

"I wasn't, either."

"And how'd that work out for you?"

"Honestly? I struggled for a long time. But, at some point, I decided to stop giving a fuck about what others thought of me. That's how you find the right friends — people who will accept you as you are."

"James accepts me."

"Good," Mal said.

"I think he's the only one."

Mal let that sit, using an interrogation room technique — silence — to loosen the suspect.

"What are you going to tell my fosters?" Katie asked, after breaking the quiet.

"What do you *want* me to tell them?"

"Nothing? I'm kind of on their last nerve. If I screw up again, I'm sure they'll kick me out. I really don't wanna go back to the group home or get carted off to another family."

"If I don't say anything, I need you to promise me two things."

"What's that?"

"No guy is worth going to jail over. That means, no stealing."

"Okay," she sighed. "What else?"

"I want to follow up with you. So, lunch next week?"

"You buying again?"

"If you say yes."

"Then, yes." And, for the slightest moment, Katie showed her the hint of a smile.

A miniature victory, but Mal would take every possible win.

Chapter 11 - Howard Loomis Age 10

HOWIE HAD HOPED the middle schoolers wouldn't see him if he passed across the street from the basketball courts. They got out almost forty minutes earlier than the elementary school kids, and this was the worst part of his walk home, by far.

"Hey, fat ass!" one of them called out.

Howie pretended not to hear them. Maybe they'd leave him alone this time.

He was running out of things to give them and hoped today they wouldn't demand their tax to let him pass. He'd already given them money, snacks he'd purposely not eaten at lunch, comic books, and toys. If Howie had nothing, they'd usually ask him where he wanted to be punched.

He chose the arm every time, somewhere Mom wouldn't notice. Still, sometimes they socked him in the stomach.

"That must be jelly 'cause jam don't shake like that!" one of them shouted, followed by a chorus of laughter.

Howie wasn't sure what that phrase meant, but it was probably about his belly. The doctors had said he was morbidly obese. Howie had looked up the word morbid and found two meanings. The first was what the doctor had probably meant, something to do with disease. But the other definition applied to Howie as well — an abnormal fascination or unhealthy interest in disturbing things, especially death.

The doctor didn't know that, nor did anyone else. What would people think if he admitted some of the things he thought about? What would they think if they saw the drawings he kept under the toy box in the back of his closet?

Howie hadn't always hidden his drawings. But Mom flipped out after seeing something he'd made with markers in his art pad when he was only eight-years-old. A naked lady, or his best imagining of one from what he'd seen on the magazine covers at the bookstore, anyway.

But it wasn't *just* a naked lady.

The woman was cut in half, with blood everywhere. Howie wasn't sure *why* he'd drawn her like that, other than his fascinations with both female bodies and death. Mom made him rip up the "obscenity" before she beat him with an old leather belt until he renounced Satan's influence in the midst of his screaming. But Howie didn't think it was the Devil. He was interested in women's bodies and death because they were both so mysterious to him.

But Mom was never wrong. She said it was Satan's influence, so it must've been.

Howie tried hard not to think about either women or death anymore. And every time he slipped, he prayed for God's forgiveness even harder than the last time.

"Hey, fatty!" one of the kids called again.

Just keep walking.

He walked as fast as he dared without breaking into a

run. They'd be on him in seconds if he tried, then they would *all* get a shot at him.

That's how it usually went.

He heard footsteps moving fast.

Oh, no!

Howie turned and saw his usual five tormentors running toward the basketball court gate.

He couldn't let them catch him but was too slow for escape.

So, he stopped, turned around, waited. He didn't know their names. Howie knew one of them. The redhead, an older brother of a kid in his class. Liam always picked on him, too.

Apparently, the redhead was their leader. "Hey, fat ass. What you got for us today?"

The other boys laughed as they eyed him up and down. Howie wasn't good at reading people's faces, but he knew enough to understand they were mean, despite their laughter and smiles.

"I don't have anything." Howie shook his head.

"Lemme see." The redhead held out his hand. "Gimme your backpack."

Howie took off his backpack then handed it over.

The kid started yanking everything out of it, tossing his books and notepads onto the sidewalk. Wind blew the loose papers. Howie went to chase them, but one of the other kids stepped in front of him and thrust a finger hard into his chest. "Let it go."

Howie obeyed.

The redhead looked up at Howie. "What the fuck, man? No comics?"

Howie shook his head. "I don't have any more. My mom stopped letting me get them."

"Well, tell your mom she's a cunt."

The others laughed.

Howie didn't know what a cunt was, but it had to be a bad word.

The redhead got up in Howie's face, so close Howie could smell his hot and reeking breath. "Well, this ain't gonna do. You can't pass."

"But I need to get home."

"Then you'd better give me something."

Howie looked at the ground. His pencil case was a *Star Wars* one Mom's boyfriend had given him. It was special to him, even though he wasn't allowed to see the movies.

"You want my Star Wars pencil case?" Howie offered.

The redhead looked at his friends. They were all being quiet. Howie wasn't sure what they were thinking.

"No, I don't want your fucking pencil case!" shouted the redhead.

Howie looked around for something else. He couldn't give them his school books. And his notepads had his schoolwork in them. He'd get in a lot of trouble if he gave those away.

He felt his pockets then dug inside them, hoping to maybe find some change or something of value.

The redhead looked down at Howie's empty hands, then at his pants. "Give me your pants."

"What?"

"If you want to pass, give me your pants."

"Um, I can't give you my pants," Howie said, laughing nervously.

One of the other kids stepped forward, a skinny one with a blue T-shirt, long brown hair like a curtain in his face. "Give us your pants or we'll kill you."

Kill?

Howie stared at the boy. Surely, he didn't mean *kill* kill, did he?

"Kill?" Howie repeated.

The redhead nodded. "We will kill you and your cunt mom. Give us your pants."

He couldn't let them hurt his mom. She was strict and Howie was scared of her, but he didn't want anything bad to happen to her.

More laughter as he unbuckled his pants.

He struggled to get the jeans over his sneakers, but then finally got them all the way off. Howie was afraid if he removed his shoes, they'd ask for those instead of, or in addition to, his pants. He'd already gone home without his shoes once, when they were stolen from his locker, and Mom beat him so bad he couldn't sit for two days.

He fell on his ass trying to pull off his jeans.

More laughing.

Finally, he got his feet free of the pants.

"Nice tighty-whities," said one of the kids, pointing to his underwear.

Howie stood then handed his jeans to the redhead.

He threw them to the kid in a blue T-shirt.

"Eew," he said, quickly tossing it to someone else.

They played hot potato. Howie hoped if he sat and waited, they'd eventually get bored and throw the pants back at him.

Instead, they all took off with them.

"Next time, you better bring two things!" the redhead called over his shoulder.

Howie stared at his school supplies scattered on the sidewalk and grass, then scrambled after them, stuffing them back into his bag. He still wanted to chase the papers, but not in his underwear.

He needed to be inside before Mom got home from work.

~

HOWIE REALIZED with horror that his house keys had been in his pocket.

No, no, no, no!

Tears tickled his cheeks as he realized he'd have to wait a few hours for Mom to get back. She'd see he was in his underwear, and he'd get beaten for sure.

So, he stood on his doorstep, sobbing like a big fat baby.

That's what he was doing when his neighbor, Stephanie, walked by with her brown wiener dog. She was in eighth grade. Had long brown hair and big brown eyes. Super cute.

Stephanie did a double take when she looked at him. The second time, she laughed.

But when she noticed he was crying, she stopped and came over to him.

Howie put his hands down to cover his underwear because girls shouldn't see a hint of boys' naughty parts.

"Are you okay?" she asked as her dog sniffed at his socks.

Howie shook his head and tried to use words, but a pathetic cry was all that came out.

"What happened?"

He managed to tell her between gasps and sniffles.

"What? Oh, my God. What the hell? Come inside. I'll get you some pants."

Howie was surprised by her kindness. And that she had pants to lend him. Did Stephanie have a brother he didn't know about? Or was she going to give him something that belonged to her father? He was tall and skinny, so his pants probably wouldn't fit.

Howie followed Stephanie to her house.

They stopped at the doorstep. Howie said, "What if your parents see me?"

"They're not home. Come in."

He followed her inside, then she closed the door behind them.

Her house was nice. A bit messier than his, but most homes probably were. Mom ran a tight ship, always demanding perfection. *Cleanliness is next to godliness*, she liked to say, and sometimes beat into him.

"Come upstairs." She took the steps two at a time as her dog stood at Howie's feet, still sniffing him.

He followed, her dog at his heels.

Stephanie handed him a pair of purple sweat pants with a heart on the front, and told him to try them on. "Sorry, I don't have anything more masculine that would also fit you."

Howie went into her bathroom to put them on. He was surprised to find they fit him.

He left the bathroom then walked to the open door at the end of the hall. She was standing there in a bra, slipping into a T-shirt.

He'd never seen boobs in real life. "Um … I'm sorry."

Howie ran down the stairs.

Stephanie followed him, laughing. "It's okay. It's just a bra."

He nodded, unsure of his words. He was thinking impure and evil thoughts, picturing her bra and what her boobs might look like underneath.

Dear God, please forgive me.

Please forgive my wicked thoughts.

I am a wretched sinner who does not deserve your forgiveness. But please forgive me, anyway.

Howie closed his eyes, repeating the prayer in his head

as he tried to think of pure things and forget the beautiful girl in front of him.

He felt his naughty place stiffen.

No, no, no, no.

He scurried to the couch then sat down, trying to hide it, working to think of anything else that might eliminate the wicked thoughts and the sinful feelings that chased them.

"Are you okay?" she asked, her voice closer.

Howie opened his eyes.

She was sitting next to him on the couch. She put a hand on his shoulder.

"Um, yeah, just … I'm sorry. I should go home." Except he didn't have his keys. "But … I can't get into my house."

"The keys in your pants?" she asked.

Howie nodded.

"You can hang out here until your mom gets home."

"Are you sure? Your parents won't mind?"

"They wouldn't care. Besides, they don't get home until later tonight."

"They won't care if you're here … alone with a boy?"

She looked at him for a long moment before finally smiling. "No, they won't care. Why would they care?"

"Because girls and boys shouldn't be alone together. It's a sin."

"What?"

"Mom says boys can't be around girls because girls will lead them into temptation."

Stephanie laughed again. "What?"

Howie nodded. "It's God's will that girls remain chaste and that boys wait."

Stephanie's eyes widened. "Wow. Um, okay. Do I tempt you, Howie?"

She did, but he didn't dare say it.

Howie wasn't used to lying, but he felt a deep shame in this particular truth. He shook his head. A headshake was slightly less than a lie.

"Don't worry, Howie. I won't lead you into temptation with my whorish ways." Then Stephanie laughed again.

Howie wasn't sure why she was laughing, but he liked the sound of it. She was nice. Aside from teachers, she might be the first person ever to be nice to him. The first girl, for sure.

He thought about Stephanie's boobs again and felt red-hot heat spreading over his cheeks.

"Want me to order pizza?"

"You can just *order* pizza? It doesn't have to be a special occasion?"

"Wow, who are you?"

"Howie Loomis," he answered.

She laughed again, then tousled his hair. "You are too cute, Howie."

HOWIE HAD NEVER BEEN HAPPIER than in the two and half hours he'd waited with Stephanie. They watched shows on TV that Howie didn't even know existed and ate a whole pizza together. All twelve slices. She was so nice.

He'd almost forgotten the horrible moment that led him to her house.

"Well, I've got to go home now," he said at exactly ten after six.

She walked him to the door then they stood on her porch.

"Well, if you ever lose your pants again, feel free to come hang out."

"Really?" he asked.

Stephanie laughed again, but it didn't sound mean. "Yes. Or anytime."

"Thank you."

She leaned in and hugged him.

A girl had never done that before. He couldn't even remember his own mother hugging him. That was something he'd only seen other people do.

It felt good, and she smelled so pretty. Howie could feel her boobs against him. He started stiffen again. He pulled away and smiled, then waved, eager to get away before she noticed his bad part sticking straight up.

"Okay, thanks!"

Mom's car pulled up as he turned toward his driveway. She wasn't pleased, judging by her soured lips.

She made him wait on the couch while she changed out of her waitress uniform and into a long gray dress. Then she returned with a glass of wine in one hand and a cigarette in the other. "Okay, I want answers."

"To what, ma'am?"

"First, why are you wearing girls' pants?"

He explained what happened.

"And you let them take your pants?"

He felt the hot sting of shame. "Yes, ma'am."

"Why?"

"Because they said they'd kill me. And they'd kill you."

"Don't be so stupid, Howie. Nobody's killing anybody."

"I'm sorry, ma'am."

"So, that little whore just invited you into her house and *gave you* her pants?"

Howie nodded. "She's not a whore, Mom. Stephanie is nice."

"Are you talking back to me, boy?" Mom looked like she might smack him across the face.

"No, ma'am. I'm sorry."

"Were her parents home?"

"No, ma'am."

"You went into that whore's house when her parents weren't home? What did I tell you?"

"I'm sorry. I didn't have anywhere else to go."

"Because you let those boys take your keys. It's your fault. You should've stood on our porch. Or in the back yard. Could've mowed the lawn while you waited."

She let out a long sigh as took an even longer drink, then she stared at her son for a long time like she was trying to figure something out.

"What?" he asked.

"Did ... did she tempt you?"

He thought of Stephanie leaving the door open while she changed into her shirt. He'd thought it was an accident, but ... what if Mom was right? What if she had been trying to tempt him?

"What is it?" Mom asked.

It was like she knew he was hiding something. He wasn't sure how she did it, but she *always* seemed to know.

"I ... I don't want to say."

"Tell me, boy."

Howie started crying.

She set her drink down, walked over, grabbed a fistful of his hair, then yanked his head back, forcing him to look up at her, dark eyes burning into his. "*Tell me.*"

He couldn't hide from her gaze, not now or ever. If he didn't tell her, she would burrow into his head and find out, anyway.

"It was an accident."

"What?"

"She left her door open, and I saw her changing. Just her bra."

Mom pulled him up by the hair until he was standing on his tippy-toes.

"And did you look?"

Howie wanted to lie, but lying to your mother was one of the worst sins. He exploded into tears, not wanting to answer.

"*Did ... you ... look?*"

He nodded.

"And? Did you think wicked thoughts? Did your sinful part get stiff?"

Howie nodded again, wanting to disappear into his shame and die right there on the spot. He was nothing. *Less* than nothing. A worthless, wicked sinner who didn't deserve the Good Lord's forgiveness. He'd surrendered to temptation. Mom had warned him, but he'd ignored her and looked.

And now he would have to pay.

"You know what you have to do, boy."

He cried, pulling down the sweatpants and then his underwear.

Mom stared down at his wicked part, shaking her head in disgust. "I am doing this for you. Now beg for God's forgiveness."

"Please, God, forgive me for my wicked, impure thoughts. I am not deserving—"

He felt the first of the cigarette burns just above his bad part. Howie cried out as she went in for the second burn.

He went upstairs to his room in tears when she finished. Sat on the bed, removed the pillowcase from his pillow, and slid it over his head.

You are not what you feel.

You are not weak.

You are meant for so much more.

The tears stopped, and Howie found that familiar peace.

But he felt something else inside it. A kinship with something he could only sense but not yet see.

That would come years later with the first of Mister K's messages.

Chapter 12 - Jasper Parish

IT HAD BEEN four days since Jasper had stopped taking his pills, but he had yet to see Jordyn or have any visions.

Last night had been the toughest. Jurkovicz was on duty instead of Hernandez. And Jurko was even more of a ballbuster. Jasper played it docile — so sleepy, the guard didn't bother checking to see if he'd swallowed.

But now he was running out of time and pacing his pod like a crazy man.

It was almost lights out, and he'd yet to see anything. Hernandez would demand proof of Jasper's abilities if he was on duty tonight. Jurko, or someone else, might force the pills on him. It would take days for the effects to wear off.

His "symptoms" usually returned relatively soon. He'd see Jordyn or have a vision before the week was half over. More often, his daughter would return with a vision of her own. She was far stronger, especially in death, than Jasper had ever been.

Odd she'd not manifested psychic visions until after her

passing. She'd had a few premonitions during her life, but not like now.

"Don't you think it's telling that she only has strong abilities after she's gone?" The shrink had asked Jasper. "That maybe these visions are just you manifesting her?"

But how could the doctors understand his situation? They were forced to work within the parameters of fact, of what was easily accepted or understandable. They were like cops in that way, working with the most likely explanation of events. If the evidence pointed toward Suspect A, it was usually Suspect A. The most obvious answer was most often the *only* answer.

Except now.

Maybe Jasper wasn't seeing Jordyn or Carissa because they didn't *want* to see him. Jordyn blamed him for what happened to Spider and the others and had still never *really* forgiven him for what he'd done to Calum and Brianna. Carissa never approved of what he was doing, and he'd disappointed her by bringing their daughter into his need for revenge.

Their absence might be more punishment.

Please. If you're here, talk to me.

This is too much.

Still no answer.

I thought I could do this, but … I can't.

Tears bubbled under the surface, but Jasper held them back, refusing to let self-pity best him. He had to keep his mind open to the chance that maybe the meds had yet to wear off.

Hard to tell in the hole.

Jasper had been medicated ever since his sentence began. But the hole had a way of cutting through the numbness, cranking his anxiety regardless of the dulling chemicals inside him.

And now, he was moments from breaking.

Were the meds wearing off, or was Jasper losing his shit?

They'd increase his doses if he turned violent, make him even more of a vegetable, thereby making it even less likely he'd ever Jordyn or Carissa again.

He closed his eyes, sprawled in the bed, and tried to meditate himself into a better place.

Sometimes visions came when he managed to empty his mind of thoughts. But in a place like this, the images were too muddy. He couldn't clear them because they kept returning to fear:

What if I can't convince Hernandez?

What if I'm forced to stay on the meds forever?

What if I deserve this punishment? Or something even worse?

Part of Jasper wished Kozack *had* killed him. He would no longer suffer, and Kozack could have justice for his son.

No, no, no …

I can't give in to that.

Have to clear my mind.

Think of nothing.

Let go of every thought. Imagine them leaving me, floating away with each rising and falling breath.

Jasper imagined his darkest thoughts and ugliest fears coalescing into a singular black cloud, blooming from his crown then spreading outward.

Eyes still closed, he pictured that cloud dissipating above him and joining the ether.

That's it.

Jordyn?

He resisted the urge to open his eyes. She would vanish if he did — assuming she was really there, that it wasn't just wishful thinking.

He continued, clearing the thoughts of Jordyn as he

had the others, picturing them floating away. He was alone, waiting without thinking about his waiting. Or trying not to.

A flash of movement.

A teenage boy, dark hair and red T-shirt, running. People behind him, chasing.

The door buzzed and unlocked.

Whatever Jasper saw, or thought he had, disappeared in a blink and left only raw terror behind. He had nothing and prayed it wasn't Hernandez's turn in the rotation.

The door opened.

Jasper sat up as Hernandez stepped holding the cup of pills in his gloved hand.

"Well?" Hernandez asked.

I should lie.

Tell him that Jurko checked last night and reset my abilities. I need more time.

Hernandez said he wasn't going to let anyone else in on it, but maybe that was a lie. Or a test. What if he asked Jurko not to check?

"I … I need more time."

"Enough bullshit, Parish. Open up and say *ah*."

"Please," Jasper begged.

His face went red and his eyebrows furrowed as he grabbed Jasper's jaw with one hand, ready to force the pills down his throat with the other.

Jasper reached up, grabbed Hernandez by the forearm on instinct, and glimpsed a fragment of a vision.

A boy in red, running. Kids chasing him and calling out, "You're a pussy, Jamie!"

One of the boys pulled out a knife.

Hernandez shoved Jasper backward, dropped the pills, and made a move toward his baton. The first blow hit Jasper hard in the ribs before he even had a chance to raise his hands, still too shocked to process what was happening fast enough to defend himself.

A second strike to his back. Jasper curled himself into a ball and cried out, "Jamie! Jamie!"

Hernandez let up, backing away. "The fuck you just say?"

Jasper eyed the man, saw his confusion and anger-soaked expression. Noted his fist clutching the baton, waiting for an excuse to beat the hell out of him.

"I saw a young teenage boy. Dark hair, red shirt, running from some kids. They were calling him a pussy. Someone pulled a knife."

Hernandez stared at Jasper, the color gone from his face, baton shaking in his hand.

"Is he your son?"

Hernandez shook his head, then the glare returned to his red eyes and matching face. "Someone put you up to this?"

He should have called for back-up already. Would soon unless Jasper kept him talking. Hernandez was shaken, so Jasper was close to something. He needed something to prompt another vision.

"I saw it when I touched your arm," Jasper said. "Who is it?"

"Why don't you tell me?"

"I only heard them call him Jamie."

Hernandez stared at Jasper, then saw his pills on the ground. "Pick those up and take them."

"Please, I know I saw something — something important to you. Who is he?"

"Fuck you, Parish. Take your meds. I'm not buying it."

Jasper crawled to the ground, pain splintering his ribs and back, then slowly gathered the pills in his hand. "Give me more time. Maybe if I touch your—"

"Take the pills!" Hernandez barked, baton raised, poised for another strike.

Jasper was nearing his normal. Being this close only to fumble in the final yards felt like the worst defeat of his life. He'd rather die.

"*Please*. Let me help you."

Hernandez brought the baton down.

But Jasper grabbed it.

The guard moved to counter, but the prisoner was faster, sweeping his legs out from under him. Then Jasper was on top, punching him in the nose, hearing it crack beneath the impact.

His baton fell to the ground. Hernandez gasped and reached for his nose, vision likely blurred by the tears.

Jasper grabbed the weapon and held it over the guard, who looked up at him, angry and terrified, too disoriented to do anything more than clutch at his bloody nose.

"I don't want to hurt you. Just give me a minute."

"Fuck you," he grunted, reaching for his radio.

Jasper wrapped him hard on the knuckles. "Stop!"

Hernandez yanked back his hand with an incoherent shout.

"Let me help you. If I can't, then you can beat the hell out of me."

"Oh, you better believe I will."

"Put your arm out," Jasper ordered.

Hernandez begrudgingly did so.

Jasper touched his arm again, and saw another flash.

The boy on the ground as two others held him down.

"No, please," he cried as an angry-looking crewcut blond with a scar under his right eye glared down at him. The images were blurry. The boys all appeared to be around eleven or twelve, except the blond. He was older than the other kids by at least a few years.

One of the kids, a pudgy one with greasy brown hair, scowled and said, "Do it, Dom. Do it!"

The blond stabbed him, repeatedly, as the kid cried out.

Then the boys all left him alone to die in a junkyard, sobbing for his mommy.

Jasper let go of his arm.

"They stabbed the boy. Who was he to you?"

Hernandez shook his head. "I don't know who told you what. Maybe your lawyer hired some PI to look into me, but I ain't fallin' for it."

"Do you know who killed him?"

Hernandez stared at Jasper, his eyes afraid but hopeful. Whoever this kid was to him, the guard wanted to believe Jasper had answers.

"It was his last case," Jordyn said, suddenly standing beside him. Jasper wanted to cry and to hug her, but Hernandez would see him as insane.

Still, tears stung at his eyes. He was no longer alone. His little girl had returned.

"It's the case that broke him," Jordyn said. "Made him become a CO."

"It was your last case. An unsolved crime, wasn't it?"

Hernandez clutched his bloody nose in silence. Jasper ripped off a piece of his shirt and handed it to the man as a makeshift rag.

Hernandez reluctantly took it.

"I'll tell you who killed him, but you have to let this thing go. And no more meds."

"How can you know?" Hernandez stared at Jasper. "Did you kill him?"

He shook his head. "I'd never kill a kid."

Hernandez looked down at the bloody rag, turning it over in his hand before putting it back against his nose.

"Do we have an agreement?" Japer asked.

Hernandez nodded. "You tell me who did it, and it checks out, then yes. But ... if you're wrong, I won't put you back here. I'll throw you in genpop, tell them you're a cop, and let the Aryans and everyone else fight over who gets to skull-fuck you first."

"The name Dom ring a bell?"

Jasper could tell from Hernandez's face that it did.

Chapter 13 - Mallory Black

MAL WENT to work early Monday morning, checking in to see what forensics had found at the scene. She saw nothing new, then went to computer crimes and asked Aanya to check on the phone that had been left for her, hoping to trace its purchase.

A burner bought at a gas station in Jacksonville. Aanya would call the carrier and trace the number's activity, but Mal doubted they'd find anything.

She drove to Jacksonville and waited half an hour for the store manager to find the receipt. The phone was bought with cash, more than two months ago, meaning the unsub had probably been planning this crime for a while. Without a credit card number to trace, Mal asked if the manager could show her security footage from the time of the purchase, knowing what he'd say. And sure enough, the footage was recorded over every week.

She called the hospital next but there was no news on McKenna Shaw coming out of her coma yet.

Just after two o'clock, she got a call from Mike — they were running down a list of people with white vans in the neighborhood, and one of the men took off when they went to question him. He lived three blocks from the girls and, more importantly, went to their church.

They had him in the box and had begun to question him when they decided it would be better to ice the guy. Now they were stalling. Mike called Mal, even though she'd been reduced to grunt work by Barry, because he wanted her in the room. It was good to be needed, especially by her partner, and she felt guilty for questioning his loyalty.

Mal raced back to Creek County Sheriff's Office, eager for a crack at the suspect.

When she arrived, Skippy and Mike were sitting adjacent to the interview room looking through the two-way mirror at the suspect, a rail-thin dirty-blond in his mid-thirties. A long face with bulging eyes and a big black-and-blue bruise blooming beneath the left one. He kept bouncing his leg, fidgety as fuck, as he grazed the room with his eyes like an addict dying for a fix.

Takes one to know one.

"Name is Terry Watkins," Mike told her. "He's a mechanic at Vlad's Custom Imports, drives a van similar to our unsub. And, get this — six months ago, a neighbor girl, age seven, claims he was standing in his window masturbating when she and her friend walked by. Case was dropped because the kid and her parents got flakey about the details. Mom said it was a big misunderstanding, but the deputy on duty wasn't buying it. You ask me, dude looks shifty as hell. So, we went to have a little talk, asked him where he was when the girls were attacked. Terry excuses himself to use the bathroom then high-tails it out the back door on foot. Skippy caught him. Might have clocked him in the eye."

"Whoops." Skippy smiled.

"So, where we at?" Mal asked her partner.

"Forensics has his van, nothing to report yet. And we've been letting him sit and stew before going back in. Thought it might be good to bring you in halfway through, see how he reacts."

Mal nodded as the guys entered the interview room.

Mike sat across the table from Terry and dropped a Manilla folder between them. Terry glanced at it, several times, but didn't ask what was in it.

"So, how are you feeling?" Mike asked.

"Um, okay." He flinched as Skippy stepped into the corner of his peripheral vision, turned, then paced behind Terry's back in an effort to unnerve him.

The suspect shifted in his seat.

"So, before we get back to it, my apologies for taking so long," Mike said. "We're talking to a lot of folks right now, and there are only a few of us on duty. You know how it is."

"I told you everything. I know the girls from church, but … ain't ever said more than 'hi' to 'em."

"Yeah, I'm sorry. We've just got to dot our I's and cross our T's, you know how it is."

Terry nodded and shifted in his chair again, still not meeting Mike's gaze.

"Can I get you something before we get back to it? A water, soda, some coffee?"

"Yeah," Terry said. "A Coke."

"Sure thing." Mike stood and left the room.

Then he sat beside Mal in the adjacent room. The two of them watched Skippy work, still pacing behind the suspect.

Terry did his best not to look back or show his fear, but whenever Skippy made any noise — an extra loud step, smacking at the keys in his pocket, or simply clearing his throat — Terry visibly started. He was nervous for sure, but his anxiousness didn't necessarily have anything to do with the girls.

Skippy finally circled around to where Terry could see him.

"How rough did you all get with him?" Mal asked.

"Skippy just touched him up for the running. Nothing too bad."

Mike was by-the-book. He didn't like when a colleague lost control, especially Mal. So she trusted him when he said Skippy hadn't done much.

"Dude is spooked like he's expecting a beatdown," Mal said.

"Yeah, he's hiding something."

"Get a warrant for the house yet?"

"Hawthorne and Robbins are over there now."

Mal nodded.

Skippy walked the table in long, lazy circles.

The suspect laid his head down and closed his eyes. It looked like he might be sobbing.

Skippy stopped and slammed his palms on the table.

Terry jumped, eyes wide in terror, as he looked at the detective, then around the room as if he expected to see another five other cops storming in to kick his ass.

"Why'd you run, man?" Skippy shouted.

"I told you, I don't know."

"Bullshit! Innocent people don't run. You know who runs, Terry? Guilty people, that's who. You know how many times an innocent person has taken off in all my time on the force?"

Terry just stared at the table, hair hanging in his eyes.

"I asked you a question. *How many times do you think an innocent person has run, Terry?*"

"I dunno."

"Wrong answer." Skippy slammed his palms on the table again.

Terry jumped in his seat.

Inches from his nose, glaring as he bellowed, "None, Terry! Innocent people never run!"

Skippy was dangerously close to Terry, who could easily bite his cheek if he wanted to. But Skippy was clearly feeling invulnerable in the face of his cowering suspect. Mal would advise more caution. Terry looked like a loser dirtbag Life had spent decades fucking hard in the ass without any lube, but that didn't make him less of a threat.

"What's wrong, man? You look scared." Skippy took a seat across from Terry. "You thinking about what our guys are gonna find back at your place?"

Terry shook his head. "I didn't do anything, man. I told you."

"What are they gonna find? Got some kiddy porn stashed away? Maybe some pics of little children from the park or something?"

"I'm not a fucking pedophile." His brow furrowed.

"So, it was just an accident that you were cranking one out as those two girls passed by? With your curtains open?"

"They lied! I don't know why, but they did. You all came around and asked me questions. I told you the same thing then that I'm telling you now — *I ain't into fucking kids.*"

Mal stared hard through the two-way mirror and saw something rare — the suspect wasn't lying.

He was hiding something, but Mal didn't think he was into children.

Still, he might be their guy. He could have killed a kid without raping her.

"Come on, man," Skippy said, his voice syrupy sweet.

"Let me help you. Tell me what happened. It'll be *so* much easier than if you don't tell me."

"I didn't touch any kid."

"Bullshit!" Skippy smacked the table again then shot up from his chair.

Terry flinched, taking furtive glances at Skippy as the detective went back to pacing.

"Here's the thing. Right now is your only shot to get ahead of this. We're willing to go easier on you if you tell us what we need to know now. But make us wait, *especially* if you make us wait until we find whatever sick shit you've got at your house, and we're not gonna be in such a cooperative mood."

Terry's hands were cuffed and chained to the table, with enough slack to wipe at his tears.

"Then tell me why the hell you ran, brother."

Terry shook his head and pulled at his hair, hard enough to turn his knuckles white.

Why hadn't he lawyered up?

Mal picked up the two-way radio on the table then pressed a button to communicate in Skippy's ear. "Go Bad Cop. But just scare him, don't give the guy another black eye."

Skippy glanced at the mirror with a light roll of his eyes. He grabbed the Manilla folder off the table then started thumbing through it, not yet revealing the contents to Terry.

"I gotta ask, what's with the symbols?"

"What?" Terry said, his curiosity piqued.

"The symbols on the body. You a witch or something? Wait, no, dude witches aren't witches, are they? No, um, what are they called?" Skippy pretended to think. "Don't tell me. I'll get it … Oh, yeah, a warlock. You a fucking warlock or something?"

"No, I'm not a fucking warlock," Terry said, sounding thoroughly confused.

"Like this one right here." Skippy shoved a gory photo in front of Terry's face. "What the fuck is *this* symbol?"

Mal watched his eyes widen in horror, his face twist in revulsion. Then he turned, gagging.

Skippy grabbed his hair, yanked it hard. Moved the photo even closer. "Look at it, you cocksucker. Look at it!"

Terry cried out, an agonized wail like someone had shot his dog in front of him. And still he kept trying to turn away.

"Look at it!" Skippy screamed before grabbing more photos and throwing them at Terry.

He kept wailing, closing his eyes, begging Skippy to stop.

"That's my cue." Mal rushed from her room to theirs.

She threw the door open and glared at Skippy. "What the fuck are you doing, detective?"

"This fucker did it. I know he did! Look at him. Fucking piece of shit!"

"Get out of my interview room!" Mal yelled.

Skippy feigned disbelief. "But—"

"Now!" Mal pointed at the door. "And take those photos with you."

He gathered the pictures, retreated, then shut the door behind him.

Mal and the suspect were finally alone.

Now it was time to work.

Chapter 14 - Howard Loomis

TWELVE DAYS AGO ...

HOWARD LOVED TO WATCH.

He was at the desk in his bedroom, staring at his laptop screen late at night as he scrubbed through the security footage from inside the apartment of that brunette he saw at Sloppy's.

Her apartment complex provided complimentary security as part of the rent, and Howard worked for the company that installed the cameras. One on the outside of every front door and another in the living room.

Most customers kept their outdoor cams on at all times, but many only turned on the living room cameras when they went to bed. Few people liked the idea of someone recording their every move, if they bothered to even think about it.

If only they knew how easily it was to spy.

Howard had exploited a backdoor feature unknown to most, allowing him to remotely turn on cameras and record activities to cloud storage for his personal use. And he had quite the collection. He'd been watching people all over the county ever since such cameras became ubiquitous. He even found ways to hack into those installed by other companies. Howard masked all his traffic via a TOR browser so even if someone discovered an intrusion, nobody would know it was him. Not difficult, if you knew what you were doing.

Howard had spied on the wicked and the righteous alike. He'd watched all manner of illegality. Even witnessed a murder, though he never told the cops. Fortunately, he didn't need to call anything in. The police saw the same exact footage, never knowing those seven minutes were some of his favorites.

Howard felt most at home in the shadows, so that's where he chose to live. A place to stay invisible and watch without ridicule, indulge in his fantasies and wash the shame off his body.

After following the girls home from Sloppy's, Howard started recording the brunette's camera feed. Cami Rivera lived alone. The black girl was only hanging out with her.

Howard rewound the footage to last night, the part where she was sitting on the couch in just her bra and panties, talking on the phone. A single light left her looking a bit pixelated. He turned on the audio and heard her talking dirty to whoever was on the other end of the line.

As she slid her fingers into her panties, he pumped lotion into his hand then reached into his boxers. Kept his pace slow, not fast-forwarding to see where the video would go, how much Cami would reveal. Just enjoyed the show as it unfolded.

Her top came off. If only the resolution was higher or the lighting was brighter. He craved a closer look at her nipples. They were dark blurs on her otherwise milky white tits, tan-lines bold with her bra pulled aside.

He pumped faster as she moaned.

But then Howard heard Mother's footsteps approaching outside his door. His heart started racing. He flipped the lid of his laptop down and quickly raised his boxers, seconds before the door swung open and light from the hall bled into his dark bedroom.

Mother's hair was pulled back tight, making her face look even more severe than usual. She was in her night-gown, covering her body neck to ankles.

"Why's it so dark in here?" Mother flipped on the switch.

The room went bright and her eyes went from the bottle of lotion on the desk to the bulge in Howard's boxers he was awkwardly trying to cover.

"What's wrong with you?" Mother asked, shaking her head in disgust.

"I wasn't doing anything."

She approached him — far too fast for her seventy years — and glared down at Howard.

He felt the same fear and insignificance he had as a child, the same heavy coat of shame.

"You sicken me," Mother snapped. She snatched the lotion from his desk. "This is how you disgrace the Lord? In *my house?*"

"I'm sorry," Howard whined.

"You know what to do …" Another disgusted shake of her head. "Unless you want me to do it."

"No, ma'am, I will do it."

"Are you sure you're man enough?"

"I will atone, Mother."

"Good." She slammed his door on her way back into

the hall, leaving Howard alone with his hurt and humiliation.

What the hell was I thinking?

She's right.

I should know better.

He prayed for forgiveness as he reached for the lighter. Flicked it then waited for the flame to turn the metal hot. Lowered his boxers, closed his eyes. Then Howard burned himself yet again, promising God he was sorry through the agony.

Pathetic sinner!

He pulled up his boxers, got up from his desk, then went to bed.

Mister K spoke from the shadows. The entity had yet to *truly* reveal himself, appearing to Howard in layers of darkness, more of a shambling blur of shapes than any solid form.

"You going to let your mommy keep making you feel shame, *Howie?*"

"Mother is right. I am a wicked sinner."

"No," said Mister K, "you are one of the chosen. But you do nothing to command her respect."

Howard was silent except for his sobbing.

"You should show her what you're becoming."

"No," he mumbled, shaking his head.

"Then show me again. Prove to me you're worthy."

He lifted his shirt and showed Mister K the iconography carved into the flesh of his stomach and chest.

"I believe there's room for more," Mister K said.

Howard climbed to his feet then trudged to the bathroom. He reached into the medicine chest for his razor blades.

"What shall I carve?"

AFTER CLOCKING out the next day, Howard sat in his van outside Cami's apartment, waiting for her to come home so he could spring into action.

He felt an excitement and fear like he'd never experienced while working up enough courage to approach her. Howard still wasn't sure what he was going to do. Mister K had only told him where to go — he'd offer further instructions upon Howard's arrival. Getting into her place was the primary goal. Not too hard since he'd turned off her camera's recording feature.

Cami pulled up in front of her apartment.

She got out in a rush then ran inside.

His radio crackled to life with Mister K's voice. "There she *issss*."

Howard's adrenaline pumped with his pounding heart, mind conjuring images of all the many things he planned to do, starting with silencing her. Next, he'd tie the girl up, bring her somewhere else. A place where he could take his sweet time. Then he would slowly strip her, laughing as she begged him not to touch her.

But of course, he would. Too many women had denied him. But Cami wouldn't be able to.

Howard grabbed his hardening cock, squeezing it tight. Savored the pressure and pain.

He remembered the way she had looked at him with such disgust while at Sloppy's. He couldn't wait until recognition flashed on her face and she was forced to acknowledge it was him who would own her flesh and him who would decide what would happen next.

Him and Mister K.

But Cami threw a wrench into his plans. She left her apartment, got back into her car, then drove away.

What is she doing?

Where is she going?

"What do I do?" Howard asked, feeling his plans fading away.

"Follow her."

Howard obeyed.

Two cars behind Cami's, he thought about the many years since his adolescence spent searching for and studying Mister K's many scrawls, hidden in the margins of books.

He'd found the first one at age thirteen, at the pit of his suffering, the day Stephanie betrayed him and laughed at his awkward advance. The day he almost killed himself and ended things for good.

But he had a report due on Monday, so Mother had dragged him to the library instead.

That's where he found the first message, in the margins of an encyclopedia, on the letter K.

Feel like the world hates you? Want to know the truth? Follow the next message in a classic seafarer's journey.

Howard found two copies of *Moby Dick*, yet neither had any messages scrawled inside them. So, he asked the librarian for other classic seafaring tales and was told about an old book called *The Seafarers*, by John Bloundelle-Burton.

He found the next book then followed the messages from title to title, first in that library, then to used book stores. Even to a few garage sales over the years. In those messages, Howard learned what the world had always hidden from him. He discovered his power. Assembled a world history unlike anything historians ever recorded.

I've been around since The Beginning, read one of the messages. *And I'll be around in The End.*

Mister K knew the truth.

And Howard yearned to know it, too. Longed to see

the true face of the only person, or whatever he was, who had ever been there for him.

"Slow down. She'll spot you," Mister K said on the radio.

He obeyed, easing up behind Cami. "What should I do when I find her?"

"Patience, Howie."

"Am I almost ready?"

"Soon, Howie. Soon you will be ready."

"Can't you please just show me what you look like?"

"Why? Do you not have faith?"

"It's not that. I just—"

"It sounds like doubt." Mister K's voice grew angrier.

"I bel—"

"There are others to share my knowledge with if you doubt me. Those who don't share your weakness."

"I believe!" Howard shouted.

Silence, then static, followed by the braying of the AM talk show, Rich Macklin, ranting about the global elites.

Cami's car slowed down as she pulled up to a house then into the driveway.

Howard parked across the street, watching in his side passenger side mirror as she spoke to a woman at the front door.

Who is this?

Two blondes, one around thirteen and another around ten or eleven, hugged the woman before heading to Cami's car.

A friend? Babysitter?

Cami got in after the kids then pulled out.

Howard sighed. He couldn't do anything now, not when she had witnesses.

"What are you doing?" asked Mister K.

"She has kids with her," he explained.

"Perfect. I've got another idea."

"What?" Something awful turned in Howard's stomach.

Mister K made his usual demand. "Do you have faith or not?"

He was indecisive and speechless. What did Mister K have in mind? Howard didn't want to hurt any children and didn't need any witnesses to what he planned on doing with Cami. He couldn't even imagine wanting to do those things with kids around. He wasn't a pervert.

"Do you have faith or not?" Mister K repeated, impatiently. He wouldn't ask again.

"Yes," Howard whimpered.

"Then follow them."

Howard obeyed.

Chapter 15 - Jasper Parish

JASPER HADN'T SEEN Officer Hernandez for two days. Jurko left the medicine on his sink the first night. On the second day, Officer Dalton Springs walked in then set the cup on his sink.

"What's the deal you got going?" Springs asked before leaving.

"Huh?" Jasper played dumb.

"Hernandez said to just let you take your meds, that you could be trusted. *Why?*"

Springs stared at him suspiciously. Jasper remembered how quickly the guard had come down on him with the baton after Jasper shivved Kenn. Prisoners were supposed to stay subservient to their COs. He didn't cut deals.

"I just want to see my girl one more time."

"Your *girl?*"

"My dead daughter. Only way I see her is without the pills."

His eyes narrowed on Jasper. "How'd she die?"

"Suicide."

Dalton's shoulders relaxed. His face softened ever so slightly. "How old was she?"

"Sixteen."

"I lost my little boy when he was six months old."

"Shit. Sorry."

"Yeah, fucking SIDS." Springs sighed. "What's Hernandez get out of this?"

"Honest?"

"No, lie to me."

Jasper had to smile. Maybe this guy wasn't a total asshole. Hard to get a decent feel for people while his senses were dulled as a residual effect of the drugs.

"I snitched on who killed Wally."

"So, you're a rat?"

"Just desperate to see my girl again. And sorry, I don't dig the Aryans. Nothing personal if you are one."

"Not every country boy is a racist. Fuck Kenn. That asshole got what he deserved." Dalton walked out the door. "Sorry about your daughter," he said before the door shut with a buzz.

After breakfast on the third day, Jordyn paced his cell. She wore a bright pink and purple hoodie with black jeans and big black boots. A pink heart sticker decorated her right cheek, and she was singing an unfamiliar song.

"What is that?" Jasper asked.

"Indigo Girls, 'Closer to Fine.' You like?"

"I do. You have a good singing voice."

"Thanks. So do you."

"How would you know? You never heard me sing."

"You used to sing me to sleep when I was little."

"That was a long time ago."

"I still remember."

"What was your favorite song?"

"I liked when you sang 'Time after Time.'"

"Your mom loved that song. First dance at our wedding."

"I bet Mom looked beautiful."

Jasper thought back to how stunning Carissa had been in her dress and felt a sting of tears welling up in his eyes. He wished she would visit again and wondered where she was if not with him. Spending time with someone else who remembered her? Someone who made her happier? Who didn't remind her of how much pain he'd brought upon them all?

Jordyn started singing "Time After Time."

She sounded better than Cyndi Lauper. At least more soothing. He closed his eyes and imagined them back home before Carissa died, before his daughter killed herself. Jasper would do anything to rewind time and get a chance to live his life over again.

He wiped the tears from his eyes as she finished. "That was beautiful."

"Why, thank you, sir." Jordyn blushed. "So, how long do you think you'll be in solitary?"

"I dunno."

"Do you mind being all alone?"

"I did before you came back. Now I prefer it."

"Sorry you couldn't see me. I was always with you, though. Not *always*. But I saw you every day."

"You did?"

"Yes."

A horrifying thought occurred to him. One he really wished he'd considered before turning himself in. "Are you stuck with me, wherever I am?"

"No. I can go anywhere people remember me."

"How does that work?" he asked.

"I don't know. Sometimes I'm here. Other times I'm with someone I didn't even think was a friend back when I was alive. But I guess they must remember me, or else I wouldn't be there. Sometimes I'll see Bobby Hollingsworth."

"How is he?"

"He's sad," Jordyn said. "I'm worried about him. Drinks a lot. I think he blames himself for what happened."

"He *should have* done more."

"Don't start, Dad."

"Fine. So, do any of them … you know?"

"What?"

"Does anyone else *see you?*"

"Only you."

Jasper nodded. Then he thought about what the doctors had said and how the meds made it impossible to see her. "How do I know I'm not just imagining you?"

"I guess you don't." She shrugged. "I could go outside this cell and get information you wouldn't know, but you're psychic, so …"

He nodded and sighed, staring at Jordyn with an overwhelming sorrow like fire in his chest. "I'm sorry I didn't see how much pain you were in. That I missed so many signs."

Jordyn didn't respond, staring at the floor with her back to him. Jasper wondered if she was crying or pretending he wasn't there.

"Jordyn?"

"Something's happening." She turned.

"What is it?"

The door buzzed open. Hernandez entered then closed it behind him.

Jordyn disappeared.

Shit. What did she see?

"So, how's it going? The other officers treat you right?"

Jasper nodded. "How about you? That name pan out for you?"

He knew it had before the officer opened his mouth. "Yeah. Told my old partner to take a harder look at one of our suspects. Got his alibi to admit she'd lied. Landed a confession less than three hours later."

"Damn."

"Damn, indeed. How did you know about it?"

"I told you — I see things."

"As long as you don't take your meds."

"Right," Jasper confirmed. "That gonna be a problem?"

"You're good, for now."

"Let me guess, you want something else?"

"Not yet."

"What is it? Sports bet? Lotto numbers?"

Hernandez looked at him for a long moment. Jasper wasn't sure if he was considering his offer or wanting to ask something else. He strongly suspected the latter.

"But first, the warden says it's time for you go back to your pod."

"Just when I was getting acclimated to the wonderful decor."

Hernandez nodded toward the door. "Let's go."

They made their way past scads of prisoners. He heard a few racial slurs, several hoots and hollers, and a few general obscenities before they were back in the vacant pod he once shared with Wally.

"No cellmate?" Jasper asked as the door buzzed open.

"Not yet. But don't get too cozy. I've no say in who you room with."

Jasper nodded.

"Yard time will be half what it usually is, as we're splitting the Aryans and everyone else."

"So, the Nazis get rewarded with their own recess? Nice. You know they're not the ones who wanted Wally gone."

"Just tryin' to keep a riot from breaking out." Hernandez glanced back to see if anyone else was within earshot. "And keep you alive a little bit longer."

The cells were closed off with bullet-resistant polycarbonate doors. Two on either side of Jasper, and another row across from him. No one could hear Hernandez, but he lowered his voice anyway. "Just keep your head down and try not to get shivved, eh?"

Jasper nodded.

"And play along if someone tries to make you take your meds. I talked to a few of the guys I trust. But some of the others, well…"

And with that he left.

At least now Jasper had an idea what Hernandez was being so cryptic about. He didn't trust the other COs.

Why? What's going on here?

JASPER WAS in the yard leaning against the shed, staring up at the clouds, feeling the warm sun on his face while trying to remain aware of his surroundings.

Meurte Boyz occupied one of the weight areas and one of the basketball courts. 904 Mafia, and other unaffiliated black dudes, were spread out at the other stations and courts while a few stragglers circled the track. The COs and a couple of unaffiliated older men were the only white guys in the yard.

Since Jasper left isolation, he hadn't heard from Jordyn and was starting to wonder if something had happened to her. She'd seemed so alarmed right before she left. What had she seen? And why hadn't she come back to tell him?

"Maybe 'cuz it's all in your head," said a man beside him.

Lenny Barnes, his old basketball coach and mentor. Dressed in jeans and a black windbreaker, charcoal fedora tilted ever so slightly.

"So, you finally came to see me." Jasper kept his voice low so nobody saw him talking to ghosts or illusions.

"Why didn't you just stay with that nice lady and her girl?" Lenny asked.

"You know why."

"Because you can't stand to be happy?"

"Because they're better off without me. I bring pain or death wherever I go."

"You really believe that, son?"

"I do."

A long moment of silence stretched as Crazy Gary passed, mumbling to himself. He looked at Jasper and winked, then kept on walking.

"He sweet on you?" Lenny asked.

"Maybe he sees you, too."

Lenny waved, but Crazy Gary was no longer looking at them. "You know you're gonna die in here."

"With any luck."

"How's the girl?"

"She's okay."

"She visiting you?"

"Yeah."

"Prison is no place for a kid."

"She's free to come and go, same as you."

"I've gotta say, I'm disappointed," Lenny said after a long sigh. "All the work we did to keep you out of prison and here you are, exactly the same."

"Yep. I'm still great at letting people down."

"Oh, stop feeling sorry for yourself."

"I'm not," Jasper said. "I'm just finished lying to myself. Done pretending I'm a good person. I killed a lot of bad people. Saved some good ones, but in the end, the score is against me. I got my own kid killed. I could've stopped working after Carissa passed. I blamed Calum Kozack, but it's my fault for not seeing the signs and not being there for Jordyn."

"So, that's what this is? Punishment for all your sins?"

"Can't hurt anyone else from in here."

"Can't *help* nobody, neither."

"Like I said, the numbers don't add up in my favor. I hurt as—"

"This is about Spider? She's gonna be okay."

"Now you're a psychic, too?"

"That girl knew what she was getting into when she decided to work for you."

"She was a child. I recruited a crippled kid whose family was dead. I could have just given her money, I didn't have to involve her. I wouldn't have been looking for how she could return the favors of my help if it was really all about Spider, or if I was really a good person."

"The girl wanted to work, and you knew it. Didn't want to be a charity case and liked being valuable. She was working for Logic and those other dealers, anyway. She knew and accepted the dangers."

"I should've protected her. And Jordyn. I—"

"Tell me when you're done so you can get off the cross and donate it to a—"

"I'm not being a martyr, Lenny. Or feeling sorry for myself. I just want to do my time and then rest in peace. I'm done fighting."

"Did they take your balls when they brought you here? The Jasper I know would never quit so easily."

"You told me to stop my vigilante shit! You told me to retire!"

"Yeah, that's when you were with that nice woman and her kid — what were their names?"

"Alicia and Ophelia."

"Yeah, and then you just up and left them. I thought you all had something special."

"It *was* special, until I fucked it up just like everything else. I had to leave, for their sakes."

"If you say so. But why turn yourself in?"

"Kozack turned me in."

"You could've lawyered up. Got a reduced sentence for all the shit you've been through, for the ... mental problems." Lenny made a cuckoo sound and spun a little circle around his ear.

"Yeah, well I didn't. And now I'm here. So if you don't have anything useful to say, please let me enjoy the rest of my rec time in peace."

"Suit yourself, martyr."

Lenny disappeared. Jasper closed his eyes, trying to enjoy his peace. Footsteps ruined his moment. He opened his eyes to see two men approaching.

One had a broad chest, giant shoulders, and tight cornrows. The guy looked like he just finished lifting a car. His face was mean enough to frighten a pit bull. The other guy was shorter but no less fearsome — a short, skinny, lighter-skinned black man with a low afro and tattoos over every visible inch of skin, including *Young Luther* inked across his forearm.

Young Luther was short, around five foot six. He reminded Jasper a bit of Logic, who ran the drug trade in

Butler. Logic's men had helped Jasper when he tried to save Spider, and many died in the process.

After rubbing his nose, Young Luther sneered at Jasper. "So, you the rat that snitched on us?"

Jasper didn't back down, though holding Luther's gaze meant not paying full attention to the giant beside him, the one most likely to shiv him.

"I've no idea what you're talking about."

Luther laughed, looked away for a moment, then back up at Jasper. "Sounds like something a rat would say. You should'a said yes when you got offered that job."

"And why the fuck am I ever gonna kill someone just 'cuz some fucking Nazi said to? I had no beef with Wally."

"Wasn't him makin' the ask. But you knew that."

He held Luther's stare. "Someone wants something from me, they come to me, like a man."

Muscles grunted like he was begging to be let off his leash and tear Jasper from Adam's Apple to anus.

Jasper still didn't look at him, maintaining eye contact with the man in charge of 904 Mafia.

Young Luther nodded. "Think you all that, old man? Think being a cop is gonna save your ass in here?"

If Kenn knew he'd been a cop, so did Young Luther. But Jasper neither confirmed nor denied the accusation. The rapper-turned-kingpin nodded one final time, then with his back to Jasper, said, "Be seein' ya' around, rat."

Muscles followed, leaving Jasper to contemplate his numbered days.

One of the COs barked it was time to line up and return to their pods.

Jasper got in the back, behind Crazy Gary, as they were led back inside.

He turned and smiled at Jasper. "You see them, too, don't ya?"

"See what?" Jasper asked.

"The ghosts. Fucking ghosts everywhere in this place."

Jasper nodded, so the man would stop talking.

When Jasper was let back into his cell he found a dead rat in his bunk.

His days were numbered for sure.

Chapter 16 - Mallory Black

MAL RETURNED from the vending machine with two cold Cokes. She slid one over to Terry then cracked hers open. "Sorry about that."

"Thanks." He grabbed the soda. After pulling the tab, he took a long drink. It did little to settle him. He still seemed nervous, his hair sweaty, leg bouncing and body full of twitches. Slowly, he looked up and met her gaze.

Mal asked him what he was withdrawing from. As he opened his mouth for a lie, she cut him off. "Takes an addict to know one."

"Ran out of Oxy two days ago," Terry admitted. "Was gonna pick up a prescription after work. And … then this. I didn't do what they're asking me about."

"Then let me help you. Sooner you get out of here, sooner you can get your meds."

He nodded and took another drink. "You gonna ask the same thing they did?"

"Where were you Sunday?"

"Church."

"After church?"

"I went home."

"Did you see Alice or McKenna Shaw on Sunday?"

"Yeah, at church."

"Where were they?"

"Sitting two rows ahead of me."

"Who were you with?

"Myself, as usual."

"And what did you do after church?"

"Went home. Took a nap."

"Can anyone confirm that?"

"My dog."

"Are you a religious man, Terry?"

"More than some, not as much as others."

"How often do you attend church?"

"Most Sundays."

"How well do you know Alice and McKenna Shaw?"

He shifted a bit, looking away before returning his gaze to her. "See them in church. Not too well."

"And their mother?"

"Seen her around," Terry said, holding his stare.

"Did you see either Alice or McKenna after church?"

"No."

"What did you do after church?"

"I told you. I went home and took a nap."

"Right. Sorry. So, did you see anyone talking to the girls on Sunday?"

"No. I mean, yeah, their friends."

"Which friends?"

"I dunno their names. Couple of girls in church."

"And you don't know them?"

"No."

"But you know the Shaw girls?"

"Well, I see them around."

"Have you seen them outside of church?"

"I dunno. Maybe." He looked down at his hands.

"Where else have you seen them, Terry?"

"Just around, man. I dunno."

Mal sat silent for a moment. She sipped from her can and let him stew in the moment.

Terry took a drink then started rocking in his seat.

"How do you know the Shaw girls, Terry?"

He shook his head. "I told you, I—"

Mal didn't slap the table or shout. Instead she reached out, softly touched his hand, then set something inside it.

He looked up into her eyes.

She glanced at the camera to let him know not to open his palm.

He looked down with caution.

She'd given him one of her two 'Just In Case' pills.

"Please, let me help you. Just tell me what you know."

Terry met her gaze again, arching his eyebrows as if asking if she was serious. Did she really want him to take the pill?

She nodded, nice and subtle.

He leaned his head back dramatically, sighing as he put his head in his hands and covertly slipped the pill into his mouth. He washed it down with a swallow of Coke, then sat in silence, probably waiting for the pill to kick in or maybe brewing the courage to say whatever the hell he had been keeping to himself.

"What do you want to tell me, Terry?"

"I used to date Sheila."

Mal wanted to smack him. "When? For how long?"

"Last year. For about six months."

"And what happened?"

"I didn't touch those kids." Terry shook his head. "They meant the world to me."

"What happened?"

He closed his eyes and vented an even longer sigh. "*Fuuuuuck.*"

"What happened, Terry?"

"I didn't touch those kids."

"What happened, Terry?"

What the hell did he do?

"She was my dealer."

"Sheila deals drugs?"

"I dunno if she still does. We broke up after some kid accused me of jerking off in the window."

"*Were you* jerking off?"

"No. I was walking around naked. And yes, my curtains were open. But I was fucked up, out of my mind. I wasn't jacking it, especially not to some kids! *Fuck.*"

"So why did the girl accuse you?"

"I don't know! I have no fucking idea," Terry said, his eyes now wild. "The parents withdrew the complaint, but it was too late. Fucking ruined my life. I didn't do shit, but that don't stop people from looking at me like I did. I'm lucky I didn't lose my job. I couldn't go to church for four months."

He started crying again.

"I don't blame Sheila for breaking up with me. I get it. She had to protect her kids. But, man, it fucking hurt. I didn't do anything to those kids. I ..."

Mal stared at Terry, letting him have a moment to doubt whether she believed him. Eventually he'd fill the silence and give her more to go on.

"Did I get her in trouble?" Terry finally asked.

He might be guilty of something, but Mal believed his innocence about this. "We're not looking to screw with Sheila. She's been through enough. Thank you, Terry."

She got up, grabbed her Coke, then headed for the door.

"What now? Am I allowed to leave?"

"Assuming you don't have anything the detectives wanna talk to you about after they get back from your place, I'm guessing you'll be free to go soon. But you did run, so there might be some charges on that."

"Thank you," he said, looking down to his hand.

"Take care of yourself, Terry."

She left the interview room then went next door to where Mike and Skippy were waiting.

"Well?" Mike asked. "What do you think?"

"I think he's telling the truth."

"I dunno." Skippy shook his head. "Seems like a pedo to me."

"Well, I guess we'll find out when Jacobs and Taylor get back," Mal said. "Who wants to talk to Sheila about this? We need to see if Terry's story matches, then we've gotta see if she's still dealing and if there are any clients, past or present, who might have something to do this."

"Ought to lock her up. What kind of mother risks losing her kids by selling drugs? Just think of the scumbags she's exposing her kids to. How many pedo drug addicts or rapists she's probably sold her … what?" Skippy stopped.

Mal was looking at him, laughing. "*Pedo drug addicts?* You know, being a drug addict doesn't make someone more likely to be a scumbag, a pedophile, or a rapist. One thing has nothing to do with another, Skippy, so let's not rush into blaming the mom, eh?"

"Um," Skippy said with his finger in the air like a pretentious twat, "if she's dealing with the kids around, then she exposed them to bad people. Someone like that ought to have her kids taken away. Maybe Alice would still be alive if her mom wasn't a goddamned dealer."

Mal shook her head and looked at Mike. "Jesus, *this* is

who Barry thought ought to head up this case with you instead of me?"

"What did I say?" Skippy asked, offended. "You defending dealers now?"

She shook her head and turned to leave.

"I'll talk to Sheila," Mike said.

Mal turned at the door. "Don't let Skippy near her."

"The name is *Stan*," Skippy said, narrowing his eyes.

"Whatever, Skippy."

Mal headed down the hall, angry and shaking. She couldn't believe Skippy was being such a dick. How could you compare an addict with a pedo or a rapist? To lump all addicts in with the worst of humanity wasn't just wrong on a moral level. It was a dangerous attitude for a deputy to be carrying around.

Not all crimes were equal, nor all criminals. Seeing everybody in the same shades of black and white made even a well-meaning person desensitized to nuance. That was one of the easiest ways for a good cop to turn bad.

There had been enough of that under Sheriff Barry's first administration. Gloria had cleaned house of the worst of them, but if attitudes like Skippy's weren't kept in check, the department could decay from within yet again.

Mal entered the bathroom, then went into a stall.

As she sat there, she reached into her pocket where she'd been holding her two Just In Case pills. Now she had only one left.

It would be so easy to take it and make the pain go away.

No. You're fine.

You don't need it.

You want it, but you don't need *it.*

You're not anxious.

You're not on the verge of a panic attack.

You're just pissed, and you can deal with that.

117

Put the pill away, Mal.

She did so with a sigh.

Then her phone buzzed with a text.

She grabbed it and looked at the screen.

Katie: Remember how you offered to help me?

Mal: Yes.

Katie: Well, I don't really have anybody else and don't know what to do. Can you come get me so we can talk?

Mal: Where are you?

Katie: At school. Supposed to be walking home, but I can't go back to that house.

Mal: What happened?

Katie: Can you come or should I find someone else?

Mal pondered all the many things that might have gone wrong as fear chewed at her gut. Did Katie get into more trouble? Had she been raped again? Was it an average teenage drama or something much worse?

Mal: I'll be right there.

Chapter 17 - Howard Loomis

HOWARD FOLLOWED Cami for several days, tracking her schedule and getting to know her.

She went to college, worked some nights as a waitress at a nice steak house, and babysat three days a week for the Shaws.

Last Sunday, he followed Cami to their house then to church.

That's when Mister K decided to test him.

Howard was sitting in his van, watching them walking back to their house together, when Mister K's voice crackled over the radio. "Are you truly ready for The End?"

"Of course."

"I need you to prove it by helping me send a message to the others."

"What kind of message?" Howard asked.

"A message the right people will understand. A message for the Truth Knowers. The ones waiting for my word, to bring the new world into fruition."

"Okay," Howard said, eager to hear and know more.

Mister K had been promising to reveal great secrets to him for so long, sometimes it felt like it might never really happen. That Howard wouldn't ever be ready or worthy of trust.

"I can do it. I'm ready."

"We will see," Mister K said.

Chapter 18 - Jasper Parish

JASPER'S DOOR buzzed open just before lights out.

Hernandez entered with his paper cup full of pills. He walked to the sink as the door closed behind him, then set down the cup before turning to Jasper.

"Tell me more about your abilities," Hernandez said, in barely more than a whisper.

Jasper put his book of Robert Frost poems aside and sat up on his mat.

"Like what can I see?"

"More like, how does it work?"

"I sometimes get flashes, visions, or dreams that come true."

"When I was a detective in Vero Beach, I was working a missing kid's case where months went by with no suspects or evidence. Just a whole lot of nothing. The parents got desperate, turned to this TV psychic promising to help find the kid if they'd give her an item of clothing or something. So, they gave her a shirt, then the woman apologized and said he was dead. She couldn't say exactly what happened, or even where to find a body, only that he died quickly."

Hernandez looked at Jasper. "That something you can do? Touch an item and get a vision or something?"

"Sometimes, yes."

Hernandez nodded. "If I gave you an item, you could tell me about the owner?"

"Maybe. Like I said, I don't always control what I see. Sometimes I get nothing. I can't make any promises."

Hernandez nodded as he dug into his pocket. He pulled out a pack of Marlboro Red then tossed it to the prisoner.

Jasper looked at him curiously. "I don't smoke."

"Tell me about the owner of those cigarettes."

Jasper turned the pack in his hand. It wasn't a fresh pack, despite never being opened. The corners weren't sharp, and the edges were worn beneath the plastic wrapping. He closed his eyes, searching.

A glimpse of memory — an old man picking up the pack off the counter then walking outside. Then another nearly identical scene.

He met Hernandez's eyes. "They were yours. But your father took them. He picked them up off your kitchen counter. Said they were poison and you ought to quit — if not for your stupid ass, then for your son's."

His expression fell somewhere between amazement and anger. Perhaps Hernandez was angry Jasper could so easily peer into his tragedy.

"It was the last time you saw your father alive. A few hours later, you were pulling him out of his car after it blew a tire then slammed into a tree. Your cigarettes were on the passenger side floorboard, along with all the contents of his glove box. Your father died instantly."

Hernandez snatched the pack of cigarettes away from Jasper and shook his head. "I don't know what you've got, but it ain't right."

"You're right." Jasper nodded. "A lot of people would love to have whatever this is, but it wasn't there when I needed it most. I've seen winning lotto tickets, sports scores, and people dying. Even managed to save a few. But I couldn't see shit for the two people that meant everything to me. Didn't see my wife getting cancer and dying and didn't see my daughter being abused or killing herself. So, yeah, it ain't right."

Hernandez stared at the cigarettes in his hand, likely thinking of his own loss. But he wasn't just mourning his father, Jasper could feel it.

"Who is Frank?"

Hernandez looked up, eyes wide before narrowing on him.

"You're thinking about him. Frank Tagliano. He … he worked here, didn't he?"

"I swear to Christ, if you're fucking with me, I'll kill you myself," Hernandez spoke through gritted teeth.

"I'm not fucking with you. You know nobody here knows about the cigarettes. You didn't even tell your wife, did you?"

He shook his head.

"You're here because of Frank, right?"

Hernandez nodded.

"What do you want to know?" Jasper asked.

He reached into his pocket, grabbed a metal pen, then handed it over. "What can you tell me about this?"

Jasper turned it in his hands. A Parker. He wasn't sure if the pen was expensive, but its quality felt high. "You said you wanted to write a book, so he gave you this and a fancy leather journal to write in."

Hernandez said nothing.

"And he's dead now, isn't he?"

Hernandez nodded.

"It happened here, didn't it?"

Another nod from Hernandez.

"I … I can't see how, though. Do you have anything from when he died?"

He shook his head. "No, you didn't say I needed something a person had on them when they died."

"I don't always. But I'll need something else. He gave this to you. I'm getting more of your feelings than his."

Hernandez took the pen back, wiped it off on his shirt as if Jasper had tainted his friend's possession, then shoved it in his pocket.

"You want to know who did it … they got someone, but you don't think it was really the guy, do you?"

Hernandez glanced back at the door, then at Jasper. "Keep your fucking voice down."

"If you can get me something else of his, a badge of something he had on him, that might help."

"I'll see what I can do. But I had another idea."

"What's that?"

"Could you get anything by touching someone here?"

"You got a person you're thinking of?"

"You might wanna bump into some of 904 Mafia."

Jasper smiled. "Funny you should mention that. Ran into Young Luther today. He left me a rat in my bed. Knows I'm a cop."

"Well, see what you can get. If things heat up, find a way to get yourself in the hole again."

Jasper nodded.

Hernandez tipped his chin toward the paper cup, reminding Jasper to toss his pills.

"What happened with the hit on Wally? Anyone give up Young Luther?"

"Nope. They're blaming Kenn. And I don't expect

they'll press further charges for defending yourself. For whatever that's worth."

Jasper felt something coming. Whatever it was had bothered Hernandez. "The brass is just letting it go, aren't they? They don't care who was really responsible."

"They like neat bows. It's in your best interest to leave it alone." He turned to leave.

"Hey, what happened to that missing kid?" Jasper called out. "They ever find his body?"

"Yeah, but he was alive. Found him a year later, taken by someone who spotted him at a park. That psychic was full of shit. Would love to have locked her ass up, maybe teach her not to fuck with a family's hopes. But worst of all, she made me feel stupid for believing her lying ass."

Jasper nodded. "At least the kid's family had a happy ending."

Hernandez stood in the doorway. "Don't make me look like a fool."

Then he left, the door clanging shut behind him.

"Lights out!" shouted one of the other COs.

Then Jasper's pod was plunged into darkness.

Chapter 19 - Howard Loomis

HOWARD WAITED inside Cami's pitch-black bedroom.

The door was closed, and he was sitting on her bed, wearing his black balaclava.

There was a certain clarity and calmness he found in these silent moments before striking.

It shouldn't be this way, he shouldn't feel so serene. A mask made all the difference.

Howard had spent most of his life an anxious, frightened mess, terrified of most every social interaction. He could only do his security job by putting on a figurative mask of who he felt he needed to be. It was almost as if he was someone else at work — confident, unafraid of greeting people, shaking their hands and looking them in their eyes, speaking directly as though their judgments couldn't destroy him. He was known at work as one of the few installers who could handle even the most difficult customers.

But Howard was something else outside of work. Any attempts to wear that work mask felt hollow and false. He was a nervous wreck who could barely handle confrontation, from a random man looking to start a fight at Walmart to a drunk at a restaurant or the loan clerk at his bank. Howard avoided confrontation at all costs and yet was now actively seeking it for a second time.

The real mask made him feel like who he was truly meant to be. It allowed him to do his job without fear or feelings getting in the way.

It was a mask he learned to wear early, to get through the hell of growing up in that house. Disconnection was the only way to survive Enid. A mask he was perfecting with Mister K's help, one he needed last weekend when taking that child and carving a blade into her flesh.

He would have lost his nerve without that mask. Would have stopped and responded to her pleas. But Mister K ordered the work done and said God required it.

Howard voiced his lone objection just before he ended her life. "She's just a child."

"Children will be the first to suffer in The End. You are sparing her something worse than death. Granting God's mercy and allowing her entrance into Heaven before the gates close forever."

"Are you sure?" Howard had asked.

Mister K grabbed his hair tight and forced him to stare into the child's terrified eyes. "End her suffering or condemn her to the hellfires."

Howard cried, but only for a moment as the girl begged him not to.

Then he lowered the mask and followed his fate.

Howard was six years old again.

Mom caught him looking at a woman's cleavage in church. It was the first time he'd seen so much of a woman's chest. Her breasts were so round and milky when compared to that tanned neckline. Howie had felt an instant mix of titillation and shame, curiosity and condemnation.

He shouldn't look, but Howie couldn't help it. He had to know more, to *see* more.

But then Mom had seen him and pinched his ear so hard he let out a startled yelp and drew the entire congregation's attention.

More shame.

Mom grabbed his hair tight and dragged Howie into the shower at home. Made him turn the water scalding hot, then forced him to undress and get in.

"It hurts! Please, no!" Howie's cries turned into sobs.

But still, Mom held him under the water as she yelled, "This pales in comparison to the constant hellfire burning your soul!"

Afterward, she took him to the kitchen and tenderly applied cream to relieve the pain.

"I only do this to prepare you for the cruel world. I love you, Howie. You know that, right?"

"Yes, ma'am."

He went to his bedroom and cried into his pillow. But those tears only made him feel more shame. Howie wasn't sure what compelled him, but he removed his pillowcase and put it over his head as a makeshift mask.

Only there could he be someone else, someone who wasn't in so much pain. Someone who felt nothing and only observed.

In the mask, Howie was safe. From others and his weakness.

The sound of Cami's car brought him back to the present.

Howard stood and patted at his belt. His knife and pistol were ready in case he encountered a problem.

He grabbed the bottle and the rag, readied it as he waited for her bedroom door to open.

"Soon," Mister K whispered in the darkness. "Soon, The End."

Howard stared at the door and waited.

Chapter 20 - Mallory Black

MAL NOTICED clusters of kids outside the school and in the parking lot, hanging out. But Katie stood alone, leaning against the fence, a black Twenty-One Pilots hoodie pulled low to cover most of her face.

Mal rolled down her passenger side window of her SUV. "Hey, kiddo."

Katie looked around, her face flushing. "Sheesh, I thought you'd have your other car."

"Oh, shit. Sorry. I didn't even think how it would look rolling up like five-oh."

"It's okay," Katie said, begrudgingly, climbing into the truck and closing the door. "Not like I care what any of them thinks of me, anyway."

Mal seriously doubted that. Katie's makeup, edgy hair style, and choice of clothing said otherwise. But she wasn't about to point that out. The girl would only deny it, and Mal could remember how difficult it could be to fit in at that age. Criticizing a kid for craving acceptance was a shitty thing to do.

"I guess it's a good thing I didn't flash the lights and siren," Mal teased.

Katie laughed.

"I still could," she said, reaching for the buttons.

"Please, God, no." Katie sank down in her seat, pulling her hoodie even lower.

"Buckle up, it's the law."

Katie rolled her eyes as followed the order.

Mal pulled away from the curb. "The eye-rolling — that something you kids are born with, or they teaching it in school?"

"Oh, we learn it. Same place you learn your lame jokes."

"Touché." Mal drove without direction. "So, what's up? Am I supposed to feed you again?"

"Not sure I can eat now. But you can if you want. I've got nowhere to go." Katie put a hand on her stomach. "And I'm feeling anxious."

"What do you mean you've got nowhere to go?"

She stared out the window, her jaw clenching and unclenching, fists clutching her sleeves and pulling them across her chest.

"What happened, Katie?"

"I'm pregnant."

"*What?*"

"When Ben first accused me of sleeping with James, I hadn't even done anything. But he still said he'd send my ass back to the group home if I got pregnant. Because he 'refused to raise a slut.'"

"Wow," Mal said, stunned by both the news and her foster father's response.

"So, what are you going to do?"

"Are you asking if I want an abortion?"

"Something like that."

"I don't agree with my dad. Or the religion, on a lot of things. But I still can't bring myself to kill a baby."

"Does the father know?"

Katie shook her head.

"And he's your age?" Mal asked.

"He's eighteen. It's legal if we're within a few years of each other, I think."

"You *sure* he's eighteen?"

"Well, I never carded him. But does it matter? It's not like I'm pressing charges or anything. And if *you* try to charge him, I'll just deny it."

Mal wasn't going to argue that if she was pregnant, they wouldn't need her permission to press charges. The baby would be evidence enough.

But a back and forth would be pointless. Katie was defensive, and an argument wasn't the way to reach her. She would only close down. Besides, there was too much Mal didn't know about the situation, like whether he was her peer or some old scumbag preying on the girl's need for attention and continuing the cycle of abuse in her life.

Mal always erred on the side of caution in situations like this, and she'd rather be overprotective than turn a blind eye to any bright red flags. Still, the best thing she could possibly do right now was to simply listen and be there for Katie.

"So, are you going to tell him? What do you *want* to happen?"

Katie smiled, looking almost dreamy as she thought about him. "Well, I'd love it if we got married and moved in together, but I don't know if that's possible."

"Why not?"

"He's kinda living with someone else."

Ah, scumbag.

But Mal said nothing.

"He's not in love with her, anymore. James is trying to find the right time to break things off. But she's emotionally fragile, and he's afraid she'll hurt herself."

Mal had heard that line plenty of times before. She tried to hide her disbelief and disgust. She wasn't judging Katie, the girl was desperate for connection. Growing up sheltered and in an abusive situation, she needed something good in her life.

But this guy didn't sound like the person to take care of her.

"So, what are you going to do? Stay at the foster house until he can live with you? Does he make enough to support you and a baby?"

"I don't know," Katie said with a long and frustrated growl. "I was hoping you'd be able to give me some advice or maybe tell me what to do."

"Let me talk to Ben and Sarah."

"*That* is a horrible idea. I wouldn't want to go back and have my kid there. He's so judgmental. He's a terrible father figure. I'd rather live on the streets."

"Well, that's not going to happen. You can go back to the group home."

"I don't want to go back to God's Mercy."

"Why?"

"The kids there are awful. Girls would hit me, call me names, and steal my stuff. The boys were all the worst, making sexual comments and stuff ALL the time. It's like I run into assholes wherever I go."

"I can talk to the people there."

"The people who worked there weren't much better. I doubt it'll do any good."

"Did *they* hurt you?"

"No, nothing like that. They were just really mean."

"All of them?" Mal asked.

"Enough of them. They ignored me when I told them what the other girls were doing to me. Sister Agnes was the only one who seemed to care. But she was old and way too nice, so the other girls walked all over her."

"Can you go home for tonight and keep the pregnancy to yourself? I'll talk to a friend of mine and see if she can help me figure something out for you."

"I guess," Katie said. "Thanks."

~

AFTER DROPPING Katie off at home, Mal left a message with Carrie Thompson in Victim Services, then she checked in on the Shaw case.

McKenna was still in the coma. Aanya had tracked the cell phone's GPS coordinates with the carrier. After being activated in Jacksonville, it hadn't pinged another location until the church where Alice's body had been discovered.

The number used by the unsub to call Mal was also a burner, which she'd tracked to another gas station. She sent a detective over, but he got nothing they could use to track the unsub. That phone's GPS pinged near the church the day he called Mal but hadn't surfaced since.

Back in her hotel room, Mal grabbed a cold bottle of water, sat on the couch, then called Mike to follow up on his progress with Sheila.

He was on his way home to Gina and the kids.

"Yeah, she was a bit reluctant, but her story matches Terry's. Says a cook who used to work with her got her into it to help make ends meet. She only had a few clients when he got busted. Got spooked and stopped. Claims she hasn't sold since and never used."

"You believe her?" Mal asked.

"Yeah."

"And Skippy?"

"I interviewed her alone, sent him to follow up on interviews with people at the church."

"Any new leads?"

"Nothing else."

Mike updated Mal on some other details from his conversation with Sheila, along with a few dead-ends he'd been chasing. There was a long, awkward pause once he finished, and Mal thought about what Sheriff Barry had said about him keeping an eye on her.

"What are you thinking?" he asked.

Ask him. Ask him if he made a deal with the devil, and if so, why?

"Just thinking about that Katie kid," she lied, then updated him on what was happening with her adolescent disaster.

"So, what are you gonna do?"

"I put a call in with Carrie to see if she knows of any other options."

"Bet you're glad that you didn't adopt her."

"I told you about that?"

"You were feeling awful about what happened with her parents, so I understand. But it sounds like a handful."

"She's definitely working through some shit. And I've got enough of my own."

"How *are* you doing?"

This your way of checking up on me for Barry? Or do you really want to know?

"What do you mean?"

"Just checking in. Ever since you came back, you've been, I dunno ... *different*. I know you went through hell. I guess I'm just trying to ask if you need anything. We don't talk like we used to. I mean, *really* talk."

"I'm good." Then she answered the question lurking between the lines. "And yes, I'm still sober."

"Good," he said, following a pause.

"Yeah."

"I know I don't ask often because I don't want to be too intrusive. You can get a bit ..."

"Bitchy?"

"I was gonna say 'hard to love,' but sure, bitchy works in a pinch." Another pause, then, "I just want you to know I'm always here for whatever you need. To talk, cry, make me listen to your godawful taste in music — *whatever*."

Her tears were welling up. A part of her *wanted* to talk to Mike more than she did, to open up about how difficult everything had been, how lonely she felt, and how hard it was to get over murdering a man in cold blood, even knowing he was the monster who destroyed her life. She wanted to unburden her soul with confession, tell him how she'd gone on a vigilante spree of her own to deal with her rage. Admit she'd mutilated a man without flinching.

But it wasn't fair to put that all on him. Mal didn't think Mike would ever rat her out, but she didn't want to make him choose between upholding the law and protecting her. Best to keep her partner at a distance.

Nobody could understand that side of her, except maybe Jasper Parish, a crazy murderer who saw and talked to his dead daughter.

It also felt weird discussing her loneliness. For the most part, it was a choice. She had him, and Tim Brentwood had tried to connect with her plenty of times. But some part of her needed to keep the world at a distance. Every time Mal started to feel something for someone, she sabotaged it.

Why? Was she self-destructive garbage? If so, Mike was too sweet of a guy to burden with her bullshit. He had his own family to worry about without having to wonder why she was never happy, no matter what.

Best to keep him at a distance, like everyone else. He wasn't going to have the answers she was looking for, so there wasn't any point in dragging him down to her level.

"Thanks, Mike. I'm gonna find something to eat."

"Alrighty, see you tomorrow."

She hung up then looked in her fridge. Leftover Chinese with cartons of an undetermined vintage. So, room service it was.

The phone rang before she could call — the one left by the unsub.

"You've got twenty-four hours, detective," said the voice when she answered.

"Twenty-four hours for what?"

"To find her."

"Find who?"

But the call went dead.

Seconds later, a text with an image. A closeup shot of a brunette in her twenties, a gag in her mouth and eyes wide with terror. A gloved hand held a blade above her.

A text followed.

Twenty-three hours and fifty-nine minutes, detective.

Then another library of congress call number.

Mal found the book, *Pilgrim's Progress*, then went to the library and located the page number listed. But instead of an address, she found a message in the gutter.

Hello, detective.

Mal slammed the book, buried her terror, then did what had to be done.

Chapter 21 - Howard Loomis

HOWARD PACED the abandoned motel in the dark.

The place was relatively close to a gas station off I-95, but it was well concealed behind vegetation that had claimed both the building and the road leading to it. His van was parked in the rear, obscured if not invisible.

Nobody ever came here. It was one of those abandoned buildings passed by thousands of people each day with only a few ever looking over. It wasn't a destination. Even homeless people never squatted here since a lone gas station was the only other thing around.

Cami was still sleeping, gagged and bound to a chair, reeking of piss and sweat.

He shined his flashlight on her lacy bra as he sat on the dusty old bed beside her, rubbing his crotch.

She opened her eyes, startled by the light, squinting same as the last couple of times. Cami looked down at her lowered tank and squirmed, but there was nothing she could do.

She mumbled something Howard couldn't make out. Probably more pleas to set her free.

He set the flashlight down. It shined against the wall, bouncing back on them both.

Cami mumbled something else.

Howard stood, drew the knife from his belt sheathe, and presented it to her. A massive, machete-sized blade. "I'll cut your throat if you scream. Do you understand me?"

She nodded and he removed the gag.

"Please ... I need some water."

How grabbed a bottle from the floor, unscrewed the cap, then offered her a mouthful.

Cami swallowed as fast as she could.

He pulled it away before she felt too quenched, allowing some of the water to spill on her bra and shirt, making him harder.

"What do you want? You want to fuck me?"

"You wouldn't fuck someone like me, would you?"

"You never know," she said, an obvious fucking lie.

"You laughed at me. You and your bitch friend."

"Oh, shit. I remember you." Her eyes widened with realization.

Howard's worry lasted only a moment. Even if she could describe him to a sketch artist, even if she knew his full name and address, she would never get a chance to spill a word of her misery to anyone.

Mister K's directions were still a mystery, but surely they would end in her death.

"You were at Sloppy's that day!"

He nodded. "I was."

"Is that what this is about?"

Letting her wonder why she was here, Howard said nothing.

"Oh, God. I'm so sorry we laughed at you. I did feel really terrible."

"Yeah, right. I'm a joke to you. She was right — you're all lying whores."

Cami looked like she wanted to yell at him, but she bit her tongue and forced a pathetic attempt at sympathy. "Is that what this is about? You want revenge?"

"This is about more than that."

"What do you want?"

"I just want the truth." Howard smiled.

"What truth?" Her voice climbed a few octaves. "What do you want from me?"

"From you? I don't know what you can give me."

"Then let me go."

"I can't do that." Howard laughed. "*He* won't let me."

"Who?"

He looked at the door behind him, where he could feel Mister K waiting in the shadows.

"Please, you don't have to do this. You're better than this."

He met her eyes with a whisper. "You don't know me. Don't pretend like you care."

"I know you're not a killer. You're just lonely. Please, let me go. I'll let you do whatever you want to me. Just … please."

"I *wasn't* a killer, at first. But … you made me."

"*I* made you? I don't even know you. What do you mean?"

"You and your bitch friend laughing at me. That's why I followed you. And that's when you led me to them."

"Led you to who?" Her eyes went wide as it dawned on her. "*You* did that to Alice and McKenna?"

"It was your fault." Howard gave her a pained smile. He tried not to hurt them and really didn't want to. But Mister K demanded it. Howard needed to prepare others for The End. He was still confused what his role in all of it was, but confusion couldn't keep him from compliance.

If this was a test of his worthiness, he intended to pass it and show Mother she was wrong. He was worthy, not wicked.

Cami cried.

"You shouldn't have been such a bitch. Mother is right, you're all worthless whores."

"Fuck you, you sick fuck!"

Howard stared, confusion unsettling him.

Did I make a mistake?

Should I let her go?

Something in Cami's anger made him want to shrink away like the frightened child his mother always turned him into.

She seized on his fear. Her expression changed. She started laughing, hysterically.

"Oh, my God. You're just a weak little incel with mommy issues! This is the only way you can get off, by tying up women and hurting them!"

He closed his eyes, tears burning them as Cami turned into his mother. She laughed and yelled even louder. "You're not a real man. A real man wouldn't have to do this. A real man ..."

"You going to let her talk to you like that?" asked Mister K from the darkness. "Or are you going to teach her?"

"I'm going to teach her." Howard stood and looked down at Cami.

He reached into his pants pocket then pulled out the mask.

She shook her head, eyes darting around in their sockets, her fear like a nectar to savor.

He slowly slipped on the balaclava, his fear and doubts

all disappearing. Only power remained as he grabbed her bra and ripped it off of her body.

Cami screamed, thrashing within the confines of the chair.

"I told you to stay quiet." He wagged his finger while shaking his head.

He punched her in the face, hard enough to rob her consciousness, then he shoved the rag back in her mouth and tied the gag around it.

Howard sat on the bed. Unzipped his pants with one hand while pinching her nipple hard with the other. He'd never touched a girl's tit before and it made him come too quickly.

Mister K laughed from the shadows.

Hot shame washed over him, reminding Howard of when Mother punished him for his sinful thoughts. Not only was he wicked, but he couldn't even touch a tit without blowing a load in seconds.

"So, was it everything you'd dreamed it would be?" Mister K asked.

Howard wiped his jizz on Cami's shirt, wishing he'd lasted longer. He wanted to take his time and enjoy her more.

"Don't worry, Howard, you'll get another go before it's time to dispatch her. Take it slow and enjoy her next time. With every girl who's ever laughed at you and the way your mother treated you, you've earned this. *You deserve it.*"

He stared at Cami's tits and his heart raced faster, sin and wickedness be damned.

"Yes. Yes, I did." Howard reached down, coaxing the power back into his body.

Chapter 22 - Mallory Black

THE STUDIO LIGHTS WERE BRIGHT, making Mal anxious as she sat at the desk across from her old boss. It was the first time Mal had seen Gloria Bell since Barry's reelection.

Gloria had gone from sheriff to host of a Sunday morning political talk show on the local cable network where she tackled issues involving race, women's rights, gay and trans rights, or any topics typically ignored by the press in a mostly conservative county. Her show didn't have a big audience, basically being a step above public access. But the right people watched it, and Gloria was finding a way to influence local leaders and help people despite her recent loss.

Mal thought Gloria was far more suited to this career than she'd been to being sheriff. Here she could actually make a difference. She was terrific at talking on camera and interviewing guests.

She called Cameron Ford at first, hoping he would broadcast a message out about the missing girl. He did the bare minimum, a photo and a hotline number, saying it was late and he'd touch base with her in the morning.

He also said, after conferring with the sheriff, they ought not to mention the twenty-four-hour deadline, not knowing if this was a legitimate crime or a prank. No need to spook the citizens unnecessarily. They didn't want people to think there was a serial killer out there. That might make the sheriff look like he was allowing it to happen on his watch, and Barry fancied himself a tough-on-crime bad-ass where criminals quaked in their boots and never dared to challenge his authority. As if God himself had appointed him Sheriff of the World.

Frustrated, she called Gloria and asked if they could get a segment on the news, knowing local politicians would pay more attention if it was on her show and might even pressure the sheriff to do his fucking job. The segment would be live tonight then replayed in the morning another four or five times. Hopefully, the extra press would get word out on the missing girl and maybe someone would come forward with a name or any helpful information.

"You look great, Mal. Everything good?" Probably Gloria's way of asking if she was sober.

"I'm doing better. You look five years younger. This job really suits you."

"I hated losing the election, but everything happens for a reason. This feels right."

The producer — a tall, redheaded trans woman named Jasmine — came over and double-checked Gloria's notes. "We're live in one minute," she said before backing away from the set, donning her headset, then giving direction to the control room.

"You know he's going to fire you for this," Gloria warned.

"Let him try." Mal glanced across the studio at the

main news desk where the co-anchors were prepping themselves.

Gloria gave her a smile. "It's good to see you again."

The producer said, "Live in five, four, three, two, go!"

"We come to you tonight with an urgent plea to help identify this missing woman," Gloria started.

The photo the unsub sent Mal appeared on the screen as her host spoke over it.

"If you know who this woman is, or have seen her, please call the Creek County Sheriff's Office hotline immediately. At the time of this airing, she may only have twenty-two hours to live." Gloria looked soberly into the camera. "Tonight, I'm joined by Creek County Sheriff's Office Detective Mallory Black, who helped bring several high-profile killers to justice, including Paul Dodd, the man who kidnapped and murdered her daughter. Welcome, Detective Black."

"Thank you for having me."

"So, tell me what happened. And how is this connected to the murder of Alice Shaw and the shooting of her sister, McKenna?"

"We have reason to believe our suspect in the Shaw case is behind this disappearance. He called me on a phone left at the scene where we found Alice and said we have twenty-four hours to find this young woman."

"In the earlier statement released by the sheriff's office, there was no mention of these cases being connected. Does the sheriff's office believe we have a serial killer at large?"

This was Gloria's diplomatic approach — to put the information out there without leveling any accusations against Barry. She could have gone on the attack, asked Mal why the sheriff hadn't made this more of a priority, but she was playing it right. Better to have Barry playing ball than turning him defensive.

"It's a bit early to call him that, but we do believe the cases are connected."

"What can you tell us about the suspect?"

Mal delivered the little info she had.

Gloria showed the photo again, this time asking Mal for more details about her call. "And why do you think he reached out to you?"

Mal looked into the camera, knowing the man was watching. "I'm not sure. Killers who target girls and women are often insecure little men who have trouble fitting in with society. They blame women for their lack of success or for their lives sucking. They target those they see as weaker than them, when these girls and women are always stronger because they aren't pathetic cowards."

She was taking a chance in pissing him off, but she'd do anything for a call. Aanya was running traces, same for the people running the station's lines. If he responded and lashed out, and if she managed to keep him on the line long enough, she might get a trace.

"Do you think this girl will die if you don't find her?"

Mal looked somber. "We have to take him at his word."

"What about the reports, from less reputable news sources, that there were Satanic carvings on Alice Shaw's body?"

"Those reports were inaccurate," Mal said, enjoying the opportunity to take a shot at Cameron's shitty blog. "While it claims sources inside the department had provided the information, I assure you — although there were carvings in the body, they were not Satanic in nature."

"Will the department be releasing photos of the drawings?"

"Not at the moment. We've reached out to experts for their assistance."

Gloria kept asking questions about the case, and Mal kept delivering answers, doing her best not to say anything the sheriff's office should still be keeping quiet.

Her phone buzzed in her coat pocket several times during the interview, but Mal ignored it every time. Once the interview ended and the show went to commercials, Jasmine came over and thanked her.

"No, thank you," Mal said. "Thank you all. I hope that gets us some leads."

Gloria walked Mal off the set as she checked her messages. First, her partner had texted.

Mike: What are you doing?"

Then there were all the missed texts from Ford.

Ford: What the fuck are you doing?

Ford: You are NOT authorized to be talking about this case.

Ford: Call me ASAP.

"Looks like I'm in deep shit." Mal smiled, showing her phone to Gloria.

"Well, it's not like you needed the job."

"True."

Mal was about to check her voice mail — Ford had called her, too — when her phone rang. Sheriff Barry.

When she answered, he screamed into the phone. She could practically smell his alcohol-laced breath. "What the fuck are you doing? You weren't authorized to discuss this case. I did not clear any of this, *Deputy*."

Mal resisted the urge to snipe back. "With all due respect, Sheriff, we don't have long. This girl's life is in danger. And I tried with Cameron first, but he wasn't listening. I assumed you'd want to do everything possible to get this girl back alive."

"That doesn't mean going on that fucking show and telling the county we've got a goddamned serial killer out there!"

"I never said that. In fact, I specifically said—"

"You may as well have! You are not the lead on this case. And you don't have permission to break protocol and go straight to the fucking news. That's why we have Cameron."

"Well, then maybe you should find someone more capable of doing his job, Sheriff. The fucker could barely run a goddamned blog."

A long moment of silence. Mal imagined his face burning red and puffing up like it might explode. She traded a smile with Gloria.

"I want you in my office first thing in the morning, Ms. Black," Barry finally responded. "Do you think you can follow those instructions?"

"Yes, sir."

"Good. You're off the case until then."

"We need all the people on this that we can get right now, not tomorrow. The clock is ticking, sir."

"You are off this case until further notice," Barry repeated before hanging up.

"So? What's the verdict?" Gloria asked.

"I'm probably fired. Gotta see him first thing in the morning. He wants me off the case 'until further notice.'"

"Fuck," Gloria said.

"Fuck, indeed," Mal agreed.

"Well, at least you can catch some sleep tonight."

"We'll see about that. I have to call Mike back. I'm sure he's pissed at me."

"You did the right thing, Mal. And I'm sure Mike will come around if he's not on board already."

"Thanks," Mal said.

Gloria gave her a hug.

Then Mal left, calling Mike as she walked to her car,

expecting a lecture. She wasn't prepared for how exhausted he sounded. *With her.*

"What the fuck, Mal? Why?"

"Because Dipshit Cameron can't do his fucking job."

"You had to go on *her show?*"

"What was I supposed to do? Wait for another body then wish we'd done something—"

"No, but—"

"It's done, Mike. There's nothing to say."

He vented a long sigh. "I'm trying to save your job."

"Yeah? Is that why you agreed to keep me on a short leash?"

After a pause, he murmured, "What?"

"Barry told me you said you'd keep me on a short leash. Is that why you're always checking in? Keeping tabs on me so you can report back to the big boss?"

"I had to fight tooth and nail to keep you from being demoted to traffic duty, to keep you as my partner. Barry wanted to make your life a living hell."

"Well, fuck him. And fuck you, too. I don't need anyone keeping me on a leash. I'm not a goddamned dog."

"It's not how it is. But let's be real for a minute, Mal. You *were* out of control. I'm not blaming you. Anyone in your situation, who went through the hell you've gone through, would be hard pressed to stay sane, to not fall off the wagon, but you were doing God only knows what drugs, drinking, and getting into fights. You can understand their concern."

She clenched her jaw and tightened her grip on the steering wheel. Mike was right, but Mal still hated being called out by him. Or anyone else.

"Then why the hell did you ask me to come back? If you were so concerned?"

"Because you're damned good at your job. When

sober. And I was worried what you'd do if you didn't come back."

"What does that mean?"

"I'm not stupid, Mal."

"What does *that* mean, Mike?"

"You *know* what it means. And I'm not saying it."

Does he know about my vigilante activities?

Does he think I was suicidal, or is he thinking I was going to overdose and die?

Fuck.

Mal couldn't ask, not on a line Barry or one of his gestapo might be listening in on.

"Get some sleep. I'll see you in the morning." Then he hung up.

Mal felt a sharp pain in her chest, like her only remaining friendship in her sad little world was suddenly doomed. It made her fondle the pill in her pocket and imagine swallowing it dry.

She drove home hating herself instead.

Chapter 23 - Jasper Parish

JASPER WALKED THE TRACK. Better to keep moving and make himself a harder target.

Jordyn walked beside him, hoodie pulled low and hands stuffed into her pocket. Crazy Gary eyed them both as he passed.

"Stay away from him," Jasper said.

"You forgot, Dad?"

"What?"

She ran her hands up and down her body as if the truth should be evident. "Um … I'm dead."

"Sorry … the longer I'm off the meds, the more I forget."

"It's okay. I figured you're just getting senile." She laughed.

It wasn't the same cute, raspy laugh she had as a little girl, but it was still endearing. And Jasper was glad that he could hear it again.

He looked around the yard, searching for some signal that might get him closer to the truth of what happened to Frank. Maybe if he could get near enough to the right person, he'd either find the guilty party or someone with enough information to take Jasper the rest of the way. If he had something of value to offer Hernandez, he could go without his meds a little longer, maybe indefinitely.

"You getting anything?" Jasper asked.

She looked over at the weights where Young Luther and a few of his men were lifting and hanging out. "Not really. They're all bad dudes, but I can't tell which one of them did or even ordered the hit."

Jasper didn't think Young Luther would've done it himself. He'd been sentenced to twenty-five years but would likely get out earlier. He still had fame and money, plus the record label was being run by a cousin and doing phenomenally well. Prison boosted his status as a legit gangster, but his best bet was getting out soon, even if it meant turning snitch.

"I think we should move closer," Jasper suggested. "Hang back here."

"Okay." She passed Crazy Gary who looked their way.

Jasper walked toward the basketball courts where there was a four-on-four game going on. A familiar-looking thin young man with sleepy eyes and a low curly fro stood off to the side.

Jasper approached him with a nod.

The man nodded back and gave him a whisper. "Hey, Professor."

Professor?

It took a moment, but then Jasper realized it was one of Kim's men, the guy in the Heat jersey, who had driven Jasper to meet her at the RV in the middle of nowhere.

"D'Andre's the name."

"What got you in here?" Jasper asked.

"Oh, you know, some bullshit after the Butler PD raided all of Logic and Kim's houses."

"They okay?"

"Moved operations north. They all good."

Jasper was glad to see a familiar face, but he had to keep things on the down-low. Never let people know who your friends are until you know where they stand. Alliances in prison were chess games played with shivs and duplicity.

"You want in?"

"Yeah," Jasper said.

He could feel Young Luther and Muscles watching from the weights.

D'Andre looked back at Young Luther then at Jasper. "Nah, man, you better get."

"What?" Jasper said before getting the hint. He was kryptonite in here. "Okay."

He turned to leave, but D'Andre bumped him, hard.

Jasper turned, surprised.

"Yo, back the fuck off, rat!" D'Andre said, shoving him with both hands, eyes glaring like an enemy.

As D'Andre's touched his chest, Jasper got a burst of memories — the man being visited by Young Luther, who knew of him by way of Logic's reputation. Young Luther made D'Andre swear loyalty if he wanted in on their operation — whatever that was.

Jasper backed away, raising his hands in apology.

The game stopped, the men now watching the scene as Jasper walked away.

Young Luther laughed with a chorus of echoes, then got off his bench and started walking toward Jasper, Muscles by his side, with another pair of men right behind him.

"What's up, pig?" Young Luther got in his face.

Touch me so I can see inside your soul.

"Just trying to play a game."

"Yeah, well, you ain't welcome here, pig." Young

Luther's voice swelled loud enough for everyone to hear him call Jasper a pig, just to make sure — in case everyone wasn't already aware — the convict had once been a cop.

Energy from the others — and the entire situation — was surging. Excited particles slammed into one another, as if they alone might escalate the violence.

"Break it up," said a guard before Jasper could respond.

Young Luther shoved a finger into his chest. "You're lucky, but your good fortune's 'bout to run the fuck out."

A flash of memories accompanied the jabbing finger — Young Luther talking to an unfamiliar CO, who handed the prisoner a package. Payment, contraband, something else?

The memory faded as more officers came to break it up and to send everyone back to their pods. Jasper fell in line behind Crazy Gary, who looked back at him with a subtle shake of his head. Maybe a signal. Or the guy might be off his meds.

Jasper accidentally bumped into his back and felt an unexpected flash.

Crazy Gary circling the track, just minutes ago, talking to a young man in all gray. The prisoners wore orange and the guards dressed in black. No one here was ever wearing gray.

The man was looking up at the tower, telling Crazy Gary how things had changed so much.

"Things are always changing," Gary replied.

"Suppose you're right," said the man in gray, turning and meeting his crazy gaze.

He saw someone walking just beyond the man's stare of insanity — Jordyn.

"Who's she?" asked the man in gray.

"His girl." Crazy Gary pointed to Jasper, about to get toe-to-toe with Young Luther.

The vision broke and Jasper found himself staring at the man in confusion.

He can see her?

How?

"What is it you see?" Crazy Gary whispered.

Jasper looked back at him, saying nothing.

"I see. You're playing normal so they don't make you take yer' pills." Crazy Gary winked then turned his attention back to the front, peeling off the line with the guy ahead of him then sauntering down the hall to his pod.

Jasper sat on his bunk and stared at Jordyn, leaning against the wall, hands still stuffed in her pockets.

"You almost got yourself killed, Daddy."

"I needed to get close to them, see what I could get."

"And, what did you get?"

"Not much to work with … yet."

"You're gonna do that *again?*"

"Might have to think of some other way. Or maybe if Hernandez gives me something of Frank Tagliano's, I'll get something from that. Maybe you can help me."

"Okay," she said, uncharacteristically quiet.

"What is it?"

"I know what you saw with Crazy Gary."

"You knew he could see you?"

She nodded.

"Did he say anything to you?" Jasper asked.

"He said *hi.*"

"And? Did you say hi back to him?"

"Yeah."

"He heard you?"

"Yes."

"He's the first person, other than me?"

Jordyn nodded.

"And … how does it feel?"

"I dunno. Is it wrong that I want to talk to him?"

"Do *not* talk to him."

"Why not?"

"He's crazy."

"People say *you're* crazy."

"You know what he did to get in here?"

"No."

"He killed people."

She started to interrupt.

"And before you say so did I, he killed his next-door neighbor, an old woman who never hurt anyone."

"Why?"

"Robbery gone wrong, needed money for drugs. She came home and saw him. He did it so she wouldn't call the cops."

She stared at the ground.

"Still want to talk to him?" Jasper asked.

Jordyn still didn't answer.

Jasper felt a pang of guilt. "Listen, I understand you're lonely."

"No, you don't. You have no idea what it's like. I can't talk to anybody but you."

"I think I know exactly how you feel, Jordyn."

"No," she said, pulling her hands free so she could use them to talk. "Maybe if I was stuck somewhere like you, at least there'd be someone to talk to. Maybe you don't have the best options, but at least there are other people you can have a word with. I'm stuck around people I used to know, but they can't see or talk to me. I may as well not exist. I can't go to Heaven or Hell, if there is such a thing. And every time I ask myself why I'm stuck here, I get more and more certain it's all because of you."

"I don't think you'd want to go to Hell."

"I feel like I'm already there."

Jasper felt that same ache he used to feel when his daughter was alive and dealing with problems he didn't know how to solve. He was her father. It was his job to make her problems go away. But all too often, he felt powerless. Just like — or perhaps even especially — now.

"You can talk to him. But ... just be careful."

"Gary can't hurt me," she said.

"Don't tell him what Hernandez did for us or is having us do."

"Thank you."

Jasper nodded. He assumed that was the end of it, but she kept staring at him. "What is it?"

"You don't see it?"

"See what?" Jasper asked.

Jordyn approached and put her hands on his face. "*This.*"

Flashes of a giant of a man murdering a child then fixing her to a cross. Mallory inside the church. The killer calling her.

Another flash, this one of the man with a knife standing in front of a girl tied in a chair, her minutes numbered.

Jordyn removed her trembling hands. "We need Mallory to come here."

Chapter 24 - Mallory Black

ANOTHER DREAM, this one making her feel like Alice in Wonderland.

Mal found herself moving through a giant dollhouse full of plastic furniture. She'd gone from room to room in search of an exit, now she was stuck in a loop in a dark hallway with four doors, one on each end and two on either side.

The hallway was ink black except for bright red flashing above, throwing crimson blotches of light on the wall. The house felt familiar, though she wasn't sure why.

Mal was trying to escape the hall, but every time she came to a door, it would deposit her back into the very same hallway. Even when she turned to try and leave out the door she'd just entered through, Mal was turned back around in the same spot, now facing forward.

She moved faster, more and more desperate to flee, walls closing in on her and the ceiling drifting down, grinding like thunder as she was squeezed from all sides.

Mal kept moving until she was forced to start crawling across the floor.

A door appeared to her right, too tiny for her to squeeze through, though she had to try anyway. She scurried toward it as the walls, ceiling, and floor crushed the hall from existence.

She fell face first on plush carpet into a well-lit room, still inside the doll house filled with plastic furniture. A set of two eerily familiar dolls sat on the bed, staring.

Mal moved to get a closer look at the porcelain faces before the dolls became Jessi and Ashley, both frozen in time. Her daughter's doll eyes blinked open, and a muffled cry bleated from her porcelain lips.

"Mommy,"

Mal hugged the doll, hard enough to turn her human. But it didn't work, and from the other side of the door came a terrible scratching, followed by an agonizing howl.

"Don't let the wolf get us!" the Jessi doll screamed.

Mal turned as the door exploded open and Paul Dodd came growling into the room, his wolf's mouth wide and frothing between rows of jagged, twisted teeth.

"Come to join the girl?" Dodd asked in the voice of a nightmare.

Mal raced toward him, her hand in a claw, ready to tear his flesh apart.

Then the phone rang, yanking her out of the dream.

It took her a moment to realize she was awake and holding her phone, her blankets kicked off the bed. Startled, heart racing and lungs short of breath, she answered without looking to see who it was.

"Hello?"

"Detective Black? It's Sheila Shaw."

Mal sat up, shivering in her cold sweat. "Of course, yes, how can I—"

"That girl on the news. I know her."

"The missing girl?"

"Her name is Cami Rivera. She sits for the girls."

Mal's racing heart jolted stop. Cami was one of the names on her list of people she'd been trying to contact. "Are you sure it's her?"

"Yes. I've been calling and calling her but can't get an answer."

~

OF COURSE IT WAS RAINING.

Mal was lights on, siren off, flying faster than she should down the rain-slicked roads, struggling to see through deluge pelting her windshield. She was racing to the station to meet Mike and Skippy. She'd called her partner on the way, left Skippy to him. Almost hoped he didn't get the call, but they needed every hand on deck to work this case — assuming Barry would let her anywhere near it.

She got to the sheriff's office in time to find the night shift deputies pulled from road duty, an additional three detectives, a few deputies brought in early, and Captain Lummock.

They met in the briefing room where Lummock and Mike went over all the new details they'd gotten since learning the victim's name. Mal took a seat in the first row, not presuming to go up front with the others.

Lummock cleared his throat. "The sheriff will be in soon, but in the meantime, I want the girl's apartment searched and anyone who knows her interviewed. We need everything we can get and have to work fast. Aanya's digging into her social media and tracing her phone's last location. I've sent a PDF to each of you with people to interview ASAP."

Mal checked her phone for the file, saw nothing, and raised a hand.

"Yes, Black?" Lummock said.

"I don't see the email."

"The sheriff has asked that you wait until he gets here."

She glanced at her phone: 4:15 AM. No telling when the fat ass would roll in. He usually made it somewhere around the crack of noon.

"No offense, sir, but we need everyone we can get on this. At least let me work the phones, check the tip lines, and see if anything else came in."

"I appreciate your dedication, Detective, but my hands are tied."

"This girl is going to die today if we don't find her. We don't have time to punish me."

"Maybe you should've thought of that before you broke protocol," Lummock said.

"If *I* didn't break protocol, you all wouldn't even have this tip!" Now Mal was on her feet. "Sheila saw *me* on TV, not that weak, glorified press release you all released."

The other deputies stared at her. She felt suddenly exposed, alone on a ledge and wanted someone else, particularly Mike, to speak up for her. But it was a room full of crickets.

Lummock lost patience with her as he lost a sigh. "Will there be anything else, or can I get on with the briefing?"

"If anybody needs me, I'll be waiting for our fat fucking sheriff to show up and do his goddamned job." Mal stormed out of the room.

She strode down the corridor then sat on the bench Barry would have to pass on his way into work.

Mal got on the phone, contemplating calling Gloria and telling her they had a name, but then she decided to follow the rules. The killer might be counting on them not knowing the girl's identity yet, and that could maybe give them an advantage.

Still, she was linked to the Shaws. It was only a matter of time before someone else recognized the missing girl. Mal needed to be certain she was doing the right thing before breaking protocol again. And right now, she was far certain.

But she was terrified for Cami's life and knew all too well what it was like to be the prisoner of a sadistic killer. There wasn't any evidence of sexual abuse on the first scene, but that was a child, not an adult. The killer's M.O. might change with someone older. Whether she was being sexually assaulted or tortured, every moment Cami was held by the monster had to be another lost to hell.

There were a million things Mal should be doing other than sitting here on her ass.

She stood and paced, trying to think of something she could manage on her own without incurring the wrath of Barry or the other deputies.

The Sheriff entered the lobby, holding a box of donuts and a huge Bubba thermos full of coffee, or knowing him, something with more bite. Never too early to tie one on.

"Ah, Detective." His furry brows cinched together like a pair of caterpillars crawling above his disapproving eyes. "Let's go to my office."

Chapter 25 - Mallory Black

MAL FOLLOWED Sheriff Barry's waddling ass down the hall into his office, the whole time telling herself, *Don't blow up, don't blow up, don't blow up, don't blow up.*

He sat at his desk, opened the box, then and slid it across the desk. "Donut?"

"No, thank you." She sat across from him, too anxious to eat despite the tempting scent of fried sugar. She wanted to get this over with, kiss Barry's ass, do whatever it took to get her back on the streets and working the case.

"Suit yourself." He eyed her as he licked frosting off his pudgy finger. "Not like you need to worry about your weight."

Are you fucking serious?

She hid her contempt. Said nothing.

"So ..." He took a bite of his donut, probably the first of all twelve. "What the hell was that shit last night?"

"I'm sorry, sir, but I felt it was a matter of—"

"I don't care what you *felt*. It's not your job to feel. It's your job to follow instructions. Why is it people — well, some people — can't follow simple directions? Used to be so much easier around here. Folks knew their jobs and did what they were supposed to do. Now everyone thinks they know better than the boss."

"I just—"

"You used to be a good deputy, back before Ms. Bell poisoned you with her bullshit. Now you're out starting fights, whoring around and getting caught on tape, doing drugs, and God only knows what else."

She wanted to scream. Wanted to take all eleven of his donuts and shove them so far up his ass they'd give his brain stem diabetes.

He looked at her as he polished off the first donut then washed it down with a big swig of coffee. "If I were to give you a drug test right now, would you pass it?"

"What?"

Barry licked his fingers again, reached into his pocket, fished out some keys, then opened his desk drawer. He pulled out a manila envelope then dumped the contents on the desk.

Photos of Mallory, shots taken from afar, some from when Cameron had run his hit piece on his blog, but others from after.

Mal drinking at the hotel bar and at clubs around town, at an NA meeting, taking pills in her car. And the one she had to mask her reaction to — a photo of Mal going into the club where she'd mauled the rapist.

Does he know what I did?

Barry stared at her.

Her heart was racing, chest tightening as dozens of horrifying scenarios played out in her head all at once. What else had he, or whoever he had following her, witnessed? Had they seen her with Jasper? Did they know about her other crimes?

If so, Barry could arrest her on the spot.

And she could end up in jail, same as Jasper.

Life over, just like that.

Her pulse raced faster. A cold sweat tickled her neck. She wanted to wipe her clammy hands down her pants but knew it'd be obvious. She was going to faint or puke. Maybe both.

"What I see here is a reckless accident waiting to happen."

If he had more, he would have led with that … I think.

"You're having me *followed?*" Seemed like the best offense was a good defense.

"I need to know what the hell I'm dealing with — what kind of lawsuits you're gonna open me up to."

"You worried about lawsuits?" She laughed. "That's rich."

"You are placed on administrative leave immediately until further notice."

"You can't do that. That girl is counting on us to find her. Counting on me."

"We'll be fine without you."

"The killer called *me.* There's got to be some reason for that. Give me a chance to bring him in and finish my job."

"Yeah, about that — hand over the phone. *I'll* take his calls from now on."

"Are you serious?"

"One hundred percent, missy. Hand it over."

"I think it's at Aanya's work station," she lied.

"Go get it and bring it to me. Then I want you to pack up and go home until further notice."

The walls were closing in around her. What could she do while sidelined from the case? That girl was as good as dead. And who knew how many more victims there might be?

She nodded, afraid to open her mouth, scared of what

might come out of it. Then she stood and left without another word, her heart ready to explode.

In the hall, she leaned against the wall, curbing her dizziness before making her way to the restroom, stumbling inside, then collapsing into the stall.

Mal fell onto the seat then kicked the door closed. She needed a Xanax, right fucking now. A panic attack probably couldn't kill her, but it sure as hell felt like it might.

She reached into her jacket, realizing that she'd left the Xanax on her nightstand.

Fuck, fuck, fuck, fuck!

Mal could hear her own heartbeat. She gasped, trying to breathe while closing her eyes.

Center yourself.

But of course, she failed. Fuck if she could focus on anything but the goddamned pulsating in her ears. The squeezing of her chest, and now her skull.

Mal clenched her fists, frustrated, wanting to cry at what a helpless fuck she was being. Needing a fucking pill to soothe herself.

She should be able to do this on her own. Or—

Her hand brushed against a bump in her pocket.

The Just In Case pill.

No, don't do it, Mal.

You're doing good.

You don't need it.

You're six months sober.

Do not fuck this up.

The bathroom door opened.

"Are you okay in there?" asked an unfamiliar voice.

No, I'm not fucking okay. I'm a fucking train wreck!

Mal couldn't open the door, not like this. She'd never live it down. She'd have a full meltdown, maybe pass out.

And at work! Barry would make sure she never saw action again.

She reached for the pill, pulled it from her pocket.

Just once.

Once and that's it.

She shouldn't. But the alternative was worse. Mal shoved the pill into her mouth and dry-swallowed before she could stop herself.

"Mallory?" the woman's voice asked.

Great, she knows who's in here.

"Yeah, just feeling nauseated … I'm …" she made a fake gagging sound. "I'm fine."

"Okay," the woman said before leaving.

Did the woman have business in the bathroom and get scared away, or had she been actively following her?

Maybe another fucker keeping tabs on me for Sheriff Barry.

Mal closed her eyes. The wave of relief wasn't immediate, but knowing it was coming felt like solace in itself. Maybe a placebo effect, maybe not.

She fished the killer's phone from her pocket, opened it, took out the SIM, then shoved it into her pocket. She powered down, giving her enough time to get out of the sheriff's office after she handed it over. She'd be in the parking lot before he realized the SIM card was missing — assuming he didn't just open and check. Fortunately for her, Barry wasn't all that bright.

Mal left the restroom, went to her locker, pretended to grab the phone so the closed-circuit cameras would see her, then started walking toward his office, pretending to have a conversation on *her phone* as she entered his office.

Mal moved fast, and to the imaginary party on the other end, she said, "Yes, I understand, but … hold on …" She dropped the phone on Barry's desk. "Here you go."

The sheriff started to raise a finger to get her attention,

but she pretended not to notice, turning around and continuing the conversation with her imaginary partner. "No, that's not what I was saying … *you tell me*."

Mal pretended to listen as she headed down the hall, into the parking lot, then over to her car. She heard footsteps running behind her before she could get in.

Shit. He found out.

She turned and saw it was Mike.

"What the hell was that back there?"

"What?" Mal said. "You mean me trying to actually do some police work?"

"No, I mean you undermining the captain, and that whole 'fat fucking sheriff' thing."

Mal stared at him, wanting to take her partner seriously, but suddenly found herself bursting into laughter. "Oh, yeah, I did call him that."

He stared at her like he wanted to be angry, then he laughed too, begrudgingly. But then his smile faded and lowered his voice while meeting her eyes. "Are you using?"

The question, and the accusation inside it, hurt Mal more than if Mike had punched her in the stomach. She could take a hit, but not his utter lack of faith in her here in this moment when she needed him to have her back more than anything else.

"It's one thing to ask me when I was on leave, or when you were picking me up from some bar fight, but *now*? When there's a girl's life on the line? Is that what you think of me?"

Mike stared at her as if trying to decide whether he should apologize or interrogate her further.

"Fuck this." She finally broke, turning around to open her SUV door. "Fuck all of this. I'm out."

"What are you doing?"

"He sent me home. I'm on administrative leave 'until further notice.'"

"What?"

"Barry's wanted me gone for a while now. So really, it's no surprise."

"Damn." He looked down at his shoes then back up at Mal. "Let me see what I can do."

"You can't do anything, Mike. Just let it go. Maybe I can do more good on my own."

"What?"

"I'll find a way to track this fucker down. He obviously called me for a reason. I don't think he's gonna stop."

"And what are you gonna do? Go arrest him on your own?"

"No, not arrest." She smiled, got in her truck, slammed the door, then tore out of the parking lot.

Part of Mal hated herself for using. But another part hated the sheriff even more. She was determined not to lay down and surrender. Mal would find a way to find this fucker.

And just as she thought of the one person who might know something, her phone rang with an unknown caller. She answered, wondering if the killer somehow got her work number.

"Hello, is this Detective Mallory Black?" The man sounded formal, maybe a cop.

Her gut clenched. Surely someone was about to give her more bad news.

"My name is Ramón Hernandez. I'm calling on behalf of a prisoner here, Jasper Parish. He says he needs to see you."

Chapter 26 - Jasper Parish

AFTER YARD TIME, Jasper lay on his bunk, reading. Jordyn sat on the end, humming a song she was playing on her phone.

"Crazy Gary is indeed cuckoo for Cocoa Puffs," she said out of the blue, even though Jasper had forgotten to ask if she'd talked to him. "But he really does see ghosts."

"So, the people he's always talking to *are* ghosts?"

"I'm not entirely sure. I think some are. Others might be in his head, or maybe I just can't see them."

"Can you see any?"

"Not like he does, I don't think. Only glimpses of shapes here and there. I'm not sure if they see me at all."

"Weird. What do you two talk about?"

"He asks about you."

"What's he want to know?" Jasper asked, putting his book down.

"What you were in for. What you were like before this."

"He know I'm a cop?"

"I think everyone does."

"And? He not like cops?"

"He seems cool with you."

"Anybody else in here he's talked about?"

Jordyn shrugged. "Some trivial complaints, mostly about the guards always forcing him to swallow his meds."

"Wait, he is *on* his meds?"

"Oh, yeah. I'm not sure if he'd see even more without them or what, but he definitely has a few theories. Something about the government trying to control him. Like I said, cuckoo for Cocoa Puffs."

"Any idea why he always winks at me?"

"No." She laughed. "But he winks at me, too."

"Like … a pervy wink?"

"No, Dad. Sheesh, I'm dead. You can stop worrying about guys harassing me."

"I'm your dad. I'll *always* worry about you."

"Right now, I'm more worried about *you*, sir. Lots of whispering about you right now."

"About how I rock these prison garbs?"

"Hernandez treating you different has made people suspicious."

"Do they know what I'm capable of?"

"They've heard the rumors about you being psychic, so maybe they're putting two and two together. We should be thinking about getting out of here."

"Like an escape?"

"Like maybe call your lawyer, change your plea, say you were insane, get moved somewhere else — anything. If you're in danger, someone has to move you, right?"

"Unless the ones I'm in danger from are running things."

"Then you need to break out."

"I don't *want* to break out."

"You want to die?"

"Not particularly, but if that's what happens, so be it. I

171

did some bad shit, baby. Caused a lot of pain. I ruin people's lives."

"But you tried to do right. You helped people. *We* helped people."

"At first, yeah. But … then it became something else. You were the first to see it and warned me to stop. But I ignored you. And your mom. You tried to talk me out of what I did to Calum and Brianna, but I wouldn't listen to you."

"You did it for me. I understand."

"Did I?" Jasper shook his head. "I was consumed by revenge. Maybe it was all for me. I wanted them to hurt as much as I did. Killing them didn't bring you back, and it never could. All that shit with Spider and the others — that's on me, and you warned me about that, too. What kind of man would I be to hold others accountable to a justice I'm unwilling to face? What kind of father—"

"You're a great father." Jordyn crawled beside him on the bunk and met his gaze. "Don't ever question that."

"No, I let you down." Tears welled. "I wasn't there for you. I never saw how much pain you were in."

"Is that what this is about? Are you punishing yourself for what happened to me?"

"I don't know." Jasper hadn't thought about that. "I'm … I'm just tired of running. Tired of causing pain wherever I go."

"You can't give up, Dad."

"Why not? Maybe I'll be better off dead. I'll see you and Mom again."

"But …"

"What?"

"Never mind."

"What is it?"

"I don't think it works like that."

"What do you mean?"

"I don't see Mom anymore. I did for a while, but now I only see you and other living people."

"You never see her at all?"

"No." But then a realization turned the corners of her lips down. "Maybe I don't see her because she's gone on to Heaven and ... I'm in hell or purgatory because I killed myself?"

The door buzzed, lock tumblers clicked, then the door opened.

Jordyn sat up, her eyes on the door, afraid.

Hernandez entered and shut it behind him. "That detective is here."

"Oh?" Jasper said.

With all they'd been through, Mallory Black was the closest thing he had to a friend these days — even if she didn't feel that way about him.

He stood, but Hernandez raised a hand. "Wait. I wanted to show you something first."

He reached into his pocket, pulled out a black cloth, unfolded it carefully, then handed the badge inside to Jasper.

"This Frank's?"

Hernandez nodded. He could've been a smart ass and said, "you tell me" or something, but he apparently no longer doubted this prisoner's gift.

Jasper closed his eyes, opening himself to whatever delivered the visions and memories. He saw Frank Tagliano getting ready for work, kissing his wife, Whitney, and their seven-year-old daughter, Violet, goodbye.

Then he was at work, staring at the back of a prison laundry truck where he was helping to unload boxes of contraband smart phones.

As the vision faded, he saw Frank talking to someone

Jasper couldn't see. The world darkened at the edges, but he could still hear Frank saying he was out, he hadn't signed up for this.

The person told Frank opting out wasn't an option.

Then Jasper was inside Frank's point of view, walking through the cafeteria as a fight erupted among some members of White Nation and 904 Mafia.

He was trying to break it up when he felt the shiv enter and exit his body a dozen times, so lighting fast, he never had a second to see who had done the deed.

Pain splintered through his back before he snapped out of the memory and into the present.

Jasper's expression must have terrified Hernandez.

"What do you know about boxes of cell phones on the prison laundry truck?"

Hernandez shook his head.

"Sounds like your guy was in on something, maybe smuggling contraband in? He wanted out, but they had him killed instead."

"Who?"

"I didn't see. But for my money, I'd say it's your own people. Sure you wanna know?"

"Of course I do. A good man died."

Jasper considered saying he wasn't sure how good a man Frank had been but thought better of it. He knew all too well how easy it was to slip into a world of compromised integrity. "If you want to leave the badge with me, maybe I'll get something later?"

"No." Hernandez snatched it away then gingerly wrapped the badge back in the same black cloth. "Someone finds this in your cell, you're fucked. We both are."

"Fair enough. I've got another idea."

"What's that?"

"I haven't been able to get near Young Luther without his goon nearby. Given how I stabbed that Nazi fuck, I'm guessing they're not gonna let me get close enough to touch him. So … if you can get something from his cell, maybe I can find out if he had anything to do with it. He probably knows who ordered the hit, even if it wasn't him."

"I don't think this is a good idea." Jordyn shook her head. "You're both gonna get killed."

If Jasper started talking to her in front of Hernandez, it would probably be too much and might undermine anything else he had to say. Probably get him back on the meds.

Hernandez nodded, still looking shaken, maybe trying to come to terms with his pal being involved in shadier shit than he'd realized. "Let me see what I can do."

"Okay," Jasper said.

"Let's go. The detective is waiting."

Jasper followed Hernandez, with Jordyn right beside him.

Chapter 27 - Howard Loomis

THE BIGGEST PROBLEM with Howard's plan was that he couldn't stay with Cami all day. Three people at work were out with a bug, and he was the back-up. And sure, Howard could've called in too, but that wasn't really an option for him.

Howard wasn't the kind of person who called in sick, even on the rare occasion when he fell ill. Despite being morbidly obese, he was otherwise healthy and dependable. He'd used exactly one sick day in all his years on the job. He liked being someone his bosses could count on. That helped him stand out from everyone else. Most of the workforce was clearly only there to collect their check.

Mother had instilled that lesson in him at a young age. No matter your job or how low your position, a good worker gave it everything he had. If you mopped jizz at a peep show, then you should be the best jizz mopper that ever mopped jizz.

Not that Mother would've approved of that job. Nor would Howard. But if that was the only work he could get, then he would've poured his whole heart into it.

But being a great employee today meant he had to ensure Cami couldn't go anywhere before he got back to her. He paced the motel, considering just killing her now, but Mister K reminded Howard he had given his word — *twenty-four hours.*

It didn't really matter. He didn't expect the cops to find her. Nor did he want them to. But Mister K must have had reasons to lay out his rules. And Howard was an obedient servant.

One more test to show I'm worthy.

A man who looked like Howard was always having to prove himself. He had to be that much better, work that much harder, demonstrate beyond any possible shadow of a doubt he wasn't the moronic fatass people assumed he would be.

Fortunately, Howard came prepared. He approached Cami with the hypodermic needle.

"I need you to be still."

Her body rattled in the chair, eyes full of horror. Her mouth was muffled, and she shook her head violently back and forth.

He grabbed her chin and peered into her eyes. "I have something to do. This is to make sure you don't try and escape. Now relax, or I'll be forced to knock you out in a less desirable way. You understand?"

Cami nodded, eyes still terrified.

He tied her arm off then injected her, careful to administer what he believed to be the right amount. He wasn't experienced with these drugs, but Mister K had told him how much to use.

As he capped the needle and cleaned his supplies to put them back inside the bag, Cami's eyes rolled back into her head before her lids finally closed.

She smiled.

"See, it wasn't so terrible. Was it?"

Howard secured her ropes, grabbed his stuff, then climbed inside the van.

His wheels rolled over the gravel, grass, and dirt on the way to smooth pavement. He could feel Mister K in back, gathering his strength in the shadows.

"Soon," he said.

"What are we going to do?"

"You'll see. Patience, Howard. Patience."

HOWARD WAS on his way to give someone a quote when he got a phone call from Mother.

"Howard?" She sounded different, almost frail.

It was surprising how fast the fear washed over him.

"Yes, Mother?"

"Can you come home? I think something's wrong."

"What is it, Mother?"

"Just come home," she said, crying.

"Are you okay? Did something happen?"

Mother hung up.

Howard raced home, running stop signs and red lights whenever he could, the entire time his fear like a kaleidoscope showing him all the things that might have gone wrong.

Did she fall and hurt herself?

Was she having a heart attack?

Did she have a stroke or something worse?

Mister K's voice crackled over the radio. "Ah, your poor mother. Her time is coming, at last. She's finally on the way to meet her maker."

"No … she's going to be okay."

"Oh, Howard … Why are you always concerned for her when she was so horrible to you?"

"Because, despite it all, she loves me."

Mister K laughed.

Howard hated when Mister K laughed at him. It was almost even worse than when Mother did it. Almost as bad as when any number of girls had laughed at him over the years.

"She *does* love me."

"Of course she does, when she remembers. Your mother's been slipping and you know it. She's getting dementia."

The static gave way to talk radio.

But Mister K was right. Howard didn't want to admit anything. His mom was all he ever had. Yes, she could be terrible, or downright terrifying, but Mother only did what she did because she loved him, because she was trying to prepare him for this world's cruelties while ensuring his place in the next one.

Funny that Howard had wanted to be free of her so often, yet at the moment she seemed most susceptible to some disease that might take her away, he wasn't ready to let go.

He loved his mother. But he also wanted her to be there with him in The End, so she could see how special he was, so she could know Mister K had chosen him.

Then she would see he truly was worthy and wasn't some horrible wretched sinner.

Howard pulled into the driveway, killed the engine, then ran inside to find Mother sitting in the living room, staring out the window in a daze, as if she couldn't even see him.

Is she dead?

"Mom?" Howard felt more vulnerable than he had in years.

She turned and eyed him like a stranger. "Howard?"

"What's wrong, Mother? Why did you call?"

Confusion twisted her face, tears welled up in her eyes. "I ... I don't know, Howard."

She started to cry. Howard had never seen her do that before.

Then Mother did something else she'd never done. She went to embrace him.

He hugged her tight, feeling all the pain he'd ever felt as an ignored child coming forth and melting all at once.

She does love me.

I'm so sorry for all the horrible things I've thought, for all the times I wished you would just go away.

I'm so sorry, Mother.

The two of them hugged each other as they cried.

Howard prayed she would live long enough to see The End with him.

Maybe there would be a place for Mother in what was coming next.

Chapter 28 - Mallory Black

MAL ARRIVED at the prison just after noon during visiting hours.

She sat a table in the visiting hall, waiting for Jasper Parish to be brought inside.

Mal was surprised by how much older he looked than the last time she'd seen him. It had only been six months or so, but he seemed years older, his hair already starting to gray.

He sat across from her and smiled. "Hello, Detective."

"How are you?" She pointed to her haul from the vending machine — a couple of Cokes, a Mountain Dew, some bags of chips, and an assortment of candy. "Help yourself."

"Thanks." He took a Coke and a bag of Doritos. After opening the bag, he selected a chip, took a bite, smiled at the crunch. "They don't have these in the canteen. Got them generic ones."

She popped the tab to one of the Cokes. "So, you wanted to see me?"

"I saw something, a dead kid on a cross."

"What else?" Mal was hoping that Jasper had called because he had some vision that might help her with the case.

"The killer called you."

"Yes."

"Did you bring the phone?"

"The sheriff has it. He took me off the case. Why?"

"I was hoping to get something to help you find the man. But I need to touch it."

"You see anything else?"

"He has another girl now, doesn't he? A woman?"

"Her name's Cami Rivera. Do you know where they are?"

Jasper shook his head. "No, I had a flash, but ..." He paused and looked to his right. "Okay, I'll ask her."

Talking to his daughter?

"Jordyn wants me to hold your hand. She's going to hold both of ours. Thinks maybe it'll help."

Mal felt weird, like she was playing into Jasper's delusions, but then she reminded herself of all he'd witnessed so far. Hadn't she seen enough to set her skepticism aside, to humor him for a moment if it might help her?

"Okay." She took another sip of Coke, wishing it had a healthy splash of Jack.

He placed his hands palms up on the table.

"What do I do? Hold 'em or—"

"Just lay your palms on top of mine," he said.

Mal did, flashing back to the last time she'd seen him, in the hospital after Oliver Kozack had nearly killed him. She'd gone to visit and urged him not to confess. Asked him if he thought she'd ever be happy again.

He'd predicted she would be, and that she'd have another daughter. An older one, maybe adopted. But he also predicted someone worse than Dodd would come for her.

Six months had passed and she still hadn't adopted. Meanwhile, she'd become even more closed off from potential suitors. Like Tim Brentwood.

She found herself thinking back over their relationship as their hands touched. Jasper had started off as a voice on a phone warning Mal her daughter was in danger. Then he'd become the man who saved her — not once, but twice. Her and Jessi both.

But Jasper was also a serial killing vigilante. For a while, she tried to find and arrest him.

Mal was glad she didn't. Because this man had always tried to help her, from saving her life to putting a winning lottery ticket in her house.

There was a kinship she'd tried to deny for a while. One she felt in Mexico, and a little when she found herself on a similar path — hunting down bad guys, same as him.

He'd been a cop before this. Something else they had in common. They'd each sought justice both within and outside the law. Either of them could easily end up behind bars for what they'd done. But Jasper got caught and confessed to his crimes.

"So, what now? Am I supposed to feel something? You expect to see something else?"

"We wait. You can keep talking. Maybe it'll bring something up."

She looked around, sensing other guards, prisoners, and visitors eyeing them, probably all wondering what the hell they were doing.

"So, how's prison life?"

"Well, let's see. The days are boring and the nights are long. A gang put a hit on me, which means I might not be around much longer. So, all good."

"Your lawyer can arrange a transfer."

"I'll figure something out. I always do." His hands jerked beneath hers.

"What is it?"

"The man I warned you about when you came to visit. He's the one who killed that girl."

"You said he was coming for me — how?"

Jasper closed his eyes. "We can't see that. Not yet."

"Well, you also said I'd have a daughter, so ..." Mal rubbed her stomach. "Nothing on that front yet."

Jasper kept his eyes closed, focusing. "She's in your life now."

"Who?"

"I don't know. But she's in trouble."

"From the same man?"

"No. Different. Something to do with a baby or ..."

"Katie?"

"Yes, Katie. She needs you. She's in trouble, and she's afraid to tell you how much. But ... first ..." His face tightened. "I see them."

"Who?"

"The man and the girl."

"What does he look like?"

"Big. Very big. Wearing a mask. And ..." Jasper's face looked troubled.

"What is it?" Mal asked.

"He's not alone in what he's doing."

"There's two of them?"

"That doesn't feel right ... wait a second ... I see him ... I see where he is."

Mal's pulse raced as she waited for Jasper to give her something to find this man and save Cami.

"There's an abandoned motel, been like that for a while. Near the county line, by a gas station."

An image flashed through her head, a place Mal had passed a thousand times, if not more. "Is the gas station a Shell, just off I-95?"

"Yes. And you need to hurry. She's in bad shape."

"Is there anything else?"

Jasper withdrew his hands. "I don't think he means to kill her yet. He's coming back. But … you might be too late."

Mal got to her feet. "Thank you."

Jasper stood as well, waiting for the guard to escort him away. But Mal hugged him first, despite the officer's objection.

She called Mike on her way to the parking lot and gave him Cami's location.

"How'd you get it?"

"I'll tell you later. Just call it in and say it was an anonymous tip. Leave me out of it. Also, call EMS. She's in bad shape."

"What aren't you telling me, Mal?"

"Just call it in. I'll see you there."

MAL RACED down I-95 toward the county line to the crumbling motel. Six deputy vehicles were already there, along with an ambulance.

People milled about in front of the motel. Whatever happened was already done.

Mike and Skippy were talking to two EMT workers when she pulled up. The ambulance van doors were open. A body bag inside.

They were too late, unless it was the killer.

"What happened?" Mal asked, looking past them and into the back of the ambulance.

"Aren't you on suspension?" Skippy glanced at her sideways. "What are you doing here?"

"Relax." Mike raised a hand to Skippy before heading toward her car. "Walk with me."

Mal followed.

"We got here and she was already dead," Mike said.

"And the unsub?"

"Nowhere to be found."

"Goddamnit. How'd she die?"

"Looks like an overdose. Probably heroin. Tried to revive her, but … yeah."

"Any insignias or anything?"

"No."

"Mutilation?"

"No. Find anything in there?"

"Still working the scene." Mike turned to face her. "You wanna tell me where you got this tip? The killer call you again?"

"No."

"Tell me." Mike was sharp, clearly annoyed Mal was involving herself in the case when she was supposed to be serving her suspension.

"Jasper Parish called, asking me to visit him in prison."

"Seriously?" Mike rolled his eyes.

"He got it right."

Mike sighed. "Don't suppose he gave you anything *useful?*"

"Said he was a big guy and wearing a mask."

"Well, that narrows it down."

"He also said something else."

"What?"

"I went to visit him in the hospital after his arrest. He warned me then that someone else would come after me, someone worse than Dodd. Today, he said this is that guy."

"How is he a threat to you? And why?"

"Maybe he's targeting me because Dodd did." She shrugged. "A copycat, even if his methods or victims aren't the same."

"And you think he's coming after you?"

"I'm hoping he does."

"Wait a second … Jasper said he didn't mean to kill her yet. He was coming back." Mal looked back at all the sheriff deputy vehicles and the ambulance. "We need to get everyone out of here."

"What?"

"He's coming back. If he sees that we've been here, we'll lose him for good."

Mike shook his head. "We can't leave while we're working the scene."

"The evidence isn't going anywhere. Trust me. Shut this down. Use it as bait."

Mike got on his radio and commanded everybody to wrap it up.

"What are we doing?" Skippy asked, appearing out of nowhere and clearly irritated.

Mike explained that they had reason to believe the killer would be back soon. Skippy stared at him before turning to Mal. "He's already killed her. Why would he come back?"

"But the scene isn't staged," she explained. "No carvings. Nothing to indicate he killed her, that this wasn't an OD. I don't think he knows she's dead."

"Or she died and he got the fuck out because it ruined his ritual," Skippy argued.

Mal looked at Mike, hoping he had her back.

"We move out and wait for him to return," he said without flinching.

Chapter 29 - Howard Loomis

His day kept yawning into forever.

Howard had an install on a house he could barely gain entry to because the owner was the worst hoarder he'd ever seen. Then he had to troubleshoot a department store malfunction where everything that could go wrong did. No break or escape until after six.

He hoped Cami was still tied up like he left her.

Howard entered the details into the computer, closed out the job, then started his drive to the old motel. But first, he really needed something to eat.

He stopped at a Sloppy's, seemed only fitting, and ordered his same meal from the day he spotted Cami with her friend. Maybe he'd bring her a True American to eat before killing her.

After parking in the lot, he went into the back of his van, sat on the floor, then turned on the laptop he used to monitor people.

"You're wasting time, Howard," said Mister K from the speakers, sounding broken and distorted even though the computer was fine. "It has been twenty-four hours."

"I need to eat." Howard dug into the bag, fished out a wad of salty, hot fries, then shoved them into his mouth.

"You could stand to skip a meal or two."

"What are we going to do to her?" Howard asked.

"Why? Do you like this one? Have you gone soft, now that you've touched her? Are you giving up on our mission now that we're so close?"

"No. I'm not soft. I'm still committed."

"Good."

"What are we going to do?"

"This will be one to remember. We shall flay her, putting our symbols only on her face, our message to the others that The End is almost here."

"And what will happen at The End?"

"You've always been so impatient," Mister K whispered. "What is it, Howard? Do you not trust me?"

"Yes, I trust you. I … I'm just curious about what's next. I've always wanted to know."

"Yes, you are a very … *curious* human. You should cherish patience as much as you enjoy sating your curiosity."

"Can you blame me? I've been waiting to be something more than what everybody else said I was for all my life now. You see how people look at me."

"Yes, but they don't see what I see — the intelligence, the power, the righteousness that so many weaker beasts lack. Your mother is wrong about you, Howard. You are so much more than these fools can ever see. But they will see, soon enough. Stay the course. Help me deliver these messages, then all will be revealed."

Howard felt better, even something approaching joyous. He just needed to hear the occasional affirmation that what they were doing was the proper path indeed.

"I'm sorry." He was foolish for his doubts. Mister K

had already done so much for him, revealed so many truths others had hidden away. He showed Howard how to situate himself into a position of knowledge, working at a place with unfettered access into so many homes. Now he knew the secrets of people who didn't even know he existed.

He thought about that scandal with the sex ring from six months ago, blowing up and ruining so many lives, sending all those rich and powerful into hiding. Howard didn't have *that* kind of dirt, but he knew who was cheating on who, had seen secret meetings between politicians outside of the Sunshine law, and witnessed enough crimes to blackmail some important folks, if he were so inclined.

But for Howard, the power came in just knowing and keeping the secrets. As others had discovered all too often, history wasn't always kind to those who knew that which was designed to stay hidden. People hated those who unearthed their ugliest parts. And erased them whenever possible.

So, Howard did as Mister K advised and kept everything to himself.

He tuned into the camera feed he'd set up across from the motel and scrubbed through the day's events, just to make sure Cami hadn't escaped.

He bit into his first burger, moving through the footage at 72X speed.

Movement caught his eye, several swallows in. Not just movement, but sheriff's vehicles appearing on-screen. Howard froze, a bite of True American in his mouth, blood turning cold.

"No, no, no." He spit out the burger and slowed the fast forward to normal speed, then to rewind.

"What the hell did you do?" asked Mister K, his voice boiling over the speakers.

"How?" Howard said to himself. "How did they find her?"

He rewound the footage, searching for some wayward person on foot or in a car who might have stumbled upon the motel. But he saw nothing, not even a sign that Cami had gotten loose all by herself.

The sheriff's deputies arrived out of nowhere, approaching the building with their weapons drawn. Who had tipped them off?

"Who did you tell?" Mister K asked.

"Nobody," Howard whined, confused. He returned to the footage, searching for clues. Watched as they carried Cami from the motel in a bodybag.

"You ruined my grand plan!" Mister K snarled.

"I'm sorry," Howard cried, still so confused, scrolling until he saw a familiar face appear onscreen. The detective, Mallory Black.

"She knew," Mister K said.

"What? How?"

"I don't know, but *she* did this."

He stared at the screen, then at the pretty detective who had ruined his plan. Howard had followed her story ever since her daughter was abducted. He'd actually felt bad for her.

But, the more that came out about her on the blogs and news, the more certain he became she was a wicked woman. Mallory Black's child was taken because she was a wretched sinner. Her daughter paid the price for her being a drunken whore.

It was a shame, children should never have to suffer for the sins of their parents. Howard had nothing but disgust for Mallory Black now. And somehow, she'd soiled all of their plans.

"That whore has to pay," growled Mister K.

"But how?"

"We find a way to break her. But first, we'll make up for this loss and find someone else. Someone who can really make them hurt."

Chapter 30 - Jasper Parish

JASPER STOPPED READING in his bunk when he heard a commotion in the pod below.

He went to his open cell door then looked down over the balcony to the tables. A brawl had erupted between D'Andre and one of the Latinos. The fight would spread like a virus in moments.

D'Andre was trying to get in with 904 Mafia.

The COs moved in as D'Andre egged them on, screaming, "Fuck you, pig!"

But then he got the beat down. D'Andre laughed like a maniac as they shoved his face into the ground.

The alarm buzzed for a lockdown.

Jasper returned to his bunk and sat with his back against the wall, pretending to read while staying alert in case anyone decided to use the commotion as fuel to attack him.

"Back in your cells," guards shouted as they broke up the fighting with relatively little resistance, judging from the riotous symphony.

Jurko walked by Jasper's cell, looked inside, then kept

walking, checking the next one. The buzzer went off again a few minutes later, and the cells all slid shut in unison.

Jasper resumed his reading.

Jordyn sat at the end of the bunk, listening to her music, humming something vaguely familiar and surprisingly sad. She hadn't spoken since telling him the deputies had found the girl but were too late.

Neither had Jasper.

The other inmates were pissed about lockdown and talking shit to one another from their cells. More mouthfuls from the guards on duty, baiting them. Whoever started the fight would be answering to whomever was king of their group. They'd get a hard bruising, be forced to surrender an even higher tax on their canteen funds for a while.

Jordyn stopped singing, pulled out her earbuds, and lowered her hoodie. She had that look in her eye, the one that suggested a memory but was really her trying to fine tune an oncoming vision.

"What is it?" Jasper asked.

She held a finger to let him know he needed to wait, then she leapt off the bed, landed in a crouch on the floor. Her eyes burned with intensity as she looked around the cell.

Jordyn was spooking the shit out of him. It was even stranger since he wasn't feeling so much as a hint of whatever she was sensing.

She scrambled on all fours toward the toilet. Jasper was sure she was about to puke, but she leaned forward, straining to look behind it. Then she looked back at him and motioned him toward her with the same finger she'd used to silence him before.

Jasper stood over her, trying to see what had gripped her attention. Then he saw it — a tiny metal disc attached to the back of the toilet. He reached down, pulled it out, and raised it to eye level, slowly inspecting the thing.

"Is that a bug?"

He nodded, mouthing the words, *They're listening.*

"How long have they been listening?" Jordyn asked.

The longer he contemplated his answer, the clearer Jasper's conversations with Hernandez formed in his head.

Fuck. They know.

He had to warn Hernandez before whoever planted the device discovered what he knew.

As Jasper was placing the bug back behind the toilet, his door buzzed and the pod unlocked behind him. He turned, feeling caught red-handed, as his cell slid open and Young Luther entered with Muscles.

Jordyn backed up on the bottom bunk, pushing herself into the corner. "*Daaaaad,* what are they doing? Who let them in?"

Jasper had only his hands and a prayer — a weak plea to an indifferent God against a beast like Muscles.

Young Luther looked him up and down. "Well, well, well, old man, not many people surprise me, and you have most certainly surprised me."

How much did Young Luther know? And who else might be sharing the knowledge? Who among the guards was on his side or his payroll?

Jasper clenched his fists, preparing for a fight, surveying his enemies and searching for any obvious weaknesses or possible weapons. Empty hands meant shit inside. Prisoners hid shivs everywhere, beneath benches in the yard, buried outside, one of any dozen places inside the kitchen. Sure, the guards found them, but there were always more to be made, and no way Young Luther and Muscles were coming into Jasper's pod unarmed.

"So, what are you? Some kinda Miss Cleo or some

shit?" Young Luther asked with a sneer.

No point in lying if Young Luther had heard his messages.

"I see things sometimes."

"What sorts of things? Like sports scores and shit?"

"Sometimes."

"And maybe shit you're not supposed to see?"

"Sometimes." Jasper narrowed his eyes on the man, waiting for an attack, a threat, or hopefully, an offer.

"Like a certain guard getting got? You see who did that?"

Jasper shook his head.

"Which is why you wanted Hernandez to get somethin' of mine, eh? So not only are you a fucking pig rat, you're also a psychic motherfucker snoopin' in people's heads and shit. That ain't right, man. I can't have you peepin' in on my shit, ya' feel?"

Jasper nodded.

"So, here's what's gonna happen. Whatever Hernandez brings you, whatever you see, or whatever you fucking *think* you see, you're gonna be keeping that shit to yourself. And you gonna tell him somethin' else."

"What would you like me to tell him?"

"You tell him that White Nation did that shit. It was all Kenn, and since that motherfucker's already gone, the case is nice and closed."

"And what do I get out of it?"

Young Luther looked thoughtful. "What do you want, old man?"

"I want out," Jasper said.

"You want out?" Young Luther laughed. "Then why the fuck you go and give yourself up?"

"I wasn't in my right mind."

"Now that's something we can both agree on. But you

gettin' out?" He shook his head. "Nah, I don't think that's in the cards right now. Things are kinda tight around here with you and that pig lookin' into shit you ain't got no business even blinking at. But I think you and me can be a great team, ya' know? You've got lots of knowledge up in that nappy ass head of yours. You like the crunch berries in my cereal. And maybe, just maybe if you help me for a bit, I can get you out ... when doing so makes sense for me. It's gonna be a minute, you feel? I need to recoup my investment. How's that sound?"

Jasper had thought he was ready to die, but losing his life to this pair of fuckers would be an insult to his memory and the man he was. He wouldn't go down without a fight, but Jasper planned to stay smart about it. Tell them what they wanted to hear until he figured out his escape.

"You agree to help me get out, I'll play ball."

Young Luther nodded then turned and left the cell.

Before Muscles followed his leader, he stared Jasper down to remind him he was nothing but a punk ass bitch in their eyes.

JASPER'S DOOR opened before lights out.

Hernandez entered and dumped another cup of his meds into the toilet. Jasper handed him a scrap of paper, torn from his book and written on with his fingernails, before the guard could utter a word.

Hernandez opened it in his palm, keeping his back to the door, and read the note.

THEY BUGGED MY CELL.

YL knows what you're doing. Told me to lie and say Kenn ordered the hit.

Play along with me.

HERNANDEZ STARED AT THE PAPER, jaw clenched.

Jasper could see his wheels turning, probably wondering who bugged the cell and what other guards were part of it. If he had any sense, he was also worrying about his family. Young Luther probably had more pull outside than anyone in the prison, and it wasn't just Hernandez in danger. Anyone he loved was a possible target, as well.

"Get anything from Young Luther's cell?" Jasper coached him with a nod.

Hernandez reached into his pocket, pulled out a thin metal shiv, and handed it to Jasper. "Got this."

Jasper had a flash of Young Luther crafting the shiv from a piece of fence, then followed the thread until he saw what he was looking for — Young Luther ordering the hit.

Jasper nodded. "Kenn ordered the hit on Frank."

"Are you sure?" Hernandez asked.

"Luther knew about it, but he didn't have anything to do with it. I'd drop it if I were you."

"Yeah?" Anger brewed in the officer's eyes.

"Yeah, dude is dead. No point in making a thing of it."

"Thanks," Hernandez said, wadding up the paper and tossing it into the toilet.

Jasper mouthed the words, *Be careful.*

Hernandez nodded then left.

"Lights out!" bellowed a voice over the speakers in the hall.

The lights died, but Jasper wasn't anywhere near ready for sleep.

Chapter 31 - Mallory Black

MAL DROVE AWAY from the crime scene, boiling mad at being forced to abandon her mission, suddenly impotent with no way of taking this fucker down.

She was on administrative leave — her punishment for not shutting up and being a good girl. For doing what the corrupt fucking sheriff was too incapable of doing.

The anger reminded her of being a kid and struggling to get picked in flag football games at the park. Mal was one of the only girls who liked to play and none of the boys wanted her on their teams. Short, scrawny, and, worst of all, a girl, she was always the last one picked. Mal had to play ten times better than anyone else just to prove her equality.

She remembered playing running back when she was nine when this asshole, Troy Baumgartner, had missed a tag on her as she ran right past him to score a touchdown. He tackled her the next time she got the ball. Sent her hard to the ground.

Mal spent more than a minute gasping for air. It was the first time in her life when she thought death might be coming. But she couldn't let any of the boys see her fear. So as a mass of people rushed over to check on her and Troy clutched his stomach in uncontrollable laughter, Mal had to battle the tears and force herself to stand.

She did, still refusing to cry.

A few plays later, Mal got back in the game. Another kid, Robby Meade, was running the ball. Troy ran to tackle him, but Mal came out of nowhere, lowered her shoulders and slammed into him hard enough to send Troy flying backwards.

He was more stunned and embarrassed than actually injured, but none of the other players ever questioned her ability again. Some even cheered.

But still, for the rest of her childhood and all these years later, whenever Mal went somewhere new, whether that meant playing with children or working a job, she had to prove herself all over again. It required her emotional overtime to earn the respect that was simply given to men.

Mal had proven herself as a detective under Barry's first administration, then again under Bell's. Now she was having to do it all over again with Barry and his cronies now that he was back in power. She was exhausted by this tired game and of having to prove herself repeatedly.

Sure, she had made plenty of mistakes. But so had plenty of other officers. Men with much more egregious errors in judgment. They never had to pay penance, kiss the ring, or beg forgiveness.

Fuck that.

Mal was done with the bullshit and jumping through hoops. She was an excellent cop and a good person. She shouldn't have to tolerate this crooked sheriff's agenda. She had the resources to start over and knew what she was capable of.

Mal could become a P.I. — or maybe just move the

hell out of Florida and enjoy life somewhere else. Anywhere had to be better than Creek Fucking County, the breeding ground for most of her misery. She had a fortune, so why not live in some little hamlet in Ireland, maybe go to Canada and learn to like hockey.

She called Katie and left her a voicemail. "Hey, Katie. Was hoping you were in the mood for pizza when you get out of school. Let me know, 'cause I'm starving."

Mal got gas. Then, coming down off her pill, decided she wanted the Xanax on her person, so back to the hotel it was. An overwhelming wave of exhaustion slammed her on the other side of the door, so she succumbed to the allure of her cozy bed, a plush pillow, and that down comforter she thought of too often.

I just need to rest my eyes for a few minutes.

Just a few—

The phone rang, dragging Mal out a heavy sleep and into the darkness.

What time is it?

9:10 PM, according to the clock on her nightstand.

Shit!

"Hello?"

"It's Katie," said the crying voice on the other end of the line. "Can we still get that dinner?"

"You okay?" Mal asked.

"I told him."

"Your boyfriend?"

"Yeah. Well, whatever he was. I told him."

"And?"

Katie burst into tears.

"Where are you?"

"I left."

"Left where?" Mal didn't like the sound of that at all.

"Ben and Sarah's. I should never have told him. He …

he was horrible. Said something about laying down with dogs and getting ticks or something. I'll sleep on the street before I go back there."

"Where are you?"

"Sitting at the bus stop in front of Target."

"Which Target? Never mind. Text me the address and don't move. I'll be over in about ten or fifteen minutes, okay?"

"Okay," Katie said, sniffling as she hung up.

NEITHER OF THEM felt like pizza, despite the earlier offer. So Mal drove to Sancho's Seaside Bar & Grille. They found a seat in the back, away from the crowds. Katie had been quiet throughout the ride, save for some small talk.

They ordered drinks and food as Katie stared at her paper mat. She'd flipped it over and was sketching on the back, drawing something that loosely resembled a fairy.

"That's great," Mal said into another long silence. "How long have you been drawing?"

"I dunno," Katie told her.

The server brought their drinks. Mal thanked her, then gave her full attention to Katie. "So, what happened?"

"Boys suck. That's what happened."

"What did he say?"

"That it's not his fault."

"*Not his fault?* Did you use protection? Were you on the pill?"

"Yeah, we used protection. And no, taking the pill is 'going against God.'" Katie shook her head. "How did I go from one religious nut father to another insanely pious foster family?"

Mal looked at her with sympathy but gave Katie the space to continue.

"James said it's not his fault if the condom didn't work. That I should've been on the pill. He also asked how I even know it's his. I told him he's the only person I've slept with. He laughed and said, 'Yeah, right.'"

"What a dick."

Her lips twitched with a smile. Then, as if accounting for her moment of levity, Katie sketched harder, scratching through the paper and ruining her drawing. She crumpled it up and slammed her pen on the table.

"I don't want to have a kid in that place! Maybe I *should* abort it."

"Would you have kept it if James wanted you to?"

"I know I'm young," Katie shrugged, "but I would love to have a boyfriend and a son or daughter. But he never even really liked me. How could I have been so fucking stupid?"

Katie reached for the pen. Her jacket sleeve rose and showed Mal a series of fresh cuts. She didn't try to hide them this time, either unaware they were showing or unable to care and crying for help.

She wanted to let Katie know things would be okay, maybe with a hug. But even if the girl had forgiven Mal for her mother's death, she was still standoffish and obviously hurting.

"Look at me. How am I going to raise a kid on my own? Gonna raise it in the foster system? Give it up for adoption and have it wind up with some horrible family?"

"It wouldn't be hard to find a good family to adopt your baby. If that's what you wanted."

The server returned with a tray full of food. Katie looked down, letting a curtain of hair spill over her face, crossing her arms as she leaned back in the booth.

After the server left, Mal saw Katie was crying behind her hair.

"I'm such a fuck-up. I ruin everything. Ben was right, I am a wicked person. Maybe this is my punishment."

"No." Mal shook her head, plucked a fry from her basket, then popped it into her mouth. Too hot and far too salty, but she was hungry and didn't care. "This isn't your punishment. Why would you think you deserve this? Or any punishment at all?"

"Because I make stupid choices. I slept with another guy who was clearly too old for me."

"How old is he?"

Katie sighed. "Does it matter?"

"Well, yeah. Say the word and I'll arrest his ass right now."

"He's twenty. Not some old dude like the coach. I hate him, but … I liked him, too. He was sweet for a while. I don't want to see him in jail."

"They're all sweet until they're not," Mal said, not meaning to sound nearly as bitter as she obviously did.

She held no grudge for either her ex-husband or Tim. Things didn't work out, but both were decent guys. Mal was bitter toward the kinds of men she saw on the job, the sort that preyed on kids like Katie or beat and murdered their wives.

What Jasper said about her having a daughter flitted through her mind. Had he meant Katie? She'd briefly considered adopting the girl in the aftermath of her mother's murder. But that was an awful idea. Mal was a mess and an addict.

She had almost brought Maggie and Emma into her house after that.

Mal was surprised by how much she was warming to the thought of having a kid in her home again.

She looked at Katie and thought how much the girl had changed from the innocent and naive victim she had met a year ago. Gone was that sweet kid in her modest, out-of-style clothes. In her place was a hurting, moody teen with a hardened exterior, dyed hair, dark makeup, ripped jeans, and a leather jacket.

How much more pain would it take to break her completely? What would Katie look like in six months if Mal did nothing? How about six years? An addict? A prostitute further abused by a society that stayed blind to her suffering and only saw her sexuality? A society that would use, abuse, then discard her?

Mal could help.

You've barely got your own life together! You're an addict.

No, I slipped one time because I didn't have my Xanax.

I won't take anymore.

"Would you keep the baby if you had a way to support it?"

"I dunno." Katie grabbed an onion ring from her plate then bit into it. "You said you were going to call and see if there was somewhere I could go ... did you find anyone who wants a pregnant teenager?"

"I haven't heard back yet."

"Oh," she said, now picking at her burger.

Mal wanted to make the offer and change her life, make up for the pain she had rained upon the girl while trying to help Katie and her mother escape their abusive situation.

Don't do it. You'll only fuck her life up even more!

You aren't ready! You can't even commit to dating Tim, the nicest guy you've ever met!

You really think you're ready to adopt, or ... whatever you think is gonna happen here?

Mal watched Katie poke and prod her burger, saw the cuts on her wrist.

She's fucked up. Beyond help. Pass her off to Carrie and let someone else help her. Someone more equipped than you. Face it, you need the pills, and you'll never live your life without them. Once an addict, always an addict.

Her fears weren't unfounded. Maybe Katie would be better off without her, but Mal also saw another path, one where the girl's life led to an ugly parade of disappointments and abusive situations, one after another until she was either dead or wishing she was.

Mal could be the difference in her life. Katie would need help, more than she was equipped to give on her own. But she had money and knew people who could help.

"What if I adopted you?"

"What?" Katie's mouth twisting in disbelief, an eyebrow arched.

"What if I adopted you?" Mal repeated.

"This a joke?" Katie laughed to punctuate her question. "Why would you want *me?*"

"Any parent would be lucky to have you."

"You don't even know me," Katie challenged, taking a bite of her burger. "I don't need your pity."

"You're right, I *don't* know you. But this isn't me pitying you, Katie. It's me seeing a part of me in you. I had a rough time growing up and finding my place. I'm still fighting to find it now. Being a cop and a mother, I know all too well that sometimes life keeps throwing punches without ever giving you a break. I want you to have a chance."

"Why?"

"I feel awful about what happened with your parents, and sometimes people need to help each other, when they can.

"My dad would be *so* pissed if he found out I was pregnant. But Mom was looking forward to being a grandma." Katie took a sip of her soda. "How do you do it?"

"Do what?"

"Carry on after you lose everyone?" Then the finer point and more difficult question. "How did you do it after you lost your daughter?"

For a moment, Mal was surprised Katie knew about Ashley, but then she remembered all the headlines. Local and national news — *Cop's Daughter Murdered, Cop Kidnapped by Daughter's Murderer, Paul Dodd Killed After Kidnapping Cop and Jessi Price.*

Did Katie also know she'd won the lottery? If so, was this some attempt at a shakedown? Was her scumbag boyfriend involved?

But Katie displayed no signs of deception. She was just another hurt soul trying to heal from the loss of her family.

"It's not easy. I find talking to people helps. So does a good therapist. We can find one together. I really should have done more after what happened — I'm sorry I wasn't there for you." Mal took her hand. "Let me help. Maybe I don't need to adopt you. Maybe we can get you emancipated and you can stay with me until things get sorted. Finish school, take some college courses or something. I *want* to help."

"Where would I stay?"

"I have a house with plenty of room, but for now I can share my hotel room."

"Why are you staying in a hotel?"

"It was tough going back to my house after Ashley died. But after I take care of a couple things, we can go back there. You can have your own room."

Mal didn't tell her the real reason she was offering her room for now was because of Jasper's prediction about the killer coming after her. A killer was far less likely to find her hotel, especially since she switched rooms last month and wasn't booked under her name.

"You want me to make some calls? I'll need to talk with your foster family. Even if they're dicks, we should at least let them know things are okay."

Katie considered it for a few moments before finally nodding. "Okay. Thank you."

Mal wanted to seal the deal with a hug, but the girl was still scared and defensive.

She'd be better down the road. And maybe Mal would stop being a hypocrite, craving pills while trying to help another soul stitch her life back together.

Chapter 32 - Howard Loomis

HOWARD PULLED INTO THE DRIVEWAY, his will to what had been asked of him suddenly replaced by a shaky uncertainty.

"Are you sure this is the only way?" he asked Mister K.

"She mocked you on TV and ruined our work. The woman must be taught."

"Are you sure *this* is how?"

"This is how you get her attention and respect. This is how you prove to me you are worthy of the knowledge."

"But …" Howard looked through the open window at the elderly woman, nearly blind, feeding the toddler in a high chair.

Their names were unimportant. He had found them randomly last week and knew they lived alone. There was a mother in the picture, but she was too busy getting strung out on drugs with her pimp boyfriend. Howard chose them because nobody would notice them missing. He would have more time than usual, enough to set up the second phase of the plan, his true goal.

Still, this one felt wrong. The old woman had been kind, from what Howard could see.

"Her daughter wouldn't be a drug addict whore if she wasn't a horrible mother," Mister K argued after reading Howard's thoughts.

"But—"

"Sinners must repent. The guilty must see what is coming for them all."

"But, the kid … he's just a baby. He never did anything."

Mister K grew angrier. Howard could see the shadows stirring violently in the back of his van. The radio's buzzing static matched his intensity, rising to an ear-piercing scream of feedback.

Howard covered his ears, trying to drown out the sound, but there was never any escaping it before Mister K finally relented.

He stared into the back of the van once the noise finally stopped, wondering if now was the time for the entity to reveal his true form.

But of course, it wasn't. Howard wasn't yet worthy.

Mister K's shadow shrank into the corner of the van as if he was about to leave again.

"No," Howard begged. "I'll do it."

The darkness returned to form, hunched like a gargoyle perched atop an ancient building.

"Then go and do what you were born to do, Howard. *Become* greatness."

He slipped on his gloves. Grabbed the mask, pulled it over his face. Stared into his eyes in the side mirror, barely recognizing them, then reached over to the passenger seat and curled his fist around the hammer.

Howard got out of the van, marched toward the house,

then mashed his finger onto the doorbell's illuminated button.

"Hold on …" The old lady opened the door, her security chain offering only an illusion of security. She squinted. "Hello?"

Howard shoved the door.

The chain snapped. The old woman fell back.

He swung the hammer.

A kid cried out from the kitchen.

Howard turned toward the child and raised a gloved finger to his mask.

Chapter 33 - Jasper Parish

JASPER WALKED the track with Jordyn, enjoying the warm sun on his skin and wondering if this would be one of the last times he reveled in the pleasure of being outside — something that had once been unremarkable and so easily taken for granted.

He found joy in the simplest pleasures while locked behind bars. Reading, a walk in the yard, playing the occasional game of spades, a few of the conversations with Wally — even if his old podmate never knew when to shut the hell up. A candy bar from the canteen held so much more joy than it ever had on the outside. But most of all, Jasper enjoyed this time with Jordyn, unencumbered by his mission, hours for them to talk and catch up.

But now, time itself was chasing him. Jasper felt death approaching.

What would happen once it finally arrived?

Would he be separated from Jordyn forever? If there was a Hell, surely he was on his way. If there was only a void, perhaps he'd be stuck there like his daughter. He wouldn't mind it so much. But if Heaven existed, then Carissa was there.

How did she visit you before?

Maybe that was all in my head.

"What are you thinking?" Jordyn asked.

"What do you *think* I'm thinking?"

"Wondering what to do about Young Luther and Hernandez?"

Jasper nodded.

"You need to find a way out of here," Jordyn said. "I know you want to be punished, but … I don't want to lose you again."

"They'll put me back on the meds if I get transferred. Then I'll lose you, anyway."

She looked over to the opposite side of the track where Hernandez was walking past Young Luther and his crew on the weights. The man was practically glaring at them.

"I don't think he's going to give this up," Jordyn said as her father sighed.

Suddenly, they had company.

Crazy Gary was walking beside them, still wearing insanity's smile, his eyes lit like the universe was displaying its infinite pixels only for him.

"Good kid, your daughter," he said.

Jordyn blushed.

"Thanks." Jasper gave him a nod.

"Why are you in here?" Crazy Gary asked after a long stare.

"What do you mean? I killed people."

"I mean, why the hell ain't you fight it? Daughter says you had yerself a fancy lawyer and everythin'. That Kozack man beat a confession outta ya' so they couldn't a used that shit. They ain't got nothin' much for any of your crimes, that right?"

Jasper looked at his daughter, annoyed. "You telling him my entire life history?"

"I needed *someone* to vent to."

"So, why you in here?" he pressed.

"Because I need to pay for the terrible shit I've done."

"Ha, is *that* what ya' think?" Crazy Gary laughed.

"People need to be held accountable for their actions — including me."

"That's what you were doin', man. You was holdin' people accountable, doin' the shit that Johnny Law wasn't ever gonna do."

"It wasn't my place."

"Bull fuckin' shit!" His eyes narrowed on Jasper, fury at the corners.

Is this dude about to go postal?

"What are you talking about, man?"

"I don't buy your excuses, bro." Crazy Gary shook his head. "Nah, man. You ain't in here to punish yo'self. You in here for somethin' else."

His patience was thin. Jasper traded a look with Jordyn, but she only shrugged as if to say, *Sorry Dad, I didn't know he was gonna say all this shit.*

"Why do you think I'm in here, *Gary?*"

"You in here because you runnin' scared."

"Scared?"

"Dad …" Jordyn said.

But Crazy Gary kept talking, stealing Jasper's attention. "Hell yeah, bro. You scared of being hurt. You an' me, we see things other people don't. That shit weighs on a man, like nobody else can ever understan' unless they see through these eyes." He used two fingers to point at his eyes, then Jasper's. "We feel the pain of all them people, all those ghosts."

Jasper wasn't sure they had the same problems, but he

wasn't about to engage in semantics. He just wanted the conversation over and done with.

"*Dad* ..." More urgent.

But Crazy Gary kept talking over her. "You in here 'cause you running from the pain of who you are. You need to suck it the fuck up, buttercup, and embrace that shit! Go out there and kill *more motherfuckers*, you feel me?"

"Dad!"

They both turned toward her.

"Something's wrong." Jordyn looked over at Young Luther's group at the weights.

D'Andre was out of the hole faster than Jasper had ever seen anyone get released. Young Luther must have pulled some strings. A group of his men circled a wiry dude named Red, who bent down, his fingers rooting into the grass.

The guards hadn't noticed.

"Looks like shit is about to go down," Crazy Gary said, distancing himself.

Red stood, looked around, saw Hernandez on the track as two guys started pushing and shoving each other on one of the basketball courts.

Hernandez went to break it up.

Red moved toward him.

Jasper screamed, "Shiv!"

Time froze.

Hernandez looked at him, confusion clouding his face.

Jasper pointed, trying to warn him.

But the clock had stopped for everyone but Red, still moving swiftly, shiv in hand.

Hernandez only realized it as Red buried the weapon between his ribs.

Time sped up as Red's hand moved with surgical precision and piston-fast plunges.

Hernandez fell to the ground, bleeding out.

Red ran, passing the shiv to one of his crew before disappearing into the chaos erupting among the clash of prisoners and guards.

Jasper stared helplessly as Hernandez lay dying.

He ran toward him, thinking maybe he could stop the bleeding. But a baton to his left elbow sent Jasper sprawling to the ground.

A guard was on him.

Then, to his surprise, Muscles was on the guard, shoving him aside.

No way he's helping me, is he?

Three guards converged on Muscles as Jasper turned back toward Hernandez. Someone he didn't see was suddenly on him, shoving him face first into the baking asphalt.

A man's voice said, "Stay the fuck down."

Jasper struggled, bracing for a shiv in his ribs or back, barely managing to turn as D'Andre came at him.

Fuck, they put a green light on me too. And this cat's about to do the job.

Jasper tried to wriggle free, but D'Andre cracked him across the skull and knocked him out instead.

Chapter 34 - Mallory Black

MAL SPENT most of her morning dealing with phone calls to Katie's foster father and Carrie Thompson, trying to figure out the best way forward. Carrie suggested that since Katie wasn't in a position to take care of herself, filing for emancipation wasn't the best option. Carrie had her contact someone at Florida Department of Children and Families instead, suggesting that Mal get an ex parte order to be Katie's temporary guardian until she could legally adopt her.

Mal wasn't certain she was making the right decision, and it was all moving too fast, but the situation *felt* right — for both Katie and herself. The hotel was far from a permanent solution, but now Mal wasn't sure if she wanted to return to the home where she'd raised Ashley or give them both a fresh start somewhere else.

A part of her wasn't ready to let go. It was a house full of memories, ghosts, and nightmares. But in the end, there was more good than bad. Bringing Ashley home. Her baby's first steps. Sitting on the couch with her late at night watching *Caillou* because it was the only thing that soothed her back to sleep.

Letting go of the house was like losing her daughter in a way, and Mal wasn't sure she was ready.

Not yet.

They went to Katie's foster house after lunch to gather her belongings. Everything fit into a sad little box, which they brought back to Mal's new hotel room — a premium suite, with two king-sized beds, a separate living and dining area, and more than enough space for Katie and her privacy. A balcony overlooked the ocean, which Mal told her was especially stunning at night.

Katie was captivated by the whirlpool tub.

"These are great for bubble baths," Mal said.

"I've never had a bubble bath," Katie said, sipping from a glass of Coke she'd brought up from the restaurant downstairs.

"What?"

"Dad thought they were too indulgent, wasteful."

"Then you have not truly lived. Wait in the living room, I'll get everything ready. I'm about to change your world."

"My world?" Playful doubt colored her face.

"Oh, yes … your world. From this point forward, your life will be remembered in terms of Before the Bubble Bath and After the Bubble Bath."

"Wow," Katie laughed. "Maybe we should change the calendars to ABB?"

"You mock me, but mark my words, you will come out of this a changed woman for sure."

"Um, okay," Katie said, still laughing as she left Mal alone in the bathroom.

She prepared her bath, dimming the lights, lighting warm vanilla candles around the tub, putting on Mozart, and grabbing the various body scrubs and brushes she rarely used herself.

"It's ready!" Mal called out once the tub and her promise had both been filled.

"Wow, you really take this bath stuff serious."

"Someone has to. Now get in before the water gets cold. And when you get out, I expect an apology for doubting me."

Mal left Katie to her bath then went out to the balcony and checked her messages.

Nothing from work. She called Mike but got no answer. It was odd to feel so disconnected from the thing she had poured her life into. And Mal wasn't ever sure what to do with herself if she wasn't thinking about work.

This is good. I'll devote the time to Katie. She needs me now more than work. And, seriously, fuck Sheriff Barry.

She set down her phone and stared out at the waves, then she closed her eyes and enjoyed the sun as it shined on her skin while a cool breeze whipped through her hair. Maybe Katie could help Mal remember how to appreciate some of the things she'd forgotten how to enjoy.

You think this is gonna be easy? That Katie's magically healed because you gave her a place to stay? How long before she goes back to that asshole boyfriend or finds another loser? She doesn't have the best record. And neither do you. How long do you expect to last without your pills?

Mal shoved her doubt aside. She hadn't thought much about an escape until this moment. Having something worthy of her time would keep Mal busy and give her the strength she needed. Meetings would help with the cravings.

I've got this.

We've got this.

Me, Katie, and the baby will all be fine.

The phone started ringing. Not the one in her lap, but the one in her purse on the kitchen counter. The one that belonged to a killer.

Fuck.

Mal ran inside and picked it up but said nothing, not wanting to give him the pleasure of hearing her voice. She could hear him breathing. And, for the first time, she picked up on something she'd missed before — the man was likely overweight.

"Hello, Detective Black."

"Hello mister … what's your name?"

"You and the world will know soon enough."

Music in the bathroom reminded her of Katie. She felt a chill, instantly vulnerable, flashing back to how she felt after learning Ashley was gone then again when hearing Jessi Price had been taken.

"What the fuck do you want?"

"How did you do it?"

"Do what?" Mal asked.

"Find the girl?"

"A little birdie told me. Same little birdie that said you're a sick fuck pussy, abducting children and women because they scare you. What is it, tough guy? Your mommy hurt you?"

The man was quiet, save for the sound of his heavy breathing.

"And, lemme guess, now you hate all women, blame them all because they can see what a sick fat fuck you are. That sound accurate?"

More silence. Maybe he'd slip up and say something now that she was pushing his buttons. Aanya might get something since she was tracing the line, and Mal was already keeping him on the line longer than she had before.

"That it? Mommy hurt you so now it's time to watch the world burn?"

"Oh, it will burn, Detective."

"Whatever, psycho. Why are you calling me?"

"You interrupted my masterpiece, and he isn't very happy."

"*Who* isn't happy?"

Silence. Then whispering, as if the monster was talking to someone.

"Mister K isn't very happy. But our work will continue, and soon the world will see what's in store."

"Oh, exciting. What do you and *Mister K* have in store?"

"I'm sending you something tonight at ten. A manifesto for you to read on-air."

"Call the news or the sheriff's office. I'm on suspension and don't give a fuck."

"Check your phone."

An image came through. Mal saw a little boy, one and a half or so, with a long knife to his little throat, holding a piece of paper with a scribbled address.

"What the fuck is that?" Mal's heart was already pounding.

"Have the police go to that address and you'll see. You will read my manifesto on the air, on the same channel, every word without censoring me. Only then will I allow this child to live. Otherwise, I will slit his throat. Then you and your wicked colleagues can bathe in his guilt."

The killer hung up before Mal could say anything else.

She stared at the photo, a helpless toddler completely unaware of the danger.

Her chest was tight, and she couldn't breathe.

Anxiety was crashing down on her in an overpowering

wave, surrounding and suffocating, crushing her under its violent weight.

Mal gasped for air, and stumbled toward her jacket, draped over the back of the couch. She grabbed the bottle of Xanax, took two, and washed them down with several hard swallows from a bottle of water.

She gave herself a second to recover her breath, desperate to calm herself.

The sound of crashing glass startled her, and Mal looked to see the glass of Coke that Katie had left on the counter had fallen and shattered on the floor.

An icy feeling fell over her, an uneasy certainty that she wasn't alone.

She stared at the glass as her phone rang on the patio.

"Where the hell have you been?" she yelled at Mike.

He was speechless, probably from the sound of her panic.

"Mal?" Mike sounded afraid when he finally spoke. "What's wrong?"

But Mal couldn't answer.

Chapter 35 - Jasper Parish

JASPER HAD A VISION, with Jordyn by his side.

They were in Mallory's hotel room, watching her on the balcony.

Jordyn turned to him and said something, but Jasper couldn't hear her.

He tried to ask what, but his mouth refused to open. He pawed at it with his hands, but his fingers were fused and his features were melting. Panic swelled, but then he heard a soothing sound, relaxing music coming from another door.

A bathroom. With a teenage girl taking a bubble bath. She felt familiar to him — someone Mallory had helped before.

Katie.

The name popped into his head. The daughter he'd dreamed of Mallory having.

Something isn't right. But what?

Jordyn thought in his head. *Something is off. Something is very off.*

A phone rang from the kitchen.

Jasper knew it was the killer. And now he could see the hulking beast, thick framed glasses, greasy dark hair.

But that wasn't it. There was someone else with him, a frenzied blend of darkness without shape, trying to take form. Something purely evil. *Mister K* it called itself.

It's not real, Jordyn said in his head. *It's not real.*

Jasper wasn't sure why, but he thought back to her, *Neither am I. And neither are you.*

Mal raced back into the room, grabbed her phone.

Jasper and Jordyn watched as the photo of the toddler in danger rocked Mallory's world.

Fuck, Jasper thought.

The killer issued his demands.

They had to warn her.

Jasper dug his fingernails into the skin where his mouth should be. It felt thin — he should be able to puncture a hole into the flesh to get his words out.

But the skin wasn't budging.

Jordyn tried to scream, but her mouth refused to open, despite it not being covered by skin. They watched Mallory have her panic attack, racing to the couch for her pills.

We've got to warn her. She can't take the bait!

But how could they warn her when she couldn't see them? They weren't even there. Jasper was in the hole, and the only person who could help him from inside the prison was dead.

Anguish was a scream he couldn't release.

Jasper raged, swinging his malformed hand at a glass of soda on the counter. To his surprise, he felt the impact as it sent the glass from the counter to shards in the carpet.

Mal looked at the glass, then up, as if she could maybe see them.

Oh, my God! We did it! We—

A WAVE of ice water crashed over Jasper.

He was yanked awake to find himself back in the hole, looking up to see Young Luther and D'Andre standing over him. D'Andre dropped a plastic pail on the ground.

"Wake the fuck up, old man," Young Luther said.

Jasper slowly sat up, his head pounding. Everything was fuzzy as he tried to remember what had happened in the yard. Blood dripped from a scratch in his forehead, stinging his eyes as it fell.

Then it came back to him — Hernandez shivved, Muscles trying to ice Jasper before guards got on him, and D'Andre taking him down.

D'Andre yanked Jasper out of his bunk, slammed him up against the wall, then shoved him back to the floor. "Stay down, bitch!"

Young Luther shook his head. "I *thought* you was gonna play ball with me."

"I *was* playing ball. I told the CO what you wanted me to."

"Then why the fuck he go and report to the warden? Lucky for me, warden's in on it, too, boo. Ain't *shit* that happens in here without my say so, you feel me?"

Fuck. Why didn't Hernandez just keep his damn mouth shut?

Young Luther kicked Jasper in the ribs for failing to answer.

"I said, do. You. Feel. Me?" A kick punctuated every word.

Jasper clutched at his ribcage, doubled over in agony on the floor.

"So, seeing as I can't trust yo' ass, I need to decide am I gonna kill you or make you my bitch?"

"Fuck you," Jasper growled through the pain. Young Luther went to kick him again.

Jasper sensed it coming and moved to intercept.

But he failed to move fast enough, so Young Luther's foot caught him right in the elbow — the same spot where Jasper had been bashed with the baton. More agony exploded, and he fell back to the ground.

"Man, you got a lotta spunk for an ol' man, and not the good kind, neither." Young Luther laughed. "You're like one of those young colts or somethin', all wild 'n shit. But ain't ever been a horse I couldn't break." He walked over to Jasper and grabbed him by the neck. "I asked you a question. *You wanna die, or would you rather be my bitch?*"

Jasper glared up at him through the sweat and blood stinging his eyes. He needed to get out, but damn it if he was anybody's bitch.

"Come on, Dad, just say whatever you need to say," Jordyn begged.

But Jasper glared back without saying a word.

Young Luther punched him in the cheek. Pure pain splintered through him, almost enough to make him pass out. His entire body felt like it had been run over and was now about to be tossed off a bridge.

Young Luther approached. Jasper's vision was too blurred to see anything but his feet.

Again, he grabbed Jasper by the neck and repeated his question. "Should I kill you or make you my bitch?"

"Dad! Say something!"

But Jasper kept chewing on silence.

Young Luther punched him in the back of the head, then took a step back. "That's a damned shame. But here's the thing, old man. My asking was only a formality. I ain't gonna kill you. I'll make you wish you was dead instead. You *will* be my bitch."

Jasper was doomed. No way to help Mallory now. The best he could hope for was seeing his wife and daughter again in the afterlife.

He glared up at Young Luther, struggled to sit up, blood and sweat still stinging his eyes. He squinted, wiping it away so he could see Young Luther's face. Blood coated Jasper's tongue and teeth as he smiled.

"Fuck you."

Young Luther's face contorted in rage as he wound up to take another charge at Jasper.

D'Andre moved first, and fast, shoving his shiv into Young Luther's jugular, then pulling it out and stabbing the man repeatedly in his gut.

Young Luther stumbled back, surprise in his wide eyes as he clutched at his neck, unable to stop the fountain of blood. He stood there dazed, like a boxer about to fall, trying to speak, but only blood came out of his mouth.

"Shut the fuck up, bitch" D'Andre said, shoving Young Luther into the wall.

He collapsed to the ground, wide-eyed, staring up at his betrayer. The last face he'd ever see.

"What?" was all Jasper could say.

D'Andre said, "Surprise, motherfucker. Logic sent me in to get your ass out."

"What?"

Jordyn laughed, joy filling her face.

"He made sure I got in good with 904. The rest, as they say, is history. Now, we've got to get you the fuck outta here."

"How?" Jasper said.

D'Andre reached into his pocket, pulled out a cellphone, then made a call. "Yo, it's D. Shit's done. We're ready." He returned the phone to his pocket.

"Who the hell was that?" Jasper asked, struggling, and failing, to stand.

"Jurko. He's gonna hook us up."

"So, I just have one question," Jasper said, looking at Young Luther.

"Shoot, dog."

"You think you could've stepped in *before* he beat the shit out of me?"

D'Andre laughed. "Yeah, not gonna' lie, a part of me was enjoying the show."

"What?"

"I'm just fuckin' with ya', man. I was waiting for him to tire himself out. Once the rage had him, his eyes weren't on me, ya' know?"

Jasper nodded, feeling a dull ache coming to swallow the worst of his stabbing pains.

"Come on, man." D'Andre offered a hand then helped Jasper to his feet.

Jurko met them outside the cell. "C'mon. We need to get this shit on the road."

Chapter 36 - Mallory Black

MAL WAS DRIVING to the TV studio, talking to Katie on the phone while trying to pretend she wasn't scared shitless of the monster murdering the toddler, pretending she hadn't just heard about the old woman found shredded and carved with religious iconography.

She hadn't told Katie what was happening. No need to alarm the girl. Instead, she delivered a half-truth, saying she was on the way to meet with her old boss.

"Don't wait up. I'm not sure what time I'll be home. But if you need anything, just call."

"No problem. Mind if I take another bubble bath?"

Mal laughed. "So, you've come around?"

"I *may* have come around."

"Take as many as you want. Hit room service if you need to feed yourself. Have them add it to my tab."

"Thanks! Can I also order a movie on TV?"

"No problem. Just don't stay up too late. And no porn." She laughed. "Unless you want."

Mal felt weird giving a pregnant teenager a bedtime and telling her what she could or couldn't watch. She hadn't thought much about disciplining the girl or anything beyond helping her. But people who had no expectations for their kids raised undisciplined adults. Conversely, Katie had grown up in a home where she was overly governed by an abusive father. So, she rebelled, hard. Mal would find a balance. Still, it felt odd to do so right now, over the phone.

"I want to make sure you're rested for an awesome breakfast tomorrow morning."

Katie paused, like she could smell the bullshit. "Okay. I'm kinda tired, anyway. I probably won't even watch a movie."

Mal arrived at the station, but instead of meeting her partner alone, she also found Barry and Ford waiting to accost her.

Fuck me.

Mal got out of her car and approached them.

"Hand it over," Barry said.

"Hand *what* over?"

"The killer's phone," Cameron answered. "You had no right to take it."

Mal ignored him and spoke to Barry. "He'll only talk to me."

"You would do well to remember that you are on administrative leave, young lady. You are not authorized to speak on behalf of the sheriff's office."

"I'm not here to speak on behalf of anyone. I'm here as a private citizen."

"You will not be going on the air tonight, Miss Black. That's Cameron's job. Now hand him the phone."

"The fuck I will," Mal said, pushing past them.

The sheriff reached out and grabbed Mal by the arm.

She spun around, giving him a scornful enough glare that he let go immediately.

But his demeanor didn't change. "Go on the air and I'll arrest you for interfering with an investigation."

Mal stared at the sheriff, then glanced at Cameron, who was smiling smugly, arms folded across his chest.

"He said if I do not read his manifesto on the air, he will kill that toddler. You want a child's death on your hands, Sheriff?"

"What I do not want, what I *will not* do, is cave to terrorist demands. No way in hell are we reading that psycho's manifesto."

"Then why are you even here? Why go on the air at all?"

"To deliver a message that the Creek County Sheriff's Office won't bow to any demands."

"And you're gonna have him as your representation of strength? Cameron Fucking Ford?" Mal laughed in the idiot blogger's face.

He stared at her red-faced, a glimmer of rage in his eyes.

She laughed even harder, hoping he would hit her so she could put him on his ass.

"With all due respect, Sheriff, I think Mal is right on this," Mike finally said. "He's already killed one child, shot another, and murdered that young woman. We have to take him at his word."

Sheriff Barry shook his head. "You're a good detective, Mike. But you're wrong on this. Cave in to one of these clowns and we'll have copycats coming out of the woodworks. Then what? We going to read a manifesto on the air every time one of these jokers gets a hair up their ass? How many fucking manifestos are we going to read?"

"A child will die, Sheriff. A *toddler*. Are you willing to have a child's death on your hands?" Mal stared at him. "How do you think that'll look in the next election?"

NOLON KING & DAVID W. WRIGHT

"Better one toddler than a bunch of kids getting kidnapped," Cameron answered. "Voters respect strength, not capitulation to threats. This'll be a memory by the time the next election comes. Just like your career here, you fucking junkie."

Mal lost it. She swung and clocked Cameron in the jaw. He went down like a sack of shit.

"Arrest her, Mike!" Barry yelled.

Mike put his hands between Mal and the sheriff. "Let's all just calm down."

"I want her arrested, now!"

Mal stared at the sheriff, then turned to Mike, wondering if he was actually going to do it.

"Come on, Mal. Let's get you out of here."

"Are you seriously going to arrest me, Mike?"

Cameron rubbed his jaw as he stood. "Goddamned right he is. And I'll be pressing charges, you cunt. I will *own you* when this is all done."

Mal spun around and clocked him again.

Mike grabbed Mal, dragging her back.

"Well, at least I got my money's worth" Mal laughed as Mike pulled her away. He put her in the back of his car then slammed the door.

At least he hadn't cuffed her.

Mal kicked at the floorboard, screaming as Mike climbed into the driver's seat. "FUCK HIM!"

He met her gaze in the rearview, his eyes sad and disappointed. That hurt Mal more than anything the sheriff and Cameron Fucking Ford had done.

Mike started driving.

Mal kept her mouth shut, lest she say something regrettable. Or worse, cry from frustration. A horrible thought hit her like a slap to the ear.

Katie. An arrest would surely impact her ability to

adopt. Did that mean that Katie and her unborn child would be victims of the system?

Another awful thought — would Cameron Ford sue her for everything? If so, how would she afford to help Katie?

What did I do?

Fuck, fuck, fuck, fuck!

"Why did you hit him?" Mike finally asked.

"Because Cameron Ford is a piece of shit. How can you *not* hit him? That fucker doesn't deserve to work for the sheriff's office. Neither of them does. They're total assholes."

"Sometimes it's our job to work with assholes."

"Speak for yourself. I'm done dealing with assholes. Tired of seeing assholes get rewarded with elections and lucrative gigs. What kind of self-respecting 'journalist' takes a job from the very sheriff he helped get elected? What kinda bullshit is that, Mike? Why do so many people sit by and watch the everlasting shit show that—"

"What other options do we have, Mal? To check out? Give up? Some of us try to change things from within."

"Sorry, Mister Holier Than Thou, is that what you're doing — changing it from within? How's that workin' out for ya'? And, by the way, the only reason I came back was to try and change it from within."

"And how's that working out for *you?*"

She looked in the rearview and saw a playful smile. Mike was busting her balls.

"Relax. I'm not going to arrest you."

"What are you doing?"

"Taking you home."

"And what happens when Sheriff Sphincter wants to know why I'm not locked up?"

"I'll tell him I refused, using officer's discretion. If he wants to make it a deal, I'll quit."

"You'll what?"

"I'll quit."

"You would do that for me?"

"Under the present circumstances, yes. Because despite your hot temper and reckless behavior, you're a damned fine cop. One of the best. And I'm not the only one that thinks so."

"Oh? Who else? Place is full of suck-ups and cronies."

He named several deputies, including Skippy.

"*Skippy* likes me?"

"Well, I wouldn't say *likes* you so much as *respects* you. He just thinks you're a dick to him. Which, to be fair, he has a point."

"So, what now? You know this little kid is going to die, right?"

"I hope not."

Mal stared out the window. "Well, with your hopes and my stellar track record, this toddler's good as dead."

When he pulled up to her hotel, he got out then opened the rear door for her.

"Thanks, Mike."

"Get some rest, and don't worry about the kid. I'll do what I can, and we'll find this guy."

"I hope you do it fast."

"Go to sleep," he said with a nod.

She hugged Mike, squeezing him tight, forgetting how good it felt to be embraced by someone who cared about her. "I'm glad you have my back. Sorry for ever doubting it."

"I'm sorry I didn't see all the shit you were going through. I should've done more."

"You're fine." Mal pulled away before she started to cry like a pussy. "Goodnight."

She turned around then entered the hotel. Two minutes later, she was flashing her key card above the lock. The moment she opened the door, her heart fell into her gut.

The place was trashed.

There was blood on the floor.

And sitting on the carpet was an envelope with two words on it in familiar writing.

Detective Black.

Chapter 37 - Jasper Parish

Getting out was easier than it should have been.

Jurko escorted them to the laundry area where they hid in laundry carts before getting hauled off by a service truck. Vehicles were typically searched before exiting the prison, but money must have changed hands a few spots down the line, same as always.

Jasper and D'Andre stayed silent throughout the ride until they were dropped off along a side of highway on the county outskirts. They were met by a black van. After they hurried inside, they were met by a familiar face.

Kim's hair was different, but her no-nonsense expression was exactly the same. "Well, hello, Professor," she said, looking back into the rear.

Jasper smiled for the first time in a while. "Fancy meeting you here. How did you guys pull this off. And why?"

"Long story short, Young Luther pissed off the wrong people, made enemies with the warden. Logic has been infiltrating 904 ever since he got out of Creek County. As for the why, he needs a favor."

"What's that?"

"He'll tell you himself. Right now, we're getting you out of town. Gonna drive through to Georgia."

"No," Jasper said. "I need to do something first."

Kim shook her head. "You don't get to decide. We risked a lot to make this happen. And it wasn't out of loyalty. We lost a lot of good guys with all that shit going down. Some of us are still pissed."

"Me, too. I never meant for that crap to happen with Spider. Or the rest of your crew. But all due respect, they knew what they were signing up for."

"True 'dat." Kim nodded. "Spider's okay. She's coming home in a week or so. After that, we're gonna move her up to Jacksonville where Logic's set up operations."

"She getting back into it?" Jasper said, disappointed.

"Not unless she wants back in. Can't stop someone that wants to work. For now, he's just taking care of her."

"I'm happy to help Logic with whatever he wants from me, but first I need to help someone else. A kid in danger."

"Unless that kid is yours, no beuno."

"My daughter is dead. I'd like to prevent the same thing from happening to a friend.

"Who?" D'Andre asked.

Jasper laughed. "If I tell you it's a cop, that make you want to help less?"

"Hell, yeah," Kim said.

"Then it's most certainly *not* a cop."

"Who is it?"

"Remember that detective whose kid was killed a couple years back?"

"Yeah, what about her?"

"She's in danger. Same for another kid she's taking care of. They're gonna die if I don't do something."

Kim shook her head. "Shit, what is it with you and that chick?"

"What do you mean?" Jasper asked.

"Logic did her a favor not too long ago, said she was good people."

"She is. Very good."

"Can't you just call her?" Kim asked.

"I need to track down the killer, and I can't do that without touching—"

"Hold on. I'm gonna call Logic."

Kim dialed while D'Andre rolled a blunt and Jasper wondered where Jordyn was. He was starting to worry she was stuck in prison, but that didn't make sense. Sometimes his daughter just went to wherever spirits go.

She'll be back. She has to.

D'Andre lit the joint, took a drag, then passed it to Jasper.

"Can't let it dampen this." Jasper tapped his temple.

"Suit yourself, man. *Shit*, I missed this."

"Thanks for what you did back there."

"No problem, Professor."

"You still could've stopped him sooner."

"You sure you don't want some a' this? It'll help with the pain."

"Maybe when I finish what I need to do."

"Aight," D'Andre said from behind another hit.

Kim hung up. "All right, Professor. Logic said cool, but you best not get yourself killed. He still needs you."

"I'll stay alive, but I might need to get my hands on some weapons."

Kim smiled. "We might be able to hook you up."

"Hell, yeah, we can." D'Andre laughed from behind a plume of smoke.

Chapter 38 - Mallory Black

MALLORY STARED at Katie's photo.

The girl was unconscious, gagged, and blindfolded. Despite the gash on her head, the wound didn't look nearly as bad as the blood-soaked carpet suggested.

She put up a fight. Maybe some of the blood belongs to him.

There was a phone in the envelope, but no programmed or previous history.

Mal called Mike and gave him an update. He was at the station, waiting for Barry's return.

She hadn't turned on the news or heard what Ford had said. Nor did she care. That toddler was probably already dead.

"You want me to come over?"

"Not yet," Mal said. "I need to handle this and don't want Barry cuffing me, literally. Besides, I might need you to get me some help, and it has to come from you."

Mike gave her a heavy *okay*, then hung up.

Mal stared at the photo, her world swaying underfoot. Sitting on the couch was the only thing keeping her vomit inside.

She'd led another child into danger.

Why the fuck didn't I bring Katie with me to the station?

Because I didn't think he was stalking me. Didn't think he knew anything about Katie. There was no way I could have known this.

Exactly. You can't protect anybody, Mal. Not from a determined killer. And, face it, you bring this attention onto yourself:

You put Ashley in danger.

You put Jessi in danger.

You put Katie in danger.

You are the common denominator.

Mal was terrified. Her anxiety was back, and more brutal than ever, but at least she was breathing and keeping it from choking the life from her body. Instead, it chewed at her soul.

She wasn't sure which was worse, the physical pain of her last panic attack or the mental anguish still coming in waves from this one, that feeling of helplessness that felt impossible to shake.

Three people were already dead. Four if he'd murdered the toddler.

Mal answered the phone before the first ring ended. "Where is she?"

"Patience, Detective Black. First, tell me why my manifesto was not read."

"The sheriff kept me from going on-air. I tried and got shut down. Seems he isn't a fan of your work. Please don't take it out on Katie or the toddler."

"I'm not a monster, and I don't kill innocents. The child is fine. I've sent his location to the sheriff's office."

Mal didn't bother to ask what Alice Shaw had ever done to anyone. "And what about Katie?"

"That whore is not an innocent. No surprise, with *you* as an influence."

"I'll do whatever you want."

"Of course you will. Not so tough now that I've got someone you care about, are you detective? We both know you're only pretending. That's what women like you do best, right? Say nice things to get what you want, despite how you *really* feel. What was it you were calling me last time? A 'sick fuck pussy,' I believe. Tell me, Miss Black. Do you still feel that way?"

Mal felt punched in the stomach repeatedly and hated herself almost as much as she hated him.

"No." Her vomit was getting harder to hold inside.

"Good, you're learning. But this is only the first lesson, detective. Before the night is over, you will see the glory that will be coming unto this world. You will witness my greatness."

"What do you want?"

"I'm going to send you coordinates, and you will come alone. If you bring anybody else or send anyone to try and intercept or snipe at me, I will not hesitate to kill her. Do you understand me?"

"Yes," Mal said. "What do you want when I get there? Money? Something else?"

"You'll see."

Fuck.

At least a demand for cash would be straightforward. But if money wasn't the monster's goal, and he was some wackadoo twisting religion to suit his sick ideology, then it was only a guess at what he might do.

What did he mean by witnessing his greatness? What the hell was this monster planning? God only knew what someone like him might do to make an example of his enemies or show the world his message.

"See you in two hours, detective. Don't be late."

He hung up.

Mal paced her living room, careful not to step on any

evidence in what was about to be an active crime scene and wondering whether to call Mike or not.

She was startled by a knock.

Mal grabbed her gun then slowly approached the door.

Then she opened it and saw the last person in the world she expected to see.

Chapter 39 - Jasper Parish

"Hello." Jasper waved, offering Mallory the best smile he had under such painful circumstances.

"What are you doing here?"

"I kinda got out early."

"What?"

"Well, not *officially*, or anything."

"Get in here." Mal pulled him inside then closed and locked the door behind them.

"Don't step anywhere. We've got a crime scene here."

"That's why I'm here … Katie."

She stared at him, confused for only a moment before she seemed to realize what he was saying — Katie was the 'daughter' he saw in danger.

"So, she's the one you saw?"

"Yeah, only it wasn't clear then."

Jordyn was back, looking around the hotel room.

"What happened?" Mallory asked. "How did you get out?"

"Long story and it doesn't matter. I won't be here long. I came to help you."

"Help me? I'm guessing you're a fugitive?"

"Maybe. Or maybe they faked my death. Not sure which way the warden is gonna play it."

"The warden knows?"

"There's some sketchy shit going on," Jasper said. "Crooked cops, a bunch of smart phones smuggled in, and a dude running a drug empire from prison. But none of that matters right now. I'm here to help you find this asshole."

"What do you know about him?"

Jasper told Mallory about his visions, including seeing himself and Jordyn in this room, how he'd tried to talk to her but couldn't, and eventually knocked a glass of soda over in frustration.

Her eyes widened at the mention of the shattered glass.

"How?" she asked.

"I don't know. If you're asking if I was actually here, I don't think so. At least, not *physically*. But mentally, no doubt. Your place looks exactly as I saw it. Did the killer leave something for you?"

Mallory nodded toward the table where there was an envelope, a photograph, and a phone sitting on top of it.

"You dust it yet?" Jasper asked.

"No." Mallory shook her head.

"I need to touch them. I won't leave prints."

"Okay." Mal met him at the table.

Jasper placed the back of his hand down so it was barely touching the envelope. He saw nothing and turned to Jordyn. "I need your help."

She placed her hand over his. A name popped into his head. *Howie.*

A flood of images. A young boy, fat and bullied for his appearance. Sweet and kind until the world broke him.

The one person who should have protected him from that world broke him first.

Jasper dove deeper into the man's psyche, the connection stronger than any he'd felt.

"It's like he wants us to see his pain," Jordyn said.

The boy transformed into a large, ugly man with memories of his mother harping on him, of watching naked people via his laptop as he spied and masturbated, of the shame and punishment he always inflicted upon himself afterward.

Howie's self-hatred ran deeper than most of the evil people Jasper had peered inside.

He went deeper and saw the darkness that called itself Mister K. A pure black entity that promised Howie answers, swore he could belong to something greater than himself, something that would finally make him matter.

Howie lured a child into his van then did vile things to innocent body and soul.

Jasper had seen glimpses into the worlds and minds of many monsters. He'd witnessed countless atrocities leveled upon women and children and felt the darkness in all of these souls. But nothing came close to what he saw in this man.

The blade cut into the naked child's skin. Jasper yanked his hand away in disgust, anger and sorrow boiling his blood.

"What did you see?" Mallory asked.

"Too much," Jasper said, shaking. He looked up to see his daughter crying.

"Did you get anything?" Mallory pressed.

"A little. A name, Howie. Drives a van."

"Anything more? Do you know where he is now?"

Jasper shook his head.

"We need to keep going," Jordyn said.

"Are you sure?" Jasper could barely handle the pain himself, let alone expose his daughter.

She nodded. "If we don't, Katie will die."

Jasper took her hand then they set them palms down on the phone, no longer concerned about prints. He saw too much that he could never un-see.

But he also saw something they could use. He pulled away and looked at Mallory.

"His name is Howard Loomis."

Chapter 40 - Howard Loomis

HOWARD PACED in the darkness downstairs.

The place belonged to Richard Messer, a widower who would be missed by nobody. He lived on a relatively secluded street with only two other homes. Both at the far end, and each of them abandoned. A large swath of woods threw shadows on the house from behind it.

Howard had parked his van in the garage beside Richard's car.

The slut was cuffed to the bed upstairs. Amid her muffled whimpers came the clanging of metal on metal. He considered heading up there to shut her up again but didn't want to face the temptation of her sinful body.

Mister K suggested Howard enjoy her, but he thought that was probably a test to see if he'd sleep with a whore. He had to resist the urges that came with seeing her splayed and helpless on the bed.

Howard was startled by the ringing phone. He picked it up, the hairs on his neck standing on end as if Mother had caught him in the midst of yet another shameful act.

"Howie? Where are you? It's late." Her voice was frail, not stern and cold as it had been for so much of his life.

"I'm working late. What do you need, Mother?"

"You didn't tell me you were working late. Is there a problem?"

"No, Mother, everything is fine."

"Can you …" A dramatic sigh. Or maybe she'd just forgotten what she was saying.

"What, Mother?"

"Never mind, dear."

He hated when she guilt-tripped him into doing something. This time the sigh was his. "Just tell me what you need and I'll get it."

"We need some milk, if you happen to swing by the store."

"Milk. Got it. Anything else, Mother?"

The harlot's whimpering grew louder.

"Howie? Are you with a … woman?"

"No, Mom. I'm working at somebody's house. Their TV is loud."

"You know God hates a liar."

"I'm not lying, Mom."

Loud banging from upstairs, maybe his prisoner kicking the wall.

Or she'd gotten free!

"I've got to go, Mother."

"Don't you hang up on me, Howie!"

"Sorry, Mom."

Howard hung up, raced upstairs, then threw open the door to see the whore writhing on the bed, kicking with all her might and desperately trying to destroy the wall. There were already two holes in it, and she was working on the third.

"Stop it!" Howard shouted, racing to the bed and smacking her across the face.

The succubus glared at him as she lashed out and pounded her heel into his balls.

Howard doubled over, then spat at her. "You are going to pay for that!"

She mouthed something through the rag, probably an obscenity from her filthy, disease-ridden mouth.

He shook his head as he walked to the dresser, doused the rag he'd used earlier with chloroform, then went back to the bed.

She shook her head and thrashed some more. But the tramp was small, no match for his size and weight. He held her down, forcing the rag over her mouth and nose until she stopped moving.

He stared at the T-shirt rising over her swelling breasts, the bottom pulled up past her piercing. Imagined the whore in some shop, teasing some man as he pierced her navel. Like Stephanie had teased him before laughing.

Mister K appeared in shadows behind him. "Touch her, Howie. You know you want to. Look at her lying there, just waiting. She wants it … needs a man's touch."

"No." Howard shook his head, trying to clear the impurity from his mind. He left the bedroom before he was tempted to do something he shouldn't, something that would prove him unworthy of the coming glories.

Mister K followed in the shadows. "You think I care what you do to her? Whores are only good for …" Mister K trailed off, perhaps trying to let Howard's head fill in the blanks with his perversions.

"I'm trying to keep my head clear. Can you tell me now? What are we going to do when the cop gets here?"

Mister K's shadowy form shifted from one wall to the other. "*Soooon.*"

"Can you at least show yourself to me? I've been patient."

"You're far too eager, Howie. I thought you were learning to wait." Mister K laughed.

"I am. I have. And I've done everything you asked. Always."

Silence.

Maybe he'd pushed Mister K too far. Howard felt stupid, weak, like the dumb impatient child his mother had always accused him of being.

"Sorry," he said, disgusted with both his eagerness and his meekness.

"I will reveal myself to you once this is over. Then you will know our master plan once and for all."

"Can … can you spare my mother?"

"You hate her. *We* hate her."

"I don't *hate* her. I love her. I don't want her to suffer."

"Then she will have a place in our kingdom, Howard. I promise."

"Thank you."

"It's almost time. We must prepare."

"Yes." Howard went back downstairs, slid on his body armor, then double checked his guns and knives.

Mister K, shifting in the shadows beside him, belted a long and rattling breath as if he were gathering strength from what he saw, or perhaps merely voicing his pleasure.

"Tonight, Howard. Tonight is The End of everything you've ever known. Tonight, you will finally become what you were always meant to be."

Howard smiled in the darkness. For the first time in his life, he felt he had a purpose that wasn't Mother's, or his employer's, and surely not some worthless whore's.

Tonight was his destiny.

Chapter 41 - Mallory Black

THEY STOOD ON THE BALCONY, overlooking the city lights, Mal slowly digesting everything Jasper had just told her.

She wanted to call Mike and give him the name, have deputies track him down, maybe get a location from the man's cell phone pings. Itched to call for backup, get the SWAT team mobilized, along with a hostage negotiator.

But Jasper forbade it. "You *can't* do things by the book."

"I don't know what you're thinking, but I'm doing this by the book."

"You trust your sheriff to do the right thing?"

"No, but I trust my fellow deputies. And Mike has my back."

"Doing this textbook means that Katie will die. I've seen what he has in mind, along with his security cameras. Send anyone and he'll see you. He *will* kill her. He's paranoid and schizoid."

"Pot meet kettle," she joked.

"What?" Jasper turned to his left. "Oh, yeah," he said, turning back to Mal. "You still don't think she's here. That's fine, I don't need you to believe everything I say. But *please*, believe me on this. Helping you is the only reason I'm here when I should be on the run. I'm risking a lot to be here."

"Why?"

"Because I want to make things right."

"What do you mean?"

"I should've done something myself when I found out about Ashley. I should've killed Dodd instead of leaving him to you. If I'd taken him out, then everything that happened after — Mexico, the pedo network, Spider and the others — all that shit would never have happened. All that suffering was because I didn't do what needed to be done. I suppose some part of me felt if you killed Dodd, that meant *I* wasn't so bad. But you didn't."

"I *did*. Don't you remember?"

"That wasn't you." Jasper shook his head. "I pushed you into that. And the other things you did."

"What are you talking about?"

"I know what you were doing after you got back from Mexico. And … it's okay. I pushed you to that, too. You're not a killer. That isn't you."

"I didn't kill anyone here." Mal crossed her arms, uncomfortably vulnerable.

"I know. But … you regret what you did, don't you?"

She nodded. It was weird discussing this. But she couldn't get into the depths of her feelings with Katie's life on the line.

"That's why you're back at work, why you feel a need to do this by the book, to do things right. You want to prove you're a good person. But trust me, Mallory. You can't do this 'the right way.'"

"What *am* I supposed to do then? Go meet this guy? Then what? What's his plan?"

"I've only seen a few flashes of what he's planning, or

rather what the thing he thinks is talking to him wants him to do. The thing he calls Mister K."

"What does *Mister K* want him to do?"

"He's confused and chaotic. It's all a mess. Everything running through his head is ultra-violent. He wants to send a message."

"To who?"

"To the world. He thinks the world is going to end and he and this Mister K are going to herald in whatever's coming. Lots of demons and angels and shit."

"So, he's a fucking madman with a messiah complex? Is he going to kill her? Is she already dead?"

"She's still alive. But she's dead if you go. Howard wants you to see her suffer. He wants *you* to suffer. He *really* hates you. I'd say he's obsessed."

"Perfect." She sighed. "So, what are my options?"

"I have an idea."

"Well, please, don't keep it to yourself."

"It's definitely not by the book."

Mal was waiting for Jasper to finish, then gestured for him to get on with it when he didn't.

"There's only one person he cares about, one thing that'll get him to stand down."

"Who?" Mal asked.

"His mother."

Chapter 42 - Howard Loomis

FIFTEEN MINUTES TO go as Howard watched the monitors for any sign of police activity.

The slut was stirring in the next room, still trying to break free and whimpering, but at least she was no longer kicking the wall.

Howard had resisted his urges. Now that his head was clear of her temptations, he could finally focus. He had an AR-15 on the bed behind him and a pistol in its holster at his side. There were more weapons, smoke grenades, flash bangs, and a machete for the sheath meant for his hip, opposite the holster. He had enough ammo to take out an entire police department if they were foolish enough to come at him.

Of course, Howard hoped it never came to that. If the detective obeyed his instructions and came alone, it wouldn't.

Anxiety gnawed at him because he still didn't know what he would do once she got here. Howard had a few ideas, things he wasn't sure if he'd dreamed up himself or if Mister K had sent them into his mind through their psychic connection.

Mister K wanted to test her and see if she was a good person or not. Would she really sacrifice herself to save a worthless whore?

Howard doubted she would.

Mallory Black was a selfish woman who couldn't even care for her own child and nearly got another little girl murdered. A reckless, drunken whore. People like her raised the monsters who made Howard's life a living hell.

Terrible parents raising vapid children who didn't appreciate purity or intellect, ridiculing anyone even remotely different or "weird."

Detective Black was a horrible person.

"It's almost time, Howard. Are you ready to seize your destiny?"

"Yes," Howard said, though he still didn't know what they were going to do. What if he doubted himself once he was called upon to prove his greatness? What if he'd come this far just to fail when it mattered most?

Would Mister K deny him the answers he'd been seeking all his life?

"You have doubts?"

"No, I—"

"I need you to remove all fear from this. You have lived your entire life like a scared little baby, Howie. You've been afraid of your mother, the church, and women. You've been frightened by men and everything else. Now is the time to finally shed your fear and embrace the unknown. Only by stepping through it can you become what you were always meant to be."

"What if you're wrong? What if I'm not who you think I am?"

"You are exactly what I believe you to be, Howard. You

must believe and disregard the empty shell you have been. Are you ready for The End?"

"Yes." Howard slowly slid the mask over his head.

The things that made him good and pure would no longer be a liability.

Howard would now prove himself worthy — no matter the cost.

Chapter 43 - Mallory Black

MAL KNOCKED on Enid Loomis's door with her gun drawn and ready.

Howard could be here, and armed. Jasper was around back, just in case their suspect was home and attempted an escape.

"Who is it?" An old woman's voice from the other side of the closed front door.

"Creek County Sheriff's Office." Mal held her badge in front of the peephole. "It's about your son. He's in trouble."

"Trouble?" Enid repeated, opening the door.

She was a tall woman with her hair pulled back tight, wearing a long, floral print nightgown that looked like a costume from *Little House on the Prairie*.

"Yes, I'm going to need you to come with me, Mrs. Loomis. Your son is in danger."

"What kind of danger?" Confusion and concern drew down the corners of her mouth.

"I'll tell you on the way. I just need you to come with us. We don't have much time."

"Can I grab my purse?"

"Yes, ma'am." Mal watched the woman go back inside and grab her purse and keys off a credenza. She kept her gun at the ready just in case the old woman pulled a weapon on her. No telling what Enid knew about Howard's activities or what lengths she might go to protect him. A glint of insanity gleamed in the old woman's eyes.

Mal relaxed her grip on the gun as Enid came outside.

She locked her front door then looked toward the street. "Don't you have a police car?"

Mal escorted her to the SUV. "Detectives drive unmarked vehicles, ma'am." She opened the back door for Enid.

The woman paused, suspicion furrowing her brow. "Can I see your badge again?"

Mal reached into her coat, grabbed her badge, held it up for inspection.

Enid eyed both it and Mal with suspicion. "You're that cop who lost her kid?"

"Yes, ma'am," Mal said, an uneasiness rooting in her gut.

Is this bitch about to flake?

"You wouldn't mind if I called the sheriff's office, would you?"

Jasper closed the distance and put his pistol against the back of Enid's head. "Actually, we would mind, Mrs. Loomis. Now get in the car."

Chapter 44 - Howard Loomis

HOWARD SAT ON THE COUCH, staring into the darkness beyond the living room's large open window while he waited for the detective to appear.

The dirty slut was standing in front of him, just in case any sniper tried taking a shot at him. Hands cuffed behind her back, gag still covering her mouth.

The whore mumbled something, eyes widening.

Howard put the gun to her head. "I'll remove the gag, but if you scream, there's two things you should know. Nobody will hear you, and I will pull this trigger. Nod if you understand me."

She nodded.

He removed the gag.

"I need to pee."

Mister K shuffled in the shadows behind him. "The whore can piss herself."

"Not now." Howard sat back on the couch to keep the harlot between himself and the window.

"Please, I'm gonna wet myself."

"Go ahead. We don't have time."

Howard looked down at the laptops he'd brought downstairs and arranged on the coffee table. None of the security cameras trained on a 360 perimeter of the house and surrounding area had triggered any events.

"Please," the Jezabel begged him again.

"Piss yourself, I don't care."

He heard the trickle of piss running down her legs and onto the hardwood floor. The scent was hot and acrid.

Howard shook his head.

The human disease said nothing.

He kept his eyes on the monitors. Four more minutes to go.

"Why are you doing this? You know I'm a kid, right?"

"Do you know how much you shame the Lord with what you've done to your body and with what you've let others do to it? Your virginity is sacred and you just … gave it up. To who?"

"You sound like my dad."

"Maybe you should have listened to him."

"You two have a lot in common."

"Yeah?" Howard said.

"You're gonna have something else in common."

"Oh? What's that?"

"Detective Mallory Black is gonna shoot you dead, too."

Howard glared up at her. To his shock, the whore started laughing.

"What's so funny?"

"I guess it's hilarious that there's a fat fucking loser in a stupid mask looking at me."

He leapt up and punched her in the back of the head. The whore fell, crying out as she hit the ground, awkwardly with bound hands still behind her.

She was frozen, and for a moment, Howard thought he

might have accidentally killed her too soon. But then her shoulders moved slowly up and down as she started laughing again.

"You are so fucking dead," the sinner said with a smile.

Howard grabbed the back of her hair, shoved his gun back into its holster, then yanked the slut to her feet. He shoved the gag into her depraved little mouth.

Car lights turned at the end of the street outside. A lone car, driving slowly.

"It's showtime, Howie," Mister K said.

Chapter 45 - Jasper Parish

JASPER HELD the gun to the back of Enid's head as Mallory pulled into the driveway of a two-story house at the end of a quiet cul de sac with only two other homes.

"I don't know what you think my boy did, but you're making a big mistake." Enid's voice was weaker than it had been.

He wasn't sure if she was putting on a frail old lady act or slipping in and out of senility, but she'd changed a few times during their short drive. Confusion gave way to a bitterness, her eyes sharp enough to slice right through him.

She wasn't a good person, Jasper knew that for certain. He'd seen Howard's memories of his tortured upbringing at the hands of this supposedly godly woman.

"Your son is a killer, lady. He's got a young woman in there right now, a teenager he's threatening to kill."

"Howard would never do that," Enid said with a disgusted defiance that Jasper would ever suggest such a thing.

"I want you to slowly get out of the car. *Slowly*. Don't make any sudden moves, or I'll have to spray your brains all over the driveway."

Enid harrumphed as she reached for the handle.

Chapter 46 - Howard Loomis

Howard watched as the car door opened. Then the woman stepped out.

"Go, take the whore to the porch," said Mister K.

Howard grabbed her by the shoulder. As he shoved her toward the door, he said, "Walk slowly. If you run or try to escape, I'll kill you. Do you understand?"

The harlot nodded, tears now soaking her cheeks. The bravery was gone, pure humility now in its place. Something in those tears tugged at him, made him doubt what he was doing.

"Do not let the whore's tears deceive you. She is playing you, Howie, playing you for a fool like they all do. Stay strong. The End is here. Now is the time for bold action. Not weakness."

"Yes." Howard nodded and prompted the whore forward. "Unlock the door then open it."

She did, her hand shaking as she fumbled with the locks.

After the last tumbler turned, they stepped onto the porch.

Chapter 47 - Mallory Black

Mal crouched in the brush, waiting for Jasper's call.

She was about two hundred yards away, and there wasn't any way to approach without the cameras spotting her. They would have to wait until Howard was no longer looking.

She hoped Jasper's visions were correct — that the cameras were where he said and Howard would be preoccupied once he left the house. She had no reason to doubt his visions as he'd been right so many times. But still, it was difficult.

And now, as Mal waited in the woods with Katie's life on the line, she was starting to question everything. Maybe she should've called Mike. The SWAT team was trained for this type of situation. Mal was a detective, which meant she usually arrived after shit went down, not during the hottest part of a standoff.

Jasper's radio silence grew more ominous by the moment.

Did something happen?

Her heart pounded, chest constricted. Air became harder to draw.

No.

Not fucking now.

A Xanax would help. But pills also dulled the fight or flight response, and she needed her senses razor sharp. Katie would die if she fucked this up.

The realization made it more difficult to breathe.

No, no, not now.

Mal did one of her calming exercises, inhaling deeply through her nose, then holding for three seconds before exhaling through her mouth.

But focusing on her breath while counting only made her more aware of the passing time. Every minute in the woods brought her closer to believing Katie was already dead.

She checked her signal and saw barely a bar on her phone.

What if he's already called and I missed it?

Fuck!

Heart still racing. Chest still trapped in a compactor, slowly crushing her to death.

Just go.

Now. Fuck the cameras.

No. Do it and she'll die.

You have to trust Jasper.

Mal fell back against a tree, still sucking wind, certain she was about to pass out again.

Calm.

The.

Fuck.

Down!

She took in another deep breath and counted.

One.

Two.

Her phone rang.

She answered instantly. "Yeah?"

"He's coming out the front door," Jasper said. *"Go."*

Mal ran.

Chapter 48 - Jasper Parish

JASPER WATCHED as the door opened then Katie was marched out at gunpoint.

Howard loomed behind her, dressed in black body armor, with a matching trench coat and mask. He looked like a fat weekend soldier, or any host of racist militia men whose closet was also filled with white robes and hoods.

When Howard realized it wasn't Mallory standing at gunpoint before him, he stopped in his tracks. "Mother?"

"Let her go, Howard," Jasper shouted. "We can all still walk away from this."

Howard screamed, "Who the hell are you? I told her to come alone!"

"He's gonna snap," said Jordyn, standing behind them. *Where the hell is Mallory?*

"Tell your son to let the girl go," Jasper told her.

But Enid said nothing, stubbornly shaking her head.

"You want a child's blood on your hands?" Jasper pushed the gun against the back of her skull. "Tell him."

Enid cleared her throat. "Why don't you let her go, Howie?"

"I can't do that, Mother. I have to prove I'm worthy."

Howard was talking about the thing Jasper had seen in the shadows, the thing he believed was commanding him.

"Are you doing this for Mister K?" Jasper asked, taking a chance.

If Jasper could see his face, he'd probably note Howard's shocked expression, but the beast said nothing.

Jasper needed to keep the man talking. The longer he spoke, the more time Mallory had to take him out from behind.

"Mister K is a liar, Howard. He's playing you."

"You don't know him."

"I do, Howard. Mister K showed you the messages in those books, the one that told you to kill Alice Shaw, then to take this girl. But you know what, Howard?"

Silence, then he finally said, "What?"

"He also talks to me."

"Liar!" Howard bellowed.

"He's testing you. He wants to see if you will kill a pregnant girl, to see just how far gone you are."

"Liar! He says you are lying!"

Jasper was losing him.

Where the hell is Mallory?

"Say something." Jasper pressed the gun harder into Enid's head. "Get your son in line."

"Howie, let her go. Now!"

"No, Mother. This is something I have to do."

"You're not my son if you do this. And you will burn in Hell for all of eternity!"

Howard was silent. Jasper couldn't tell from this distance if he was thinking or crying.

Jasper nudged Enid forward, just enough to get a closer shot.

"He promised you a place with me in The End, Mother. I have to do this."

"Don't be such a fool, Howie! You are being a tricked by Satan. You are allowing yourself to be the devil's pawn."

"Mister K is an agent of God. He's going to show me—"

"You stupid, stupid boy! You are such an embarrassment. You let that girl go right now and stop this before you—"

A gunshot exploded like thunder, then Enid said no more.

Chapter 49 - Mallory Black

MAL RACED through the woods to the house, her weapon drawn and ready to fire.

She made it to the sliding glass door in the back. The blinds were closed, so she hoped Howard wasn't waiting as she lifted the door off the track.

It popped off. She slid it aside then creeped into the house with her ears and eyes perked for any sign of movement.

Mal saw through to the living room then to the front door beyond.

It was open, and she could hear Howard yelling at his mother.

She raised her pistol and approached the front door.

Howard's gun went off as she reached it.

Mal crossed the threshold, her weapon aimed.

Chapter 50 - Howard Loomis

"Howie, let her go. Now!"

"No, Mother. This is something I have to do."

"You're not my son if you do this. And you will burn in Hell for all of eternity!"

"See, she doesn't love you," said Mister K in his staticky leathery voice. "She stands in your way. She's with *them*."

Howard whispered, "No, she's just saying what he's telling her to. Mother would never betray me."

Mother was tough, but only because she wanted greatness from him. She expected him to follow the Lord's path, to stay vigilant and never surrender to sin. She only hurt him for his own good, to prepare him for the ills and evils of this world.

She loved him and wanted to help him keep Satan away.

He just had to convince her he *was* on the right path. Mister K was showing him the way. "He promised you a place with me in The End, Mother. I have to do this."

"Don't be such a fool, Howie! You are being a tricked by the Devil. Allowing yourself to be his pawn."

"She lies," Mister K said. "She's never loved you. She's only tried to hold you back from your destiny. She's guilty of the most grievous of sins, being jealous of her child, trying to hold her son back from the man he is destined to be."

"Mister K is an agent of God. He's going to show me—"

"You stupid, stupid boy!"

"You see!" Mister K shouted. "She thinks you're nothing."

"You are such an embarrassment. You let that girl go right now …"

"*An embarrassment,*" Mister K repeated. "And she still thinks you're under her thumb. It's time to embrace your destiny."

"…and stop this before you—"

Howard fired his gun at Mother.

The first shot missed.

She stared at him, stunned, eyes glaring with hate and betrayal.

Fear gripped his throat, threatening to crush him as shame burned his face.

"Again!" Mister K shouted.

Howard fired, this time finding his target, twice.

The door burst open behind him as his mother hit the ground.

No, no, no!

Howard spun, raising his gun as he fired on Mallory Black.

Chapter 51 - Mallory Black

MAL WENT THROUGH THE DOORWAY, gun raised, as Katie fell and Howard spun toward her.

She fired. Hit his shoulder. Went to squeeze the trigger again.

But the fingers on her left hand erupted in an explosion of pain, bone, and blood as his bullet landed. She screamed as the impact sent her backward.

Then the behemoth was on her.

His gun jammed, so he grabbed Mal by the head and slammed her into the open door.

She crumpled to the ground in agony.

Howard screamed in rage, looming over her.

Mal looked up just as he was about to smash his boot onto her face.

Chapter 52 - Jasper Parish

JASPER AIMED at Howard the second Enid's body fell, but with Katie and Mal both in motion, he couldn't get a clear shot.

He ran to the front door as the giant knocked Mal to the ground.

When Howard raised his boot, Jasper got his shot.

He fired three times.

Howard spun around. Stared at Jasper. Tried to clear his jammed gun.

Jasper raised his pistol to fire again, but Katie was running toward him, away from the monster and blocking his shot.

He yelled at her to get down, but she either didn't hear him because of the bullets or was too panicked to understand. She kept racing toward him, then straight into his arms.

He turned and rushed Katie toward the back of the SUV. "Stay behind the vehicle and get down." When she hid, he ran back into the fray. But by the time he had a clean line of sight, so did his enemy.

Howard fired. The windshield shattered.
Something hard hit the ground in front of the car.
And smoke began to billow.

Chapter 53 - Mallory Black

MAL'S SIGHT swam in and out of focus thanks to having her head smashed into the door.

She heard Jasper fire, watched Howard throw a smoke grenade. He whipped open his jacket, drew a machete, then marched toward the smoke. Toward Jasper and Katie.

Mal looked at her left hand, quickly losing blood. Two fingers were now missing from the mid-knuckle and above.

The pain was unbearable. She was about to pass out from either head wound or blood loss.

So much blood.

She ripped material from her shirt for a makeshift tourniquet, but gunfire and Jasper's scream captured her attention before she could wrap her hand.

Howard's laughter carried back to her, followed by the *ting* of his machete hitting the metal door.

Smoke by the car was too thick for Mal to do anything but imagine the horror show — Jasper getting hacked by the sharp, curved blade before Howard turned his twisted hatred on Katie.

She crawled toward her gun — on the ground with her

fingers — and grabbed it with her right hand. It was slippery with blood, but Mal managed to grip it.

Up to her knees, slowly, carefully, terrified of passing out and hitting her head again, dying on the way down. She braced against the door frame, dizziness and pain at war in her head and in her gut as she stood.

Mal grabbed her stomach then emptied it. Vomit everywhere.

A break in the curtain of smoke showed Jasper and Katie were on the opposite side of the car from Howard. She cowered behind Jasper, who looked paternally protective.

But he wasn't armed. Howard must have knocked his weapon away.

Maybe he maimed Jasper's hand too?

Mal aimed, but Howard dropped another smoke grenade before she could fire.

She swallowed then saw how far she could make it.

Chapter 54 - Howard Loomis

HOWARD HURLED another grenade then followed with a flash bang.

The explosion and light disoriented the black man.

Howard went at him, swinging his machete in a downward arc toward his body.

The man somehow managed to dodge, but now Howard had him pinned against the car.

"Kill him." Mister K in his ear.

Howard dropped the blade then aimed his gun at the black man.

"Howard!"

He turned and saw the detective approaching him from behind a billow of smoke.

Her body was bloody, her hands were shaking, but she aimed her gun at his face all the same.

"Do it," said Mister K. "She can't hit you. Kill him, then the whore."

Howard looked down at the black man, frozen with his hands up, speaking at the edge of a crack. "You don't have to die, tonight, Howard. You can still walk away from this, maybe get some help."

"Do it," Mister K urged. "Do it or you will never see the truth."

"I know what it's like to have voices in your head, voices that won't shut the hell up. I also know what it's like to have a mother who doesn't love you. What it's like to live in a world that can never see who you really are. You did some bad shit, Howard. But you are not a monster."

Tears stung his eyes. This stranger spoke with an empathy that dipped its shovel into the open grave of Howard's pain. For the first time in a long time, he felt understood.

And confused.

"Kill him, now, you fucking pussy!"

"Shut up, shut up, shut up!" Howard kept shaking his head, wanting Mister K to go away.

"Do it. *Now*."

His head was going to explode. Howard needed a minute to think, sixty seconds in peace.

"Your mother was right about you, wasn't she? You're just a worthless little shit. You'll never —"

"Just shut up! Shut the hell—"

Chapter 55 - Mallory Black

MAL FIRED THREE SHOTS.

Direct hits to Howard's head and neck.

He fell to the ground.

And Mal right after him.

Chapter 56 - Mallory Black

MAL WOKE up in the back of her car, sick. In pain.

Confused.

They were so moving fast.

She looked up and saw the back of Jasper's head.

"What's going on?" she asked.

"You'll be okay," said a voice above her.

Her head was resting in Katie's lap, the girl holding something over her wound.

"You lost a lot of blood," Jasper said from up front. "I'm taking you to the hospital. Figured it was faster than waiting for an ambulance."

"Oh," Mal said before …

MAL OPENED HER EYES, vision blurred and hazy mind, the daylight making her blink. She eventually made out a shape sitting in a chair next to her — Katie looking at her phone.

"Hey, kiddo."

"Mal!" Katie dropped her phone and jumped up from her chair.

"How are you?"

"Good." She smiled. "I'm so glad you're okay."

Mal looked around, searching for Jasper. "Where's …?"

"Your friend? He's gone. Don't worry, he told me not to say anything to the cops."

"Oh? What did you say to the cops?"

Katie looked at the door conspiratorially, then reached into her pocket and pulled out a piece of paper.

"Your friend told me to give you this. I didn't read it, but he said it'll have everything you need."

"Um, okay." Mal went to take the note, saw her bandaged left hand, remembered losing a pair of fingers, and wanted to cry. Maybe the morphine was keeping her tears at bay.

And fuck someone's mother, now she would have to get off of opiates … *again.*

But that was a problem for Future Mal. Right now, she would enjoy the relief. And the buzz that came on like an opening riff laid on a backbeat.

She opened the letter.

You followed up on an anonymous tip which led you to Enid Loomis.

You accompanied her to the house at the address Howard gave you, hoping to talk him down.

You knew you didn't have much time to get anyone else involved.

When you showed up, Howard's mother tried to talk some sense into him. He shot her.

. . .

THE LETTER LISTED precise details of what was said, surely so their narratives matched.

It went on to explain that someone showed up, a good Samaritan who fired shots — which nobody will trace to an actual name — and that same good Samaritan drove her to the hospital after shooting Howard Loomis in the process of saving Katie.

Once he outlined the specifics, he left her with a few last words and wishes.

THANK YOU FOR EVERYTHING.

Katie is a good kid. She's really worried about you. I know you're not sure if you're ready to be a mom again. But don't do what I've done all my life and let fear hold you back from love.

Best of luck starting over.

I'm not sure where I'm going next, but I'll be in touch if I'm ever in your neck of the woods again.

By the way, Jordyn wanted me to give you this — Saturday's numbers, in case you're running low on cash:

3-15-18-25-47-51-x2

ALL OUR BEST,
J&J

SHE SMILED and wiped tears from her eyes. From the meds, the message, or maybe the blend of them together, Mal's gratitude suddenly felt ravine deep.

Katie was staring at her.

Mal felt a flush of embarrassment.

"Was he a good friend?"

"It's complicated," Mal said. "More like a guardian angel."

"No offense, but he was a little weird. He kept talking to someone who wasn't there, kinda like that psycho who kidnapped me."

"It's a long story. But he's a good guy. How are you … did Loomis … hurt you?"

"Nothing too bad. You got there in time. Thank you."

"It's my job."

"No, thank you for everything — for taking me in, and for trying to help my mom and me." Katy started to cry. "And I'm sorry I was such a dick to you after all that."

"It's okay," Mal laughed. "You weren't *that* big a dick."

"You sure?"

"A two, maybe three-incher at most."

Katie snort-laughed, then leaned in and hugged Mal, awkwardly in the hospital bed.

Mal realized how much she missed having someone to care for. She wasn't sure what would happen with Katie and her baby, but she felt good about their future.

A knock on the door preceded it opening.

"Hey, partner." Mike walked in with a teddy bear and a gift bag. "How are you?"

She held up her left hand. "On the plus side, I guess my index finger now qualifies as flipping you off."

Mike handed her the bag.

She looked inside. "No fucking way. You actually found *ABBA's Greatest Hits* on eight-track?"

"What's eight-track?" Katie said. "And who is Abba?"

"Don't ask that second question," Mike teased. "She'll make you listen to the whole album."

"Fortunately for both of you, I don't have my eight-track anymore. But I'm sure Katie can download it on her iPhone."

Mike shook his head.

Katie laughed.

"Hey, do you mind if I talk to Mal alone for a minute?"

Katie looked at her. When Mal nodded back, she left.

"You up for a statement yet?" Mike asked.

"I'm a bit loopy right now. Maybe later?"

"I was looking over Katie's. Your good Samaritan wouldn't happen to be a certain man who recently died in prison?"

"I've got no idea what you're talking about." Mal smiled.

"Of course you don't."

"He saved us, again."

"I thought *you* saved the day. You shot Loomis, right?"

"Yeah, but … the Samaritan … I couldn't have done it without him. If I went in there like I planned or called it in, Katie would be dead for sure."

"Okay." Mike nodded. "I'm not gonna push."

"Thank you."

"Barry is wondering when you'll be ready to come back."

"Oh, now he wants me back?"

"Well, you're a hero."

She shook her head. "I don't think I will be."

"What?"

"That girl out there needs me. And, right now, I kinda need her. I miss having a family."

"Well, you need anything, even if it's just to talk, you know where to find me."

"Thanks, Mike."

"I'll call you later for an official statement. Or … I could just say I already took it and it's all good."

"Sounds great.

"Gotchya, Mamma Mia." He gave another nod, then he was gone.

Katie came back inside. "So, I downloaded ABBA."

"And?"

"It's not the worst thing ever."

Mal smiled. "Let me see which one you got."

Katie showed her. *ABBA Gold: Greatest Hits*.

"See, you got the better version. This one," Mal said, holding up the eight-track tape, "actually didn't even have *Dancing Queen* on it. Their best known song, their greatest hit, came out after this album."

Katie stared at her.

"Sorry. I get really passionate about ABBA. And almost all seventies music."

Katie nodded. "Is it too late to go to the group home?"

Mal laughed.

It felt good to hear the sound again.

Epilogue 1

Two weeks later ...

Mal sat in a booth at the back of the hotel restaurant, waiting for Gloria.

She'd called earlier saying she had something "huge" to discuss.

Mal wasn't sure if it was good or bad news. Things were going great with Katie. Mal had "won" the lottery for a second time. McKenna was out of her coma and doing well. And she hadn't heard a whisper about Jasper, so maybe her unusually excellent luck streak was about to flame the hell out.

But Gloria's smile suggested the good news was great, indeed.

She sat down, looked around to see if anybody was watching, then slid an iPad across the table. "You know anything about this?"

"What?" Mal asked.

"Turn it on."

The screen was open to the iPad's files, showing several folders with months, dates, and two specific names: *Sheriff Claude Barry and Cameron Ford.*

"What is this?" Mal asked.

"Someone sent this to me anonymously. Sure it wasn't you?"

"This is the first I'm seeing this. What's on here?"

"*Good shit.* Enough to bury both of these fuckers. We've got Barry accepting extortion money, making racist comments with a city commissioner, and mountains of coke and blackmail for Ford."

"No fucking way."

"Yes fucking way."

"Where'd this come from?"

"Howard Loomis had a room full of this kind of stuff. My guess is someone bagged this as evidence and made me a copy."

"Someone at the sheriff's office?"

"I'm thinking someone else. Maybe a certain friend of yours. A certain dead friend."

"This is the first I'm seeing it, but … awesome? What are you doing with it?"

"It's tomorrow's six o'clock news story. We're going to vet a few things, but yeah, they're both going down."

"And … do you want back in?"

"I'm done with the department. I can do more good here. Less political bullshit. But you should run."

"Hell no. I'm taking a much needed vacation."

"I heard you won the lotto again."

"Yeah," Mal said. "What are the odds?"

Gloria smiled, shaking her head. Mal wasn't sure if she'd tied it to Jasper or not.

"Then I'm pushing Mike to run."

"What? Mike? No, he's too nice. He …" Mal thought

about how well he had navigated through so much of the bullshit. "Well, maybe."

"I think he'd be great."

The server came to take their order. They ordered, then he left.

Gloria said, "So, how's the hand?"

"Okay. Bandages will be off soon."

"And ... you okay?"

"You asking about the painkillers?"

"Yeah."

"I haven't taken any since the hospital. Just Extra Strength Tylenol."

"You know if you ever start to slip, you can call me."

"Thank you. But I don't think I'm gonna slip again. I've got too much going on, and people relying on me. Got a daughter now."

"I heard. That Katie kid."

"Tough exterior, but she's a sweetheart."

"Just like you."

"Aw, shit, boss, you're gonna make me blush."

"You look ... happier than I've seen in a long time. Motherhood suits you. You deserve it."

"Yes. Yes, it does," Mal agreed. "It's not the same as watching Ashley grow up and have her own family, but ... I'm looking forward to having them both in my house."

"You going back to your old place?"

Mal shrugged. "Might be time for a change of scenery. Maybe move north, somewhere with seasons."

Gloria nodded. "Well, whatever you decide, don't be a stranger."

"Oh," Mal said, "I almost forgot. I brought you a gift."

She reached down to her purse, pulled out the wrapped item, then handed it to Gloria.

"What is it?"

"Open it."

"An ABBA eight-track? Wow. Um, fuck you?"

Mal laughed. "Just don't tell Mike I gave it to you."

Epilogue 2

Jasper stood in the dark, feeling the cool breeze as leaves flitted along the sidewalk. He was standing outside a modest two-story home in a nice quiet suburban town, looking in through the dining room window, watching the woman he'd once loved sharing dinner with her daughter.

Alicia and Ophelia had started a new life in Virginia. It wasn't hard to find them. But now that he was here, he was losing his nerve to knock.

Jordyn appeared beside him. "You didn't come all this way for nothing."

"I lied to her. She probably hates me. She knew 'Dennis.' The woman's never even met me."

"What, were you planning on telling her you're an ex-cop who faked his death and spent his time hunting bad guys with his ghost daughter?"

"At least that would have been honest."

"Enough to never get a second date."

Jasper laughed.

"You lied about a part of you, but that's not all you are. You're a sweet and caring man who will do anything to protect the people he loves, even if it means sacrificing his happiness."

Lenny appeared next to Jordyn. "Here we are again, at a crossroads between what you want and what you feel *obligated* to do."

"Last time I thought this could work, I nearly got Alicia, Ophelia, and her aunt killed."

"No," Lenny said. "Alicia's sister almost got them all killed. You just ... well, you threw fuel on the fire. But you also took care of those meth bikers."

"He's right, Dad."

Jasper watched Alicia pass a bowl to Ophelia, remembering how much he enjoyed breaking bread with them, sitting at the table and talking like a normal family.

Now they were out of his life, and he wanted them more than ever.

Jasper looked down at his hands. So much blood on them.

"Monsters like me weren't meant to have love."

"Bullshit. Monsters are the ones who need love most." She met his gaze. "You can't keep living in fear, Dad. Fear ain't living, it's killing time. Nothing lasts forever, and you can't always protect the ones you love. None of us knows when our time will be up, but you should enjoy what you have while you still have it. Make their time as special as you can."

Tears stung his eyes. "What if she still hates me? What if she's happier now without me? Look at them ... they don't need me."

Jordyn looked in the window again. "That's not what I see."

"What do you see?"

"An incomplete picture. Missing you."

"What if I'm right and she hates me?"

Jordyn said, "And what if she loves you?"

"Come on, let's get out of here." Lenny turned to Jordyn. "He's gotta make this decision on his own."

"Wait," Jasper said. "I don't know if I can do this."

"Remember when you and Mom were teaching me to ride a bike … I was so afraid and kept on saying I didn't know how to do it? What did you say to me?"

"You don't know if you don't try."

Jordyn nodded. "You were right."

Then she and Lenny were gone and Jasper was alone, standing on the sidewalk in front of what he hoped might be his new house.

Every instinct pleaded with him to turn around, get out of there before they saw him.

But Jordyn was right, fear wasn't living. It was only killing time.

And Jasper had killed far too much in his life already.

He needed to start living.

So Jasper approached the door, more nervous than any of the times he'd ever entered a dark room to end someone's life.

His heart pounded as he stood on the porch. He heard Ophelia's laugh, followed by Alicia's. He'd enjoyed his time with them and needed it again.

He rang the doorbell with his heart in his throat.

"One second," Alicia said.

Jasper heard her footsteps. Then there was a pause.

Had she looked through the peephole and seen him?

Would she open the door?

Jasper swallowed the knot along with his fear.

Then the door opened.

THE END

What to read next

Want more King & Wright on your Kindle and in your life? Get the complete *Hidden Justice* and get to know Frank Grimm today.

Get Hidden Justice

A quick favor...

If you liked *No Fear*, then *would you kindly** consider taking a few minutes to leave a review on your favorite bookselling site. If you're a book blogger, we'd love any mentions on your blog or YouTube channel, also. Every bit of word-of-mouth helps to introduce us to new readers.

As always, thank you for reading,
   David Wright (and Nolon King)

(* *Bonus points if you got the* Bioshock *reference.*)

About the Authors

Nolon King writes fast-paced psychological thrillers set in the glitzy world of entertainment's power players with a bold, insightful voice. He's not afraid to explore the darker side of human nature through stories featuring families torn apart by secrets and lies.

Nolon loves to write about big questions and moral quandaries. How far would you go to cover up an honest mistake? Would you destroy your career to protect your family? How much of your soul would you sell to get the life of your dreams? Would you cheat on your husband to keep your children safe? Would you give in to a stalker's demands to save your marriage?

David W. Wright is the co-author of edge-of-your seat thrillers including the best-selling post-apocalyptic series *Yesterday's Gone*, the paranoid sci-fi *WhiteSpace* series, and the vigilante series, *No Justice*, as well as standalone thrillers *12*, and *Crash* which was recently optioned for a movie.

David is an accomplished, though intermittent, cartoonist who lives in [LOCATION REDACTED] with his wife and son [NAMES REDACTED.]

He is not at all paranoid.

He is "the grumpy one" on the *The Story Studio Podcast* with fellow Sterling and Stone founders, Sean Platt and Johnny B. Truant.

You can email him at <u>david@sterlingandstone.net</u>

We swear, he almost never bites. Unless you feed him after midnight.

Also By Nolon King

Hidden Justice

Hidden Justice

Hidden Honor

Hidden Shame

Hidden Virtue

No Justice

No Justice

No Escape

No Hope

No Return

No Stopping

No Fear

Once Upon A Crime

Once Upon A Crime

Twice Upon A Lie

Three Times a Murder

Dead For Good

Dead For Good

Left For Dead

Dead Of Night

Wake The Dead

Dead For Life

Stand Alone Novels

Pretty Killer

12

Blown

Miserable Lies

The Target

Secrets We Keep

Close To Home

Heat To Obsession

A Simple Kill

Tell Me No Lies

Red Carpet Black

Fade To Black

Victim

Also By David W. Wright

Hidden Justice

Hidden Justice

Hidden Honor

Hidden Shame

Hidden Virtue

No Justice

No Justice

No Escape

No Hope

No Return

No Stopping

No Fear

Karma Police

Jumper

Karma Police

The Collectors

Deviant

The Fall

Homecoming

Yesterday's Gone

October's Gone

Yesterday's Gone Season One

Yesterday's Gone Season Two

Yesterday's Gone Season Three

Yesterday's Gone Season Four

Yesterday's Gone Season Five

Yesterday's Gone Season Six

Tomorrow's Gone

Tomorrow's Gone Season One

Tomorrow's Gone Season Two

Tomorrow's Gone Season Three

Available Darkness

Darkness Itself

Available Darkness Book One

Available Darkness Book Two

Available Darkness Book Three

WhiteSpace

WhiteSpace Season One

WhiteSpace Season Two

WhiteSpace Season Three

Stand Alone Novels

12

Crash

Emily's List

Threshold